PRAISE FOR

'A joyful, roma[...]

Rea

'Laura Jane Williams combines sharp, relatable wit and bold, joyful sincerity'
Dolly Alderton

'Hilarious, heart-warming and truly authentic – your modern rom com must-read'
Hello!

'A fresh, smart, modern rom com. This is romance seen through the wry eyes of a cynic, and that's what makes it so special – and, ultimately, so uplifting. It had me totally gripped'
Beth O'Leary

'LJ's honesty and voice are unique'
Stylist

'Laura Jane Williams offers another dose of smart, sisterly storytelling . . . You can practically feel modern romance evolving as you're reading it'
Emma Jane Unsworth

'A perfect summer read that will leave you grinning'
Closer

'Tender, energetic and authentic . . . Such a current love story, but so timeless too'
Daisy Buchanan

D0428000

THIS IS NO LONGER THE PROPERTY OF THE SEATTLE PUBLIC LIBRARY

'Uplifting and witty, filled with so much real emotion'
Health & Wellbeing

'Laura Jane Williams' writing *sees* you, and gives you so much . . . Exactly the joyful escapism you need for your next beach holiday'
Lucy Vine

'This is the laugh-out-loud love story you need to read this summer'
Glamour

'So funny and wonderful and life-affirming'
Lorna Cook

'We devoured this book in one sitting!'
Bella

'This is the feminist rom-com of the summer'
Holly Bourne

'A cult hit'
Grazia

Laura Jane Williams was born in 1986 in Derbyshire, England. Her 2019 debut novel *Our Stop* was an international hit, and she is currently adapting it for screen. Her non-fiction includes *Becoming, Ice Cream for Breakfast* and *The Life Diet*, and she has contributed essays and articles to the *Telegraph*, the *Guardian, Marie Claire, Cosmopolitan, Grazia, Red* and more, as well as to a collection by *Stylist, Life Lessons from Remarkable Women*. You can find out more about her work on www.laurajaneauthor.com.

Fiction by the same author

Our Stop

The
LOVE
SQUARE

LAURA JANE WILLIAMS

avon.

Published by AVON
A division of HarperCollins*Publishers* Ltd
1 London Bridge Street
London SE1 9GF

www.harpercollins.co.uk

A Paperback Original 2021

First published in Great Britain by HarperCollins*Publishers* 2020

Copyright © Just Show Up Ltd 2020

Laura Jane Williams asserts the moral right to be identified
as the author of this work.

A catalogue copy of this book is available from the British Library.

ISBN: 978-0-00-841403-0

This novel is entirely a work of fiction. The names, characters and
incidents portrayed in it are either the products of the author's imagination
or used in a fictitious manner. Any resemblance to actual persons,
living or dead, events or localities is entirely coincidental.

Typeset in Minion 11.25/14.5 pt by Palimpsest Book Production Limited,
Falkrik, Stirlingshire
Printed and bound in UK by CPI Group (UK) Ltd, Croydon CR0 4YY

All rights reserved. No part of this text may be reproduced,
transmitted, down-loaded, decompiled, reverse engineered, or stored in
or introduced into any information storage and retrieval system, in any
form or by any means, whether electronic or mechanical, without
the express written permission of the publishers.

MIX
Paper from
responsible sources
FSC® C007454

This book is produced from independently certified FSC™ paper
to ensure responsible forest management.

For more information visit: www.harpercollins.co.uk/green

For J & A
Your love inspires me

Prologue

'That's the last of it, then,' he said sadly, looking into the boot of the small hire car loaded with pillows and chairs, vases and lamps. 'Everything that's most important to you, packed and ready to go.'

What he meant was: *me. Take me. Ask me to go with you. I'm important. I'm yours, too.*

'Great,' she replied, not meeting his eye. She said it too loudly, too brightly. She was over-compensating. 'Thanks so much. That was a lot. I'm knackered already!'

What she meant was: *I don't know how to say goodbye. I wish things were different. I'm scared.*

Francesco Cipolla and Penny Bridge stood looking at anything but each other, both wishing they were back in the flat together, making brunch to sit with knees knocking and tasting food off each other's forks, like yesterday morning, or in bed, twisting the sheets around them as they giggled, like last night.

It had only been three weeks. How could this all be ending after only three weeks? It was like leaving a play at the interval, or stopping after the first sip of a salt-rimmed margarita. They were wasting themselves, wasting the potential of what they had. They could be drunk on each other, they could finish falling all the way until they were in love. They were almost there anyway, and god knows Penny had searched hard enough for a man that could make her feel like this. But she couldn't see how she could physically leave and mentally stay with him – and she really did have to leave. She owed it to her uncle. Trying to stay in a relationship with Francesco was a set-up for failure.

No, she reasoned with herself. *I'm ripping the plaster off. Long-distance doesn't work, and no way will he leave London for the countryside. I don't even want to leave London for the countryside.* She thought of his touch, his nimble fingers exploring her, how he tasted. He was so, *so* hot. And kind. And thoughtful. And he listened when she talked and made her laugh and didn't treat her like a delicate doll that might break, and all of that made him even hotter.

No, she repeated to herself. *We can't.*

Francesco cleared his throat.

'Are you sure you're going to be okay driving?' he forced. 'Shall we get coffee first, or snacks . . .?'

Take me with you.

'Nah,' Penny replied, knocking her shoulder against his and focusing on the edge of the pavement. 'I think I'll get upset if we go back in there to be honest. And I don't want to have to stop for a wee until I'm at least at the Watford Gap.'

'But you will stop,' he said.

'Yes, Francesco. I will stop.' She was amused at his caring, and so finally looked up at him, halting the world on its axis.

Francesco couldn't fully explain why he'd be willing to give up his life to go with her, but he would. Penny had no reason to believe he'd be different than every other man who'd left her when things got hard, though. They were in a stand-off. Francesco could only prove he'd stick around by being able to show up for her in the first place, and Penny was holding him at arms' length, denying him the chance to try.

'Well,' she said, eventually. 'I suppose I'll see you when I see you.'

'This is so weird.'

'Nah,' intoned Penny, inwardly screaming the opposite. 'Just give me a hug and that's that.'

Francesco obliged, holding her tight. *Even the way she smells turns me on,* he thought. Maybe friendship would be impossible after all.

'Here's to what's next, then,' he said into the top of her head, inhaling the scent of her.

Behind them Stuart appeared, lingering in the doorway of the café. He scowled a bit, a way to ask Francesco if he should interrupt or hang back. Penny sensed him, though, and so squeezed Francesco's waist twice, a little morse code of release, and then pulled away.

'Don't ruin my café whilst I'm gone,' she mock-taunted Stuart, who stepped forward to issue his own hug.

'You have my word, boss,' he smiled, doing a captain's salute at her. 'I'll send updates all the time, and you can look at the accounts whenever you want.'

'You're a legend, Stu. Thank you for this.'

She opened the driver's door and started the engine. As she slammed the door shut, she could see Francesco panic that that was it, that their goodbye was over and she would be gone. She laughed through both her tears and the glass, winding down the window.

'Don't look so worried,' she insisted. 'Everything is going to be fine.' She wiped her eyes, all pretence of not crying disappearing. Then: 'Tell me it's all going to be fine.'

'It's all going to be fine,' Francesco nodded, his own eyes stinging, his own vision blurring.

Isn't that how falling in love so often works? Some stranger appears out of nowhere and becomes a fixed star in your universe.

- Kate Bolick

1

A few months ago, in March

It wasn't so much that Penny Bridge was unlucky in love as it was that love seemingly didn't know she existed. It had been five years since her last proper relationship – five years since romance, prolonged passion, or even since a bloke had stayed interested for longer than a week. It was getting pretty hard to pretend it might ever be any different, and keeping positive was really starting to take its toll, especially after last night.

'I just can't believe I'm here again,' she sighed, explaining to her head barista Stuart about the text she'd received after getting home from her date. It had read:

Hey, so I didn't know how to say this earlier but my ex is kind of back in the picture. I don't want to string you along or anything, so I don't think we should see each other again. All the best!! xx

'Ah,' replied Stuart. 'That really sucks.'

Cristian had been a Romanian mathematician who

worked for Virgin Galactic, and for their second date they'd gone to a very promising sing-along showing of *La La Land* at the Hackney Picturehouse and then next door to the Wetherspoon's. Penny had already decided that it was the night to have sex with him – she'd shaved her bikini line especially, and changed her bed sheets – but on her way back from the bathroom at the pub she'd seen the familiar yellow interface of the dating app on his phone, and realized he was obviously messaging somebody else whilst she was having a wee. Why had he lied after? He didn't need to say that his ex was making moves on him. She was a big girl. She could withstand the truth. Obviously he was just not that into her. But why? Why weren't any of them just not that into her? And why hadn't she called him out on his terrible etiquette right there and then instead of finishing her drink and making vague grumbles about it 'getting late'?

She knew the answer to that, actually. It's because it felt like she was in an episode of *Sex and the City* – the one where Charlotte screams at a sky that should have been raining men, 'I've been dating since I was fifteen! I'm exhausted! Where is he?!' Penny was too exhausted to teach Cristian about basic manners – that's why she'd finished the drink she'd paid for and left without bringing it up. She simply couldn't be arsed. His text message after was unnecessary salt in the wound.

What is so wrong with me that no bloke wants to be my boyfriend? she wondered.

Last month she'd spent five nights in a row with Trevor, a deputy head of maths on half term who, once school started back up again, fell off the face of the earth until a random 1 a.m. text asking if he'd left his protractor at her flat. Before Christmas there'd been an Iraqi estate agent from Camberwell who'd really made her laugh – and she, him – but who was so inexplicably embarrassed by what he'd asked her to do to his prostate when he was drunk that he blocked not only her phone number, but everything across all social media, too. Before *him* there'd been a string of first dates that never seemed to become second ones, a summer off dating entirely, and three trips to the Skirt Club to sate her light bi-curiosity but that didn't lead to much dating, either – Penny had figured out quickly enough that she was doomed with an attraction to men. (She did, though, get the name of an amazing seamstress in Canonbury, and made friends with two women who were now a couple and who she still saw every couple of months for drinks.)

Penny thought of herself as an entertaining date – interesting and interested. She had friends and family she loved, a business she was proud of, some fun stories and – so she'd been told – eyes that danced with mischief. Did she spit when she laughed, and nobody had ever mentioned it? Did she talk about herself too much? Was it her cup size, or her dress size, or her hair colour? Weren't redheads supposed to be a novelty? Was it because she asked too many questions?

She didn't know how to be anybody but herself, and yet herself, Penny Bridge, was apparently repulsive to all mankind because none of them wanted to actually be with her. She had half a mind to text Cristian back and ask him straight: why didn't any of her dates ever pan out? If the definition of insanity is doing the same thing over and over and expecting a different result, Penny was officially bonkers. She kept hoping that the next date might be different, that the next man might be different, but they never were. Maybe Cristian could tell her what needed to change. Would it be weird to ask him? He was, after all, one of the people best placed to make suggestions. What did the other women on the dating app have that Penny didn't?

'You don't need to change a thing,' urged Stuart, kindly. 'You only have to get it right once. This space engineer is a fool if he's blowing you off. A damned idiot.'

Penny sat across from Stuart at the serving counter, watching him arrange the grapefruit-orange crostatas and a goat's cheese double crumb cake she'd just brought up from the kitchen. This was Stoke Newington, one of the more achingly bougie boroughs of North London, so he was using breeze-blocks as support for the charcoal slate trays, all at varying heights. It was terribly hipster but genuinely quite good to look at, so she let him do as he pleased. Bridges was her café, and she cooked, but his aesthetics defined the space where the customers ate.

'But I'm so tired, Stu. I'm so sick of this feeling – of holding my breath to get some stupid validation from a stupid man, and then feeling like I need to eat a pint of ice cream and cry-wank to *The Notebook* when it doesn't happen. Do I smell like desperation?'

'You smell like burnt cream and boiled ham, Pen, like you do every day.'

'Ha, ha. Thanks.' She rolled her eyes at him playfully. She did smell, though – that was the life of a chef in a small breakfast and lunch café, to carry the faint odour of cooking from 7 a.m. until 4 p.m., Tuesday to Saturday.

'I feel like I really should plan to be single forever. Have a baby solo. I keep threatening to go for it. Maybe I should take the hint the universe or whatever is throwing at me. I just want to live my life, man. It feels pathetic to be somehow *waiting.*' She sighed dramatically. Stuart didn't need to know that before her cancer treatment she'd both harvested eggs and had them fertilized with donor sperm. Making embryos as a single woman with cancer had been a complicated decision, and one even some of her family hadn't understood. She'd have to use a surrogate when she wanted kids, but that wasn't the point right now. The point was, she really did think she might have to proceed without a partner by her side. So why shouldn't she do that sooner rather than later? Evidently that partner wasn't anywhere close to making himself known.

'I could introduce you to some friends, you know,' Stuart said, wiping down stray specks from around his display. Stuart was a twenty-five-year-old art school graduate who treated coffee like as much of a craft as his own pottery. Slim build and black skin, he wore straight-leg jeans rolled twice, socks on show, and bulky sneakers that seemingly never got grubby – as well as a t-shirt with two rolls of the sleeve and a single pierced ear. 'If you wanted somebody pre-vetted for ghosting, or lying, or general romantic ambivalence.'

Penny stood and walked behind the counter to make another coffee, her third of the morning. 'Aw, thanks. But I don't think you should be setting your boss up.'

Stuart stepped out of her way. 'You have too many rules.'

'If I dated one of your friends – who, you know, let's be fair, would be too young for me anyway – in three dates' time I wouldn't want to be running into him because he's here to meet you after your shift, but had told me he had to move to Kazakhstan for a work assignment and that's why he couldn't be with me. When I get ghosted, I really do expect to never see them again. It'd be added mortification otherwise, and I haven't got the stomach for it.'

'Just promise me you won't give up,' Stuart soothed. 'Dating is hard for everyone until it's not. You only have to get it right once, that's what my pa says. Your soulmate could be just around the corner. He could appear at any minute, and it'd be a shame to miss him because your head is too far up your own self-pitying—'

Stuart was interrupted by the sound of three knocks against the glass of the café door, forcing both of them to look over. Stood on the pavement was a dark-haired, olive-skinned man in a beanie hat and puffer vest, accessorized with an armful of sourdough loaves. Stuart immediately issued Penny a smirk. She didn't catch it.

'Ah, yeah – I meant to say,' she started, already in business mode, holding up a hand to the man outside to signal she was coming. 'The bread delivery is going to be late today because Safiya had an issue with somebody falling off a bike and so had to ask her friend to help out.' She bent down to unlock the bottom part of the door, opening it up to say, 'Are you Safiya's man-who-can? Come in.'

'Safiya fell off her bike?' Stuart said, worriedly, whilst also acknowledging the man Penny had let in. 'Alright mate?' Stuart had a crush on the bread supplier and did a terrible job of hiding it – even the way he said Safiya's name betrayed him.

The puffer-vest-wearing man put the brown paper bags down on the table by the door and happily inserted himself into the conversation. 'Not Safiya. A guy she's dating. But I'm here to save the day! I've got more in the van. Croissants, I think. Nice to meet you. I'm Francesco.' He shook Stuart's hand and nodded at Penny, who'd already walked back across the café.

Penny caught Stuart's face fall. *A guy she's dating.* That must've stung. She went back to the counter just as the coffee maker roared into life and spat hot, syrupy espresso into her cup, and Stuart busied himself by filling up the sugar bowls on each table. She watched the man outside shift several delivery trays in his van around into a more orderly fashion. His complexion and hair colour made sense now she'd heard him speak – he had a slight accent. He wore a striped apron over his clothes and paused his work to pull out a phone from the front pouch. Whoever was on the other end of the line when he answered delighted him so much that he threw his head back, laughing. Seeing somebody so elated made Penny smile by proxy. A handsome man enjoying his life. She wondered if it was his girlfriend, and then wondered why she'd wondered about him having a girlfriend. She concluded it was because of the accent. And the smile. And the heavy-lifting.

'I wish you'd let me do that for you,' Stuart said, interrupting her reverie. 'You don't treat it with the respect it deserves.'

'It's just a double espresso,' giggled Penny.

Stuart looked stern and held up a finger. 'It is never *just* an espresso, Penny.'

'My bad . . .' Penny stepped away from the machine, back around the counter, holding her hands up while giving a mocking roll of the eyes.

'This is your café – you're Penny?' Francesco said, reappearing in the doorway and dropping down two smaller paper bags.

13

'I am.'

He wiped a hand on his apron and held it out to her as he approached.

'I've read about you.'

The warmth of his palm met hers.

They locked eyes.

His smile was broad – not just wide, but all-encompassing. It was disconcerting to look him in the eye, this stranger, not least because they were stood not even a body's width apart, but Penny found that she couldn't look away. She took him in – his sprinkling of stubble and the tangy smell of coffee on his breath.

'I wish I could stay for breakfast,' he said.

They were still shaking hands.

'Leaving before breakfast and you didn't even spend the night,' Penny baited without thinking, shocking herself at how easily she'd let something so inappropriate slip out.

'I've heard great things,' smirked Francesco.

'Well . . . I . . .' Penny spluttered. She was embarrassed now. Why had she said that? Maybe *this* explained her perpetual singledom – she was a horrific flirt who, when it came down to it, didn't actually know how to communicate with the opposite sex.

'I meant about the breakfast.' Francesco laughed.

'Yes. Of course! Right. Yes, so did I.'

'Uh-huh,' he murmured, clearly enjoying her squirming.

They stood, touching, him grinning at her, looking at her, scanning her face like maybe he knew her, and Penny realized she was grinning just as widely back.

Something was happening.

Penny didn't know what to say.

His eyes were like pools of black marble.

Deep.

Penetrating.

She could count on one hand the number of times she'd experienced that. Somebody looking not *at* her, but almost *through* to the essence of her. Piercing something. The last time she'd felt like this with a hot bloke was at culinary school, when she'd met her ex. She'd felt it when she'd told her uncle about being ill, when she was twenty-five, too. Her sister Clementine could look at her that way sometimes. There was no hiding. *Jesus, I hope that wasn't his girlfriend on the phone,* Penny thought. *He's beautiful.* Not that she was going to do anything about it. Obviously. She'd probably never see him again, for starters.

'Well. I'll . . . be back,' Francesco said. 'I've got more deliveries now.'

They were still holding hands. Still staring.

'Do. Yes. We'll . . . be here,' Penny grinned, not entirely sure what that even meant. 'I mean. Of course we'll be here. Buildings don't tend to move around. Ha.' Her mouth was dry. Why was she so horribly incompetent with this? 'You're welcome any time.' She felt ridiculous.

Francesco flashed his smile once more. 'Cool,' he nodded, and dropped her hand to turn on his heel.

'Francesco?' Stuart said, and Penny realized with mortification that he'd been stood behind the counter watching as all of this happened.

'Yes mate?' Francesco replied, not making eye contact with Stuart as he spun back around, instead immediately catching Penny's eye again, grateful for the excuse to elicit another smile. She had bright red hair piled on top of her head and not a scrap of make-up. She looked tired, like she'd already

15

been in the kitchen for hours, but her cheeks had flushed to make her glow, and her voice, when she'd spoken, had reminded him of something. He felt like he'd met her before, somewhere. He wanted permission to keep staring, to keep looking.

'Are you seeing anyone?'

That got his attention. Francesco looked to Stuart. 'Ah, I'm not gay, mate. Sorry.'

Stuart rolled his eyes and motioned towards Penny. 'Not for me. For *her*.' Penny's eyes widened in horror. 'The one that's slack-jawed and dripping over there.'

'Me?' Penny squeaked.

'You're single?' Francesco questioned.

Penny looked from Francesco to Stuart, and then back again. 'Well, yes, but—'

'Oh. Cool. Well—'

Stuart cut him off by handing him an order pad and pen.

'Write your number down,' Stuart commanded.

Francesco laughed. 'God, there's no messing around here, is there?' he laughed. He looked at Penny. 'Is that . . . okay? If I do that?'

'Sure,' yelped Penny, three octaves higher than she normally spoke. 'Yes. Okay. Um . . . awesome. I will . . . use it. Yes.' She inexplicably did a thumbs-up mixed with a finger point. Later Stuart would say to her: you were *real cool, Pen. Real, real cool.*

Francesco scribbled down his digits as Penny glared at Stuart and Stuart supervised Francesco, nodding encouragingly as he handed the slip of paper over to her.

Penny smiled.

Francesco smiled.

They stood, neither of them saying anything.

This stuff doesn't happen! thought Penny. *This stuff doesn't happen to ME!*

'Okay then,' said Stuart. 'This is the bit where you both say goodbye. We've got a café to run.'

'Bye,' Francesco said, shaking his head as if he couldn't quite believe it.

'Bye,' said Penny, giddy.

'You're both very welcome,' said Stuart, ushering Francesco out. 'Especially you,' he added, for Penny's benefit, winking. When Francesco was out of earshot he added: 'I told you it could be the very next man to walk through that door.'

'Well yeah,' said Penny, lowering her voice, her eyes fixed on Francesco's bum through the window – she'd have to have been dead not to notice how his jeans hung low on his waist, his boxers peeking over the top. 'But a man who looks like that – there's got to be something wrong with him, hasn't there? Nice guys don't . . . swagger.'

Francesco gave one last look back before he got into the bread van. Penny and Stuart each raised a hand to wave at him.

'Right?' she prompted Stuart.

'Put that number into your phone right now, right this second,' he said. 'Before you lose it. If there's something wrong with him, at least find out what it is.'

'Like that's not the story of my life,' Penny replied sceptically, still waving at Francesco and his cute bum.

After service had ended that day and Bridges was closed, Penny sat outside in the unseasonably warm March sunshine. ('Fake spring' her uncle called it. 'There's three fake springs before

17

May, but don't be fooled: a week of sun does not a change of season make.') All day she'd been turning over what had happened that morning in her mind – getting Francesco's number that way. What did she have to lose by texting him? But then, what if he'd only passed along his number because he was too embarrassed not to? Penny couldn't quite engage the 'sod it' muscles it took to make a move on him. He *was* gorgeous, though. Really . . . urgh. She didn't want to use the word 'sexy' but it was the most appropriate one that came to mind. *He might be* too *sexy,* thought Penny. *If I'm a six out of ten and he's a nine, he probably wants to date another nine. That's just hot people maths.*

Penny rolled a cigarette from the pouch of tobacco in her lap, using a menthol filter. She knew smoking was bad for her, and yet that was part of the appeal. She let herself have one a day, like Obama apparently did. A good girl doing a bad thing. Lighting it, she simultaneously fished her phone out of her apron, pulling up WhatsApp to send a voice note to her sister Clementine. She held down the record button and slid it up so that it locked, meaning she could talk at length without needing to keep her finger pressed down.

'So, a thing happened this morning,' she started, thus beginning the kind of monologue that she and Clementine lovingly called 'Personal Podcasts'. Clementine was a project manager for Stella McCartney, which meant she was seldom in the country for more than one week at a time before she had to fly off to Tokyo or Helsinki or Milan to oversee the building and fitting of a new store. For the past two years their bond had subsisted mostly on these voice notes recorded and listened to at all hours of the day and night. Sometimes it was easier to be honest about their lives without the other one there – like truths whispered between lovers after dark, when it was simpler to say what needed to be said. In truth, Clementine's job had brought them closer, even though they were physically far apart.

'This guy . . . Oh I don't know. This is so dumb.' Penny sucked on her roll-up and exhaled loudly. She explained all about acquiring Francesco's number and concluded with, 'I'm going to text him. That's what I came on to tell you. I'm going to text him because I am a grown woman in charge of herself and it's not a big deal. That is what he gave it to me for. So I could use it. Which I am going to do. Use it. Me. To text him, Mr Hot Stuff, right now, in a minute.'

She stubbed out her cigarette with the heel of her trainer and gently tucked it into the side of a bay tree at the back door, in amongst all the other butts she told herself she'd 'collect all at once' to 'save time' but hadn't done in about six months.

'Anyway, tell me your news when you can. I know I just made this all about me. But, sisterly entitlement and all that, isn't it. I just needed to talk myself into being brave. Love you! Send photos from Miami! I am now going to text the handsome man!'

Except, once Penny had sent the voice note, she sat staring at her phone, turning it over in her hand, most definitely not texting Francesco. She stared at the darkening sky and let out a sigh. Cristian hadn't wanted her. Trevor hadn't wanted her. The Iraqi estate agent hadn't wanted her. Why would this guy be any different?

Dare I . . . she wondered. Images of Cristian playing on the dating app the night before flashed up in her mind, the shame and degradation washing over her once again.

'Damn it,' she said, unlocking her phone. She couldn't get the idea of feedback from another man out of her mind. She thought about it for a minute and then typed:

Oh hey – me again. Penny. I was wondering if I could ask you one thing. Not being weird or anything, but I think there's something you could help me with?

She was in luck: it came up at the top of the screen that Cristian was online, and then that he was typing back.

. . . ok??? Cristian replied.

Penny took a breath and decided to just go for it. *I saw you playing on Bumble when I was coming back from the bathroom last night,* she explained. *So obviously you just weren't that into me. I'm not saying your ex isn't back in the picture, but even if she isn't you decided you didn't fancy me. And that is totally cool! That's ok!!! But I've been really unlucky with dating, and I wondered if there was something I did to mess it up?* She hoped she didn't sound like she was begging him to change his mind. She sent another message: *Honestly, I'm not trying to be a bitch or anything. I really am hoping you can solve the mystery (to me) of my eternal singledom!*

Cristian is typing, her phone promised, before his reply pinged back.

lol. Soz that u saw that. Not that we r married or anything lol.

Lol, she replied.

Penny hated that she had replied with a 'lol'. She hated that she was even asking the question. The man couldn't even spell his texts properly! But if she *was* going to message Francesco, she wanted information first. She wanted to know how to protect herself. She wanted to make sure that if there was one thing that was turning these men off that she knew,

20

once and for all, what it was, so she could decide if she was willing to change it or not.

Cristian continued: *I mean, ur fit and everything, so don't worry about that.*

Thanks. You too!

It took everything she had in her not to add an emoji, but he didn't deserve the happy face with the jazz hands. Was Cristian always this much of a moron? Penny reflected that they hadn't really exchanged many messages before they'd gone out together – she'd just straight up asked him out, because it was draining to keep messaging and she didn't have time in her schedule to waste. He was an eloquent conversationalist – or, at least, she remembered him as one. Although . . . huh. Now she thought about it, he hadn't asked her many questions about herself, and he *did* tend to explain things to her that she already knew, even after she had said she knew them. *Bloody hell, maybe I've been so desperate to couple up that I willingly got dickmatized,* she thought, remembering what her best friend Sharon had said to her about straight women who become hypnotized into forgetting their partner's flaws at the promise of sex. 'And it doesn't even have to be good sex!' Sharon had insisted. 'Just a warm body to wake up next to!' *Bugger,* thought Penny. *Bugger, bugger, bugger.*

Penny's realization was interrupted by his reply.

If I was gonna say anyting maybe your laff is a bit loud

My laugh is too loud?

It's like confidence and that innit? You don't mind people looking and that. I like my women a bit more quiet.

Right. I'm too confident?

A bit, yeah. Sorry if I'm affending you or whatever but you asked!

How could Penny be 'accused' of being 'too confident' when literally her lack of confidence is what meant she was asking this man for feedback about herself in the first place? She started to type a response. At first she tried to make a joke about it, but then she hit the delete button and re-typed outrage at such blatant misogyny instead. She deleted that, too. Penny sat and stared at her phone and tried to reason with what she'd advise anyone else to do. If a friend told her they'd texted a date that didn't work out to ask for 'feedback' what would she say?

She took a breath.

'Bollocks to this,' she declared, and swiped left on the message thread to hit 'delete'. Then she went to contacts and hit the 'i' by Cristian's name, scrolling down to block his number.

'That's better!' she avowed out loud, a feeling of relief washing over her that she might have lost perspective for a moment, but she'd pulled it back from the brink. She certainly wouldn't be telling Clementine about this slip in judgement. There was *nothing* wrong with her. If Cristian didn't fancy her that was, like Stuart had pointed out, Cristian's problem.

Admittedly, it was a shame that Cristian's problem left Penny as the one on her own.

She put her phone back into her trouser pocket and stood to go back inside. She wasn't going to worry about Cristian, and she certainly wasn't going to get her knickers in a twist over the delivery man from this morning, either, who'd no doubt be yet another in a long string of anticlimaxes. No. It was better to swear off men altogether for a bit. She could always go on another wellness retreat, or buy a new vibrator, instead. Perhaps she'd finally join the Netball team at the leisure centre. Anything but men. Just for a little while. Maybe what she'd said to Stuart was right – that she'd plough on with her life single, and truly start preparing to find a surrogate. At least that way she'd be protected from dating disappointment. Trying to stay hopeful was costing her emotional wellbeing way too much. Couldn't there be more to life than trying to find a bloody man?

2

'Well hello, you,' Penny's best friend Sharon said in her thick Irish accent as Penny climbed into the backseat of their Uber. 'Who are you out to impress tonight? You look – well, there's no other word for it – *sensational.*'

'Oh, this old thing?' Penny asked, putting on a faux-shy voice as she fixed her seatbelt and leaned across to kiss Sharon's cheek.

Penny revelled in the opportunity to get dressed up. She spent much of her life smelling, as Stuart lovingly joked, like burnt cream and boiled ham, so to shower with her favourite oils, and style her hair and wear a dress that she'd actually taken the time to iron, felt like stepping into a different side of her personality. She was always herself, but in a ruffled red midi dress she'd picked up at one of Stoke Newington's Church Street boutiques, she felt girlish and pretty, and it was difficult to feel that way in the Crocs and chef's whites of her day-to-day. She liked reminding herself she could be both versions of Penny.

'No but seriously,' said Sharon, getting a proper look at her. 'I thought you were off men?'

'What's that got to do with anything?'

'Are you telling me you're not on the pull? That you wore false eyelashes for *me*?'

Penny reached for her face self-consciously. 'Is it too much?'

'No, no,' Sharon insisted. 'It's the perfect amount.'

'I just wanted to remind myself that I can be cute, when I try.'

'You're cute all the time!' asserted Sharon.

'You know what I mean,' Penny said. 'It's not often I go out somewhere so fancy on a school night.'

'You look gorgeous and if you wanted to tell me the same I wouldn't be offended.'

Penny laughed. This is why she found it so easy to be around her – Sharon was fun and to-the-point and never took anything too seriously.

'Sharon!' she said, as if only now seeing her for the first time. 'Look at you! You're a knock-out!'

'Why, thank you.' Sharon pushed her forearms under her boobs to emphasize the low cut of her top.

'I hope you've checked those things lately,' Penny prompted, as the driver looked at them both in the rearview mirror.

Sharon nodded. 'Once a month, in the shower, like you taught me,' she replied.

Penny winked at her.

Sharon lived around the corner from the café with her partner and two kids in a Victorian terrace her parents bought for £260,000 twelve years ago, and was now, aided by London inflation, worth a cool £1.2 million. Sharon used to work in FinTech – financial technology – but gave it all up when she had kids to become a florist, age thirty-nine. She was talented, and did the flowers for Bridges. That's how Penny had met her two years ago now.

'I'm excited,' Penny told Sharon as they arrived, joining the queue at coat check and rifling through their handbags for change to tip the porter. The women had been invited to the soft opening of a new restaurant in Notting Hill called Ecclesiast. Dofi, a colleague from Penny's days at Grayshott Hall – the first 'proper' kitchen job after culinary school for them both – had gone out on her own finally. Penny had been just as ambitious as Dofi once, but after the cancer her priorities had shifted. A little North London café was one thing, but Penny knew a whole restaurant that did lunch and dinner, could turn a hundred and fifty covers a day, employed scores of people and was probably vying for a Michelin Star, was quite another. Penny was able to be genuinely happy for Dofi though, because – perpetual singleness aside – Penny was actually really in love with how she'd set up her own life, too. They both had businesses that were right for them.

'Huh. I was sure I'd put some pound coins in here,' Penny muttered, absentmindedly still searching her through her clutch. 'Have you got two quid?'

A voice boomed over her shoulder as she looked through her bag one last time: 'Just these two please, Darius.' As a man passed two coats to the coat-check attendant, one brushed Penny's bag, tipping it out of her hands and onto the floor.

She crouched down without thinking to collect the spilled contents before they were trampled on, as Sharon bristled, 'Hey, excuse you! I think you owe my friend an apology, sir!' She said the 'sir' sarcastically, making it clear the man who'd barged past them was anything but a gentleman. Good old Sharon.

Penny stood as the perpetrator turned to face them.

'I'm so sorry, I didn't see—' the man started, a slightly odd melody to his words, like maybe English was his second language.

'Oh!' said Penny in surprise. 'I know you!'

In front of her was the bread delivery guy who'd been in the café the other week – still handsome, but cheeks flushed now. Penny literally saw his recognition of her rise up to his eyes just seconds after she'd recognized him.

'Hello,' he said, coolly, obviously taken aback to see her. 'I'm sorry about that. My spatial awareness obviously needs some work.'

'No,' Penny insisted, trying to sound kind and friendly. She didn't want him to feel uncomfortable at the sight of her when it was he who'd been brave by giving her his number. 'It was me – I wasn't looking where I was stood. I was looking for change. I'm sorry.'

God, that face. Francesco's face. And his voice, too – his voice gave Penny's body a physical reaction. Her nipples bristled under her dress. Her breathing changed. Why hadn't she texted him?

Francesco nodded, his face impassive. Penny couldn't get a read on him. The friend beside him said, 'Do you guys need tip money? I've got change.'

Sharon held out her palm to reveal two coins. 'We've sorted it,' she said. 'I found some in my bag.' Penny could tell she was waiting to have the situation explained to her – how everyone knew one another.

There was a pause as Penny and Francesco took each other in, neither really smiling or frowning, just looking, both wondering what to say.

'I didn't text,' Penny settled on, right as Francesco said, 'Well, have a great night. This should be really good.'

'Oh,' said Penny. 'Yes.'

'Don't worry about it.'

'I'm sorry,' Penny faltered.

'What did you do?' asked Sharon, looking between them, confused.

'Enjoy your night,' said Francesco's friend. It all happened so fast. Francesco was already walking towards the dining room to be greeted by the hostess before Penny could think of anything to say to keep him chatting. She watched him go. The friend half-smiled at them and turned away himself.

'Ahhh,' Penny moaned, scrunching up her face.

'What was *that*?' probed Sharon. 'Or rather, *who* was that?'

'Oh god. He came in the café a couple of weeks ago and Stuart told him to leave his number for me but I didn't use it. I think he was a bit embarrassed. Like I'd stood him up or something. I wonder why he's here, and how he knows Dofi.'

'Well,' said Sharon, taking Penny's coat from her for the porter. 'You'd be embarrassed, too, wouldn't you? If you hit on him and he said he'd call and then he changed his mind.' She slid the tip money across the counter. 'I mean, nobody died, but still. Even my ego would be bruised over that.'

'I know,' Penny said. She was still watching the space where Francesco had stood. He was even more attractive than she'd remembered. She felt awful that he'd seemed so awkward. Had she been awkward? She'd definitely been awkward.

'Is there a reason you didn't text him?' Sharon said, following her gaze. 'Because, if you don't mind my saying so, that seems a little short-sighted. He's . . .'

Penny exhaled through her nostrils loudly. 'Yeah. He is.' Then she added: 'There *was* a reason. Like I said, and, may I remind you, you agreed it was a sound idea – I'm not doing men right now, am I?'

'I'd do that one, though,' snickered Sharon, raising her eyebrows suggestively, and Penny gave her a playful shove.

'Do you think he's *too* handsome?' Penny asked, letting the waiter unroll her napkin and place it on her lap. 'Look at him. A man like that could rely on his face for his whole life, never having to develop a personality.'

'I definitely don't think a man like that is a riot in the sack, put it that way. I'll bet he's never had to even *try* to get a woman into bed,' Sharon mused.

She stabbed at the sharing plate between them.

'The best ones are like my Luke. He didn't become hot until he was twenty-nine and grew into his lanky frame and started to see a proper barber. Before that he was so unlucky in love that he didn't have sex until he was twenty-five. Not even third base. He was a proper Chris Martin type. Don't tell him I told you that.'

'Luke lost his virginity at twenty-five?' Penny said, amazed. 'How old was he when you met him?'

'Thirty-one. But because he'd never been hot, he worked really hard at sex and it was *all* about me. You know how with some men it's like, the script is three minutes kissing, one minute rubbing over your trousers, two minutes oral and then he sticks it in until he comes, because that's the objective? That he comes?'

'Depressingly, the answer to that question is yes.'

'Not with Luke. He'd be down there all afternoon if I asked him to. Just wants me to have a good time. And from the second or third time we were together I realized I was coming harder with him than anyone before because it never felt like a rush. He wasn't getting my pleasure out of the way so that he could get his own. It was as if just having me naked was the pleasure for him. I suppose because for fifteen years he didn't really have that.'

'Awwww! All he wanted was a naked woman in his bed and then he got you! I can't believe I didn't know all this!'

'Ah,' whispered Sharon. 'I don't like to brag.'

'Yes you do,' teased Penny.

'Yeah,' laughed Sharon. 'I do.'

Penny kept stealing glances back in the direction of Francesco as they chatted, so much so that she'd angled her chair in a way that meant she didn't have her back to him. She was sure he was looking at her, too.

Penny couldn't believe what had happened in the café that morning. It was so conflicting – theoretically, she knew she was worthy of being loved, or at least fancied, but in practice she was so utterly petrified of it. She was terrified of being let down, yet again. Because there always seemed to be an 'again'. And another. And another. But then, how she felt seeing Francesco this second time, how silly and nervous and electrified she felt in his presence – it was a hell of a rush. There was no way she was imagining the connection. Not now she'd felt it twice. It was this exact feeling that always made her reason, *okay. One more shot at hope. Why not?*

'Two things,' Sharon said. 'First: you're going to hurt your neck if you keep straining to see that guy. Second: try the watermelon and pecorino salad. It is very, very good.' She waved her fork into the air in the direction of the dish closest to her.

31

'I told you Dofi knew what she was doing,' Penny said, reaching over. 'I mean, everything is just magnificent, isn't it? So good. She taught me a lot of what I know about pairing flavours.'

'You need to do something like this at the café,' Sharon insisted, going in for more. 'I'd be there every day for it.'

Penny took a forkful and turned in Francesco's direction again as she chewed.

She couldn't help herself.

'Okay,' said Penny. 'Take two. I'm going to go and talk to him. You've convinced me.'

'Not that it took a lot,' replied Sharon. 'I think you convinced yourself.'

'Don't make me tell you to piss off,' uttered Penny, scowling playfully. 'Not when I'm about to be gutsy.'

'Quite right,' said Sharon, grinning, as she stood to lead the way into the lounge area for after-dinner coffee. 'Into battle we go,' she trilled over her shoulder. 'Waterloo here we come.'

'I'm saying it: piss off.'

Penny heard Sharon laugh. 'You know I've got your back,' she said, honing in on two high-backed chairs alongside Francesco and his friend.

'Are these seats taken?' Sharon asked, smiling brightly. 'Can we?'

Francesco didn't seemed surprised to see the two women, who sat down before hearing one way or the other. Penny looked nervously at Sharon for encouragement, who nodded in Francesco's direction as if to say, *talk to him.*

'Hi,' said Penny, with a small, self-conscious wave. 'How are you?'

Francesco smoothed his hair back. 'Ego-bruised,' he said,

having decided as he'd eaten dinner to address the elephant in the room. He had a feeling he'd end up talking with Penny again. Their energy was like two very strong magnets, pulling in the other's direction. 'But otherwise good,' he added, smiling. He wasn't above poking fun at himself now he'd had a drink and relaxed.

Before Penny could reply a woman walked over, crouching down to kiss both of Francesco's cheeks, saying: 'Chef Cipolla, always a pleasure. I meant what I said about needing a new pastry chef, you know!'

Oh, he's a chef too, thought Penny. *I wonder where.*

'I'll bear it in mind,' Francesco replied, grinning. 'Nice to see you, Brigitte.'

'You too darling. Goodnight!'

Penny's mind worked quickly. Cipolla. The woman had called him Chef Cipolla. She turned the name over in her mind and then it came to her. Chef Cipolla! It was *his* coconut and peach milk bun she had eaten maybe two years ago now, that was light and well-risen whilst also aromatic and deep – an exquisite example of the mastery of food, of baking. She'd always taken note of his name in food press since then and it was beginning to dawn on her that she did, in fact, know his face from promo shots and the odd feature. If she'd felt like he was familiar to her, it's because he was.

Chef Cipolla.

'Francesco Cipolla,' Penny said, understanding now. '*Conosco il tuo cibo!*' She slipped into the rudimentary Italian she'd learned on trips to Sicily with her Uncle David as a teen. *I know your food.* Francesco's eyebrows raised just enough for her to understand that her Italian had impressed him, which was exactly the effect she'd wanted. Francesco's work was quite legendary, and she'd had no idea it was he who'd dropped off the bread delivery that day. Safiya had had *Chef Cipolla* help her out. He was famous! Food world famous, but famous nonetheless.

Penny continued: *'Ce l'avevo a Bristol, due anni fa – complimenti.' I had it two years ago, in Bristol.*

'How about a little English for the cheap seats in the back?' Sharon said, looking from Penny to Francesco, understanding that the spark had caught and that she'd have to excuse herself any moment now. Sharon looked at his friend, who seemed otherwise tone-deaf, to see if he'd noticed too. He was leaning back in his armchair, his brandy about to spill, eyes gently closed. He was incredibly drunk.

'Sharon, this is Francesco Cipolla. He's one of the most famous pastry chefs in London. In England, maybe.'

'I accept the compliment,' Francesco said, eyes twinkling. Penny felt a stirring in the lowest part of her pelvis. He was grinning widely – exactly like that first morning they'd met.

'God I'm drunk,' said Francesco's friend, opening his eyes. 'Excuse me. Bathroom.'

The three of them watched him stand in silence. Sharon's phone buzzed.

'I'm just going to check on the kids, if you'll pardon me,' Sharon said, picking up her phone and taking her chance to leave them alone. 'I won't be a minute.' She reached out a hand towards Penny as she stood, squeezing it once and letting Penny squeeze it right back – their special code for 'Yup. I'm fine.' Penny turned back to Francesco and smiled again. He held his whisky in his hand, swirling it in his glass. Not knowing what else to do or say, Penny pressed the plunger of the cafetière on her table, releasing the aroma of coffee.

'Dofi said you two have known each other a long time,' Francesco said.

Penny's heart beat faster. 'Would you like any?' she said by way of reply, motioning to the coffee cups.

Francesco nodded. 'I would. Black, please.'

Penny filled the cup meant for Sharon and handed it to him. As he took it she said, 'You asked Dofi about me.' It wasn't a question.

Francesco shrugged lightly. 'I asked about you, yes.'

'Any other breaking news?'

Francesco pretended to think about it. 'You trained together,' he said. 'You opened Bridges two years ago, you don't post much on Facebook. Let's see. What else? Oh, yes. You're a terrible tipper, kick puppies, eat children for breakfast . . . have poor dental hygiene . . . and you have one of those funny heart-shaped signs in your living room that says "This home runs on love, laughter, and very cold gin".'

Penny giggled. 'What a torrid accusation!'

'Nothing a bit of mouthwash wouldn't fix.'

'I meant the sign. Did she say it was written in cursive?'

'Hey, don't diss them. I actually really like those signs. My parents have loads of them. So does my grandmother.'

'I think my mum used to have one, too,' Penny beamed. 'Anything else that Dofi scandalously revealed?'

Francesco stroked his chin in thought. 'She said you're a brilliant chef but don't push yourself – don't make that face, she said it kindly, like a proud but frustrated parent – and she said she *thinks* you're single, but let the record show I didn't ask the question directly. She volunteered that information of her own accord.'

'I should have texted you,' Penny said, guiltily. 'I am single. I'm sorry if I seemed rude.'

35

Francesco smiled. 'I'm a big boy. I'll manage. It's the name of the game, isn't it?'

'What, "Big Boy"?' Penny said. Francesco raised his eyebrows. She added: 'The name of the game, I mean.' What was it about him that made her say the cringiest things? *Big Boy, for crying out loud.* Maybe she should go to one of those flirting classes in West London, the ones that taught women how to be coquettish and cool. Penny definitely needed help.

'I can't tell if you're flirting with me,' he said.

Penny smiled. 'Neither can I.'

Francesco bit his lip, just slightly. 'I think you can.'

Penny shook her head. 'I'm not very good at it.'

Softly, he said, 'You're better than you think.'

Penny felt herself blush. 'Are you trying to unnerve me?'

'That wouldn't be very gallant, would it? No. I'm not trying to unnerve you. I think I'm actually a bit unnerved myself.'

Penny liked his forthrightness, and his vulnerability. 'Why were you delivering bread that day when you're *Chef Cipolla*?' she asked.

Francesco laughed. 'I was in the wrong place at the wrong time,' he replied.

'Meaning?'

'Meaning, I'd woken up at Safiya's house because I'd slept on her sofa the night before, after I'd got very, very drunk with her and Michael. Michael is my friend, he's the one that fell off the bike.'

'Michael. I see. And is he okay now?'

'He is, but his fragile sense of masculinity took a bashing and somehow, in amongst it all, I think he and Safiya broke up.'

Penny opened her mouth to speak, maybe to put in a good word for Stuart, but Sharon reappeared, phone in hand.

'Sorry to interrupt,' she said, barely sorry at all. 'Mia's been sick and is asking for her mama. Are you ready to go?'

Penny reached out her hand again, and as she shook Francesco's said, 'It was nice to meet you, Chef Cipolla. Again. You know. Properly.'

'Nice to see you,' he said, standing as the women gathered their things.

Penny looked at him.

'Well,' she said.

'Well,' Francesco repeated.

Sharon looked at them both, trying to figure out if they'd made good with each other or not.

'Well!' she said, impatient. She wanted to get home to her poorly child. 'It was very nice to meet you.' Turning to Penny she said, 'Sorry to make this a rush job, darling, but parenthood calls. Chop-chop.'

From the back of the taxi home Penny watched the streets of London whizz by, and took a breath.

'You've got this,' counselled Sharon, soothingly. 'It's just a text. And you have to be the one to make the move because he doesn't have your number, does he?' Penny nodded, knowing it was the right thing to do, despite saying she wasn't going to hold out for hope again. 'All you have to say is that it was nice to see him. You can do that, can't you?'

Penny thought about it.

'Yes.'

Life is about love, her mother used to tell her. Maybe that's why Penny felt so easily swayed to keep dating. She pushed thoughts of surrogates and babies and parenthood-for-one into a box in the back of her mind, a box that was labelled: 'Open In Case of Singledom'.

'Okay. Well. I'll just be sat quietly over here and scrolling my Instagram, so that you can get on with it.' She shifted her weight so that she faced away from Penny, towards the car door instead.

I'm sorry I never texted, Penny typed into a new message, thankful Stuart had made her save Francesco's number. *But better late than never, I suppose . . .*

The screen said Francesco was typing back.

I'd say so, came the reply. And then: *You're lucky I don't play games, otherwise I wouldn't be texting back until a week on Friday . . .*

Penny grinned at her screen. *I was silly not to text before. I felt scared!*

Because I'm obviously terrifying?

Yeah, obviously.

It took a moment for his response to come back. Penny jiggled her leg and let the familiar sensation of butterflies and uncertainty float up through her stomach. Her phone screen lit up. *Well, I'm thrilled to now be in possession of your number, so that a) my ego can dust itself off, and slightly more importantly b) we can, perhaps, go out? I presume that's why you've now decided to grace my phone with your digits . . .*

Penny felt a burst of glee. She was going to see him again! She'd taken a chance! She'd been a modern woman willing to believe and it was paying off! *I'd like that,* she said. *Yes.*

Okay good. I'll text you tomorrow to figure out the where and the when.

Perfect.

Islington became Newington Green, which became the

backstreets of Stoke Newington where the houses started to look familiar and soon Penny would be home.

Francesco? she added, deciding to show up to this fully since she was bothering to show up at all.

Yes Penny?

I'm really glad I ran into you.

I'm really glad I'm a clumsy oaf and knocked your bag onto the floor! he replied.

☺ *Night x,* she typed.

☺☺☺ *Talk tomorrow xxxxxx,* he said, and she truly hoped they would.

3

Give me a day and a time that you're free, and I'll do the rest, said his text, simply.

Hello! Penny replied. *All day Sunday or Monday. It's best when the café is closed.*

Please hold, Francesco typed. *Let me think of a plan. Definitely Sunday though.*

Penny sent back: *Should I pencil that in, or use pen?*

Francesco replied with the brain-exploding emoji.

How dare you. I'm a man of my word. You can write it in your diary with permanent marker.

Penny smiled. All morning she'd let herself sink into doubt as to whether Francesco actually would text her like he'd promised. Dating felt so full of booby traps that way. She hadn't texted the first time around because she'd been scared of being optimistic only for it to all come crashing down, then when she'd seen him again she'd tried to say as much because it felt like he was still interested. But was he? She kept pulling up their texts from the night before to try and calm herself down, but the thing about texts is that the tone of them depends on who is reading.

When Sharon messaged to see if they'd arranged a date yet, Penny had snapped at her by saying: *Don't tell me you don't remember that dating is psychological warfare! NO. HE. HASN'T. MAYBE HE NEVER WILL.*

Sharon replied: *Well, it is only 8 a.m. He could still be sleeping.*

Penny texted back: *I hate this!!!*

Up until the time her phone had pinged at two minutes to eleven, in the middle of brunch service, Penny had decided to write him off and, what's more, it would serve her right for being so optimistic in the first place. It wasn't even twelve hours between seeing him and his text. Traversing all of that wretched emotional landscape in less than half a day – no wonder dating knackered her.

He texted! she sent to Sharon, in between plating up an order of mushroom cornbread and accepting a delayed – and incorrect – order from the veg supplier.

Well thank god for that, Sharon replied. *I'll get the dogs to stand down* 😌

In her text thread with Francesco Penny typed out, *Blocked out in permanent marker it is, then.*

They talked back and forth for four days. Francesco's texts weren't heavy or over the top – just chatty. Penny was old enough to be wary of ending up with a pen-pal who couldn't possibly live up to the reality of himself, and was also cautious about being too clever or pithy with her responses to him. It was a fine balance. She wanted to be flirtatious and have fun, but if she spent too long thinking up what to reply to him she probably wouldn't live up to the image she was creating of herself by the time they actually met again. She tried to respond in the moment, not think about it too much, and not let her mind wander to where it could all go. That was the kiss of death with the texting thing – real life and texting life could often veer off in opposite directions and cause heartbreak.

They ended up with a sort of in-joke about prescriptions. Penny had told him at length about the supplier who had messed up the veg order and how she'd had to improvise their menu for the rest of the day at the last minute.

The doctor prescribes one menthol cigarette on the back step and a voice note to your sister, he'd texted, knowing her routine even though she'd only mentioned it once, and in the context of another conversation.

When he was home one night, buzzed after his shift, Penny had gotten up for the loo, and seen that he'd written, *Big decisions on a midnight snack: to have gorgonzola and pear in my toastie, or mozzarella and pickled peppers.*

Penny had replied: *The doctor prescribes two pieces of buttered toast and bed.*

Not long after it was decided that Francesco would come over on Sunday. He'd arrive at the flat bearing gifts of brunch, and they'd eat on her terrace under blankets if the weather was bright enough or inside if it wasn't. If they'd met on an app or dating site Penny wouldn't allow such a thing – it would be far too intimate. But since he'd been to the café anyway, and she only lived upstairs – and they'd seemed weirdly quite drawn to each other at Dofi's, not to mention how much fun it was swapping texts back and forth – well, it seemed like a safe enough plan.

'Do you want me to give you an emergency call twenty minutes after he arrives, to give you a get-out card in case you need it?' Sharon later asked, when she stopped by before closing to change the flowers in the café.

'Don't quote me on this,' Penny said. 'But I don't think we'll need it. I know it's famous last words, but, I have a really good feeling that he's not a shit.'

'High praise,' giggled Sharon as she arranged some extra-large buttercups in a big vase beside the coffee machine.

'That's what I said,' said Stuart, who was finishing up for the day and had heard text-by-text, hour-on-hour about all of this unfolding. 'I can't believe the bar for us men is that low.'

'It isn't,' said Sharon, right as Penny said, 'I know.'

'Avon calling!' Francesco trilled, as Penny opened the door to him on the day of their date.

'Good morning!' Penny said, unsure if she should hug him, or air kiss, or shake his hand. Francesco made the choice for her by handing her a bag and leaning to brush his cheek against hers as he did so.

'It's cold today,' he said, stepping over the threshold. 'I think we definitely have to eat inside.'

'You're the boss,' replied Penny, shuffling to close the door behind him. It put them in very close proximity to each other, and so when he made a hooting noise behind her it was practically in her ear.

'Ha!' he bellowed and she turned to see what he was reacting so strongly to. 'If you're offering to be second-in-command, I'll take it. Something tells me the arrangement won't last long, though.'

'You don't think I can be a deputy?' Penny said, aware of the musky, manly aroma of him. He was shorter than she remembered – not much taller than she was, and his shoulders were broad in a way that made him seem strong and self-possessed. Francesco pulled a face. 'As long as you don't ever call me bossy,' she pressed. 'Nobody uses that word for men. I prefer *instructive*. I can be an *instructive* second-in-command.'

'Oooooh,' nodded Francesco, rubbing at his stubble. 'Great word.' He looked her up and down. 'You look pretty, by the way.'

Penny was dressed in an oversized shirt and jeans, her feet bare. She'd done her make-up lightly and tried not to fuss too much with her hair – it was a Sunday morning, after all. It struck her that it was a funny time for a first date. Sunday mornings were for lovers, not strangers cooped up in narrow corridors.

'And you look very handsome,' she said, trying to remember to smile, despite her nerves. They were stood so close, and he smelled so good. She almost wanted to kiss him, just to see how it felt. But kissing can't be rushed – that's another thing her mother used to tell her. 'The best kisses happen long after you want them to,' she'd said to Penny and Clementine when they were little. 'So don't go giving them away willy-nilly. Except to me. You can always give mummy a kiss.' Penny wished she'd kissed her mother more.

'Shall we go upstairs?' he said to her. 'This bag is pretty heavy.'

Penny snapped out of herself. 'Follow me,' she commanded.

'So. Fun fact,' said Francesco as they went up to the flat. 'I actually don't know what "Avon calling" means. I just saw it in a movie once.'

Penny laughed.

'An American movie? Is that what you watched growing up?'

'Yeah, I'm an army brat. American TV was what we all

had in common – German, Greek, us Italians, even the English kids. No matter where the base was, the one constant was watching Nickelodeon together. I can barely speak Italian properly.'

'Ahhh, that explains the accent then,' Penny said.

'My mongrel accent? Yes ma'am, it does. Italy by the way of the rest of the world. I think we moved around ten times in eighteen years. I've been in London six years, now, and intend to be here six more if I can help it. It's the first place that has really felt like home.'

When they reached the top of the stairs they were side by side, Penny's home spread before them. She walked through the open-plan living room to the kitchen area.

'I ended up learning all my English slang from American TV,' Francesco continued, kicking off his shoes. 'We all did. It took me years to realize that you don't say "far out" when something is good, but that's what I learned from *That 70's Show*.'

'We don't say groovy, either . . .'

'Which I think is a shame, because that is a very nice word to say. The double-o in the middle. Groovy is a word that sounds . . . groovy. Nice place.' He took in Penny's flat. Being directly above the café, it was the exact same size and layout as downstairs. It was simply and tastefully done: lots of mis-matched framed photos and posters, a huge L-shaped sofa, wooden floors and candles and trinkets dotted everywhere. He walked through to join her at the breakfast bar.

'Okay, on the menu this morning we have,' he started, putting his bags on a chair and riffling through them, pulling things out, 'the ultimate breakfast board. Smoked salmon, smoked trout, some whitefish roe . . . everything to make my famous crème fraiche . . . sumac, for the red onion . . . and

46

these.' He presented Penny with a white bag. 'The best bagels you will ever consume.'

'Is it the Italian in you that makes everything a superlative? Ultimate this, best that . . .'

'Well, what is life for, if it isn't for having the best of everything?'

'That's literally the opposite of British culture, which is essentially "make do and don't complain".'

'Yes, I've noticed that. Very odd. Can you put this water in the fridge so it is cold when we eat? Also, I need an apron, please.'

'Yes, chef,' Penny said, remembering that she'd pledged to be his sous.

Together they pulled out plastic chopping boards and wooden serving plates and chose glasses and set the table in harmony, a playlist softly humming in the background – a playlist, Francesco had explained, that was 'the only one worth making food to. If my food tastes of love, one must hear love, too.'

'Far out,' Penny said.

'Bugger off,' Francesco smiled, enjoying how Penny wasn't afraid to give as good as she got.

'It's nice to be cooked for, instead of being the one doing the cooking,' Penny said, watching Francesco work. 'Especially in my own home.'

'It's my love language. Acts of service are my way of caring.'

'Oh, love languages – yeah, Sharon made me take a test about those once. I think the way I show I care is . . .'

Francesco interrupted, 'Wait! Can I guess?'

'Go on then.'

'There's five, right? Five basic ways most people demonstrate affection? So wait. It's acts of service, so like, doing

47

things for the other person ... quality time together ... words of affirmation, which could be yours – I feel like you respond well to words that confirm how excellent you are, since you're a chef and all. What else? Oh, the sex one ...'

'Physical touch,' Penny supplied.

'Is that your love language?'

'Maybe.'

Francesco waved a knife at her. 'It so is,' he said. 'Now I think about the other night, how you kept touching my arm ...'

Penny feigned outrage. 'I did not!'

'You totally did,' Francesco said. 'That's how I knew it was okay to flirt with you.'

'You said you weren't trying to unnerve me!'

'I lied,' he ventured, wiggling his eyebrows in a way to communicate he wasn't sorry for it, either. Penny's phone rang before she could investigate the matter further.

'Oh,' she said, looking at the screen, intending to switch it to silent. 'Do you mind? I will be five seconds.' Francesco made a gesture to signify that that was fine. Before she answered she added, 'And this conversation isn't over, mister.'

Francesco pouted at her provocatively, and then carried on with his prep.

'Penny! Darling!' said Uncle David after she answered. 'Just thought I'd catch you before lunch service!' Penny's Uncle David ran a gastro pub called The Red Panda in Derbyshire, which was where she'd learned about food and honed her natural talent for flavours and textures growing up. 'Eric's birthday next month, when Clemmie is home – shall we do it here? Or shall we come down to London for it?'

Eric, David's husband, loved a big event for his birthday. Penny said, 'Davvy? It's not a great time right now actually.

Can I take the question under advisement and let you know?'

'Yes, of course darling,' Uncle David replied. 'Just wanted to tell you we miss you!'

Penny smiled. 'I miss you too. We'll make a few nights of it for Eric's birthday, okay? Spend some proper time together.'

'We'd like that, Pooh-Bear. Let me know what you and Clem are thinking.'

'I will!' Penny sing-songed. 'Have a great shift!'

She hung up, flicked the ringer to her phone off, and made a point of putting it face down and out of reach.

'My uncle,' she said, as way of explanation.

'So nice you're close to your wider family,' Francesco replied, slicing quickly at the chopping board. 'Here,' he said. 'Try this. It's the best salmon you'll ever taste.' He offered up the flat of the knife to Penny who swiped the salmon on offer.

'That *is* good,' Penny said as she chewed. 'That might actually be worthy of the superlative. Where'd you get this?'

'I can't reveal my suppliers, I'm afraid,' Francesco replied. 'And anyway, you were saying? About your uncle?'

She hadn't been saying anything, really, and yet she confided in him for reasons she couldn't explain. Probably because he wasn't prying, he was just chatting. It felt low-stakes. Just two people swapping tales.

'He's my dad's brother, but my dad did a runner when I was a kid and so Davvy took in me and my sister. He's more of a dad than my biological one, if that makes sense. I don't see him enough though. I feel guilty about it.'

'I think everyone feels that way about their family,' said Francesco. 'Especially chefs. We work such weird, unsociable hours. We live ghost lives in a lot of ways.'

Penny nodded. She was glad he understood. Francesco

took the big board across to the table and she followed, pouring orange juice into tall glasses for them and grabbing cloth napkins from the credenza.

'He does drive me crazy though, too – so don't think I am a total angel.'

'Crazy how?'

'He's forever on a campaign to get me to move up to Derbyshire to run his pub. Doesn't understand why I don't want the pressure of such a massive place. We fall out about it every three or four months, and then make up and don't breathe a word of it until the next disagreement is due.'

'You talk about him with a lot of love, though.'

'Well, yeah,' Penny said. 'He's a legend.'

Francesco tenderly chopped some tomatoes at the table and salted them after artfully fanning them out.

'And your biological dad left?'

Penny didn't typically offer up that information to people she was dating. It was private, and she knew men immediately leaped to the conclusion that she must have daddy issues.

'My mum got secondary breast cancer when I was nine, and by the time I was ten she had died from it. I think my dad knew it was going that way, because he left before she passed away. I think . . . Well, actually, I don't know what to think, because I haven't seen him since. But in his spineless-ness I got the best father a girl could ask for. I'd walk over hot coals for Uncle David. Both my sister and I would.'

'But she travels a lot, you said?'

'She does. She's back all the time though, and we'll all get together for my uncle's husband's birthday in a few weeks. He'll be sixty-five and will milk every second of it. He's brilliant.'

They talked easily and happily, occupying the space of

Penny's home together as if they'd done this many times before, eating their brunch and drinking their tea and talking their talk. He kept looking at her intently, asking questions and listening to her answers, nodding as he processed what she said, laughing when she was being funny, and saying lovely, insightful things when Penny asked him about his life, his job, his ambitions. He seemed to be enjoying himself, and so Penny let herself enjoy it, too.

'This is good. You. Me. This,' Penny offered, letting the spring sunshine warm her face as it bounced off the water. They'd decided to walk off brunch with a meander to the reservoir. It was freezing – she'd needed a scarf and a hat – but bright, which made all the difference.

'I think so too,' Francesco answered, smiling. 'And to think it almost didn't happen because you weren't going to text me . . .'

Penny let out a 'ha!' sound. 'No! I would have done!' she said, playfully hitting his arm.

'No you wouldn't! A month had already passed!'

'I was building up to it!' she insisted.

'Lies! You were blowing me off.'

'Okay,' Penny cackled. 'I was blowing you off.'

Francesco's face fell. 'You were?'

She shrugged. 'Oh, I don't know. We'd spoken three words to each other before Stuart cornered you to write your number down. How was I supposed to know you were actually interested?'

'Ah, yes, I can see how me writing my number down and saying "I look forward to hearing from you" must have given off all kinds of mixed signals.'

Penny rolled her eyes. 'So you just . . . gave me your

51

number? How often do you do that? Because that sort of nonchalance makes me think you do it all the time.'

'Gotta take your chances,' Francesco said, moving a branch out of the way for them both.

'So you *do* do it all the time!'

'I do not often get invited to leave my number for good-looking café owners who hold eye contact for an uncomfortable length of time, no,' Francesco said. 'But it felt like there was a connection, or something. I don't know. And then when I saw you at Dofi's restaurant, too. When stuff like that happens it feels like sort of a cosmic obligation to take a leap of faith, don't you think?'

'What if the leap means you fall and break an ankle?'

'Dark,' Francesco lamented, shaking his head. He was mocking her.

'I'm serious! I'm thirty years old. I've leapt many, many times, and somehow it never pays off. I'm not like "woe-is-me" or anything, I just mean . . . How do you stay optimistic? Not the general you, I mean you, specifically. How do you, Francesco Cipolla, stay optimistic in matters of the heart?'

They arrived at a small gate and Francesco went through it, and then turned and leaned against it so that Penny couldn't. She wasn't expecting it, and so wound up bumping up almost nose-to-nose with him. She looked at him.

'How do I stay optimistic in matters of the heart . . .' Francesco replied, his voice lowered.

Her stomach lurched. He made it feel so easy. He was so comfortable in his own skin, wore the pressure of their date so lightly. Maybe he didn't feel any pressure at all.

'Yeah,' Penny said. 'Because your optimism is . . . attractive.'

'Oh?' said Francesco, so close now that Penny could feel his breath on the space between her top lip and nose. She realized she had tilted her head to the side, just slightly, ready to be kissed by him. They held themselves millimetres apart, and Penny stopped breathing altogether. She waited for him to lean the tiniest bit forward but instead he held his position, the top corner of his mouth rising up into a half-smile, and Penny realized he was waiting for *her* to kiss *him*. She had to go the last half-inch. And so she held onto the fence and pushed her weight to the front of her feet, towards her toes, to make herself reach him. She gently edged herself up towards his mouth so that her lips met his, and there they stayed, tasting one another, giving in to each other's breath until a man coughed loudly and deliberately and said, good-naturedly, 'Pardon me but, do you think I could get past?'

They pulled apart and burst out laughing.

'Sorry,' said Francesco, moving out of the way to let Penny through, and then the man with his Bedlington Terrier. 'There you go.'

'Enjoy yourselves,' the man said, and it made them look at each other and laugh again.

'Did that answer your question?' Francesco said.

Penny grinned. 'I can't tell if it answered my question or posed about eighty thousand new ones,' she countered.

'I see. Well. Only time will tell . . .'

'That's very true.'

After that they walked hand-in-hand, happy in their mutual silence. What else was there to say? Penny was happy. In that moment, everything was perfect.

4

And so their love affair began. 'It almost feels too good to be true,' Penny told her sister on one of their Personal Podcasts. 'But, easy doesn't mean bad, does it? Maybe easy just means right?'

'I think it's lovely,' Clementine had replied, somewhere north of Beijing where she'd been called in to oversee a planning issue with the local government. 'And if you're not sleeping together yet at least you're not getting – oh gosh, what word does Sharon use? Dickmatized! At least you're not getting dickmatized. I think it's actually quite romantic, taking the time to get to know somebody before you go to bed with them. I think the new sexual revolution is actually about realizing there's more to intimate relationships than sex.'

Sharon had guffawed when Penny had reported that back.

'I love your sister,' she said, wiping tears of amusement from her eyes, 'and I, too, am thrilled you're not getting dickmatized. But let's face it, you're not going to marry a shit shag, are you? It's a *bit* important.'

She held up her thumb and forefinger to emphasize 'a bit', looked down at her gesture, and then wordlessly increased it in size.

'Give me a minute,' Penny squealed, knocking her hand away jokingly. 'Five days post-kiss hardly makes me the Virgin Mary.'

'No,' said Sharon. 'You're right. Enjoy it for what it is! The world could end tomorrow!'

'Well, if the world was to end tomorrow . . .' Penny sniggered, and they both hooted with laughter, knowing that the imminent end of the world might speed things up a bit.

At home that night, as Penny lounged in her cosiest tracksuit, idly wondering what to watch on telly for the hour before bed, her phone rang, and Francesco's face popped up on screen. Penny stared at it. He was calling her? *Who calls anyone anymore?* she mused. She loved hearing from him and everything, but a phone call? At least a Personal Podcast could be listened to in one's own time. The only people who made phone calls anymore, Penny had assumed, were the boomer generation, like Uncle David. She continued to stare at it, not knowing what to do. Penny knew actual husband and wives who didn't even talk on the phone.

As it stopped ringing and 'one missed call' appeared as a notification, Penny turned over the possibilities.

Did you just try to call me? she texted.

Yeah. It's okay, Francesco replied. *I just finished my shift. I can try later if you're free?*

Penny was confused. *To talk on the phone?* she replied.

That's what normally happens when one person dials the other, and that other person picks up, yeah.

Oh. Yeah, sure. Later.

Penny switched from her WhatsApp with Francesco to voice note her sister.

'This is not a drill,' she said, down the phone. 'The Italian wants to talk on the phone with me. We have a psychopath on our hands. Repeat: we have a psychopath on our hands.'

Her phone screen lit up with Francesco's face again.

'Gah!' Penny said, holding it like a live bomb. 'Um . . . um . . .' She slid the button to answer. 'Hi!' she said, too enthusiastically.

'I don't know if I'm more offended that you'd refer to me as a psychopath, or that you don't even use my proper name to do it.'

'Ah. Yes. Well.' She could hear his smile down the line.

'I take it you don't like talking on the phone, then,' he said.

'Not so much, no. Bit retro for me. I think Uncle David is the only person who actually calls me, you know.'

'I just wanted to hear your voice.'

Penny grinned. 'Well now I've accidentally sent you a voice note, you have done.' *He just wanted to hear her voice!* Her heart leapt into her throat.

'What are you doing?'

'Pottering.'

'Uh-huh,' he said. She thought he was waiting for her to continue, but then she could faintly hear him say 'good evening' to somebody and then the hum of an engine, and she realized he was distracted by getting on the bus. She waited for him to say something else as he got settled, but he didn't. He was waiting for her to speak. She took a breath. Penny had talked to Stuart only that afternoon about being unafraid to show Francesco who she really was. That meant being cute and flirtatious with him as well as letting him get a glimpse of some of the 'realer', less sexy stuff, too.

'I get tired sometimes,' she said, deciding now was the time to tell him, cards on the table and all that. 'So I needed a quiet night.'

'I see,' he said.

'I was pretty sick a couple of years back. It still gets me, sometimes.'

Finally Francesco said a full sentence. 'You've alluded to that a couple of times actually. I didn't want to pry, but I have to admit I've been curious. Was it serious?'

'Stage two breast cancer at twenty-five. So now my body doesn't like me to get carried away. I don't think I've been getting as much rest as I need lately so, you know, I'm getting some down-time.'

'Twenty-five,' Francesco said, his shock evident. 'That's so young.'

'Yeah. About as young as my mum was when she first got it, except hers came back and . . .' Well. Francesco knew the rest.

'I didn't know you'd had it too,' he marvelled. 'That's a really shitty hand to be dealt.'

'It was. And it was tough.' It felt good to say that. It wasn't lost on Penny that for somebody who'd minutes ago said she didn't like to talk on the phone, it suddenly felt really good to be chatting to Francesco. That was the thing about him, she contemplated – all the rules she thought she had were increasingly not applicable. Stuart had said as much, too. He'd basically accused Penny of self-sabotaging every relationship she had by withholding information or affection and then blaming the other person for it not working out. It was a surprisingly insightful observation for him to make, and it had made Penny's blood boil for about ten seconds before she felt a wave of acknowledgement rush over her.

What Stuart had said had some truth. She could begrudgingly admit that. Penny could hear the shouts of lively teenagers in the background as she waited for Francesco's reaction. She put a cushion behind her head and stretched out across the sofa.

'I can't begin to imagine,' he said, as the noise behind him died down. 'Do you mind talking about it?'

'I can't say it's all that thrilling.'

'Well, one day, I want to know everything about you.' He always seemed to know the right things to say. Penny felt relieved that she didn't have to share any more, as well as a vague sense of gratitude towards Stuart that she'd shared at least a little bit. 'But for now,' he carried on, 'tell me where you are, right this second. This bus ride home is freezing and I need the entertainment.'

Penny looked around. 'Well,' she said, 'I'm sat on my couch with a bottle of water – hydration station over here – and the remote is in my hand because I've been watching movie trailers instead of picking an actual movie, and I lit a very luxurious not one but two candles. Different fragrances, too. It's called *layering* apparently.'

'Sounds snuggly.'

'It is. I'm very good at snuggly. You could even go as far as to call me the Queen of Snuggly-Ville.' She pulled the blanket off the arm of the nearby chair and put it over her legs so that she was even snugglier.

'And how does one get the opportunity to visit Snuggly-Ville?'

'Oh, well, it's incredibly difficult to get in. Very exclusive.'

'Do you want company? Somebody to do nothing with?'

Penny sat upright. Her hair was unwashed and she was hardly dressed to impress.

'I mean, I'm going to be very boring company,' she said. 'But . . . I do kind of want to see you.'

'I kind of want to see you too. Shall I hop in a cab once I've showered? I have a discount code for a Bolt.' He paused. 'Not that you're not worth the full price Uber, ha. Have you eaten? I can bring dinner? Or . . . foot lotion! I can bring foot lotion!'

Penny balked at the suggestion. 'Foot lotion?'

'I'll give you a foot massage.'

'Francesco, I'm not having sex with you. Not tonight. I am way, way, *way* too tired for that.' The idea of him naked, on top of her, made her skin prickle in anticipation – but she was serious. She hadn't fostered emotional intimacy as a gateway to a shag. Plus, she probably had about another hour and a half in the tank before she passed out.

'Just for your feet, Penny. Physical touch as a love language, remember? Can you give me some credit, please? It wouldn't be your feet I'd rub if I was trying to get you into bed.'

'You're doing that flirting thing again, aren't you?'

'Is it working?'

Penny looked around the flat. It was actually pretty tidy – she had a cleaner come for two hours once a week, to help stop the place getting really bad, and they'd been just yesterday. Penny was a mess, but her house wasn't. If she dimmed the big light a bit more and lit the lamps instead, they could lie on the sofa and drink tea and . . .

'Yes. It is. Come over. Just an hour or two.'

'Perfect,' he said. 'You just kick me out if I overstay my welcome, okay?'

'Okay,' she replied. 'Deal.'

*

60

'I can offer you water, or beer,' Penny said, walking Francesco up the stairs to her place. 'In fact, anything you can find in the fridge that doesn't require a glass and/or my help is all yours.'

'Water is fine. I'll get it. Could I just have one thing first?'

'If it's within reach, you can have anything you want.'

Francesco tipped his head to the side and licked his lips.

Penny lowered her voice and whispered, 'Oh. Well. Yes, you can certainly have *that*.'

They kissed hello and then Penny flopped down onto the sofa and watched Francesco manoeuvre himself through her kitchen. It was nice to be exhausted but to have company. It was nice that she hadn't lied about how she was feeling, or put on a show for him. She'd done that enough times before in the past – even on her worst days she'd let nobody other than her uncle and her sister know just how low she felt, how helpless and miserable and defeated she often was. That was why she didn't have hundreds of friends – it was too much hard work to hide the truth of herself and her limitations. She'd rather have a close-knit group who knew her completely than a huge group of acquaintances who knew her hardly at all. Like Sharon – Sharon accepted her, warts and all, and it was one of the most rewarding friendships of Penny's life.

'Can I get you anything?' Francesco asked, putting down two glasses of water he'd added lemon, ice, and mint from the balcony herb garden to. 'The kettle is boiling. Tea?'

'Tea,' she replied. 'Yeah. With milk, please. There's a tiny plastic carton on the top shelf of the fridge. Or there's oat milk in there too, if you prefer.'

Francesco fussed around, making tea and peering into

plastic Tupperware boxes in the fridge and asking after their contents. He tried some of her *Pasta Yiayia* and brought over the box of tiramisu that Sharon had given her.

They talked about the food, and about the playlist Penny had on. ('It's from the second season of *Master of None*,' she told him, and he said he hadn't seen it. 'You haven't seen it? Oh Francesco,' she gushed. 'You'll love it. We'll watch it here, one weekend. Okay?' Francesco had smiled and said yes, they should do. The meaningful pause afterwards meant they'd both clocked the intention to see each other again, like it was a no-brainer. Of course they'd watch *Master of None* together! Of course they'd spend a day in her house, on the sofa, doing just that!)

'It's so badass that this is your life,' Francesco said, as he pulled her feet up onto his lap for the massage he'd promised. 'This apartment, Bridges, the way you talk about your uncle and your sister and Sharon . . . you've really got your shit together, haven't you?'

'Thank you. That's a kind thing to say.'

'I'm not very happy at work. I think I'm sensitive to everyone else's lives because I'm trying to build up the courage to change some things about my own.'

Penny nodded. 'It's a horrible feeling when things don't sit right. But I'd have thought working under Anthony Farrah would have been a total dream, no?'

Francesco scrunched up his nose and lightly shook his head. 'I want my own place,' he said. 'It's amazing to me that you do. It's really inspiring.'

'What's stopping you?'

'Money,' Francesco lamented. 'And courage.'

'The first thing I understand,' Penny replied. 'I got a big medical insurance pay-out, so that's how I made this dream come true. The second thing, though – I'm fairly sure that has to come from you.'

'You mean you don't have any extra courage stored in another Tupperware that you can lend me?'

'Afraid not. Do feel free to take the pasta you liked, though.'

'No courage, but plenty of sustenance. Got it.'

Penny giggled. 'Can't climb the mountains of the mind until you've been properly fed,' she said. 'And I'm not just saying that because food is my business.'

'I don't know what I'd do if I wasn't in the kitchen,' Francesco pondered. 'If I wasn't a chef I think I'd still end up in restaurants, maybe front of house or as a mixologist or something.'

'Oh,' said Penny. 'I totally know what else I would do.'

'Go on, then.'

'Number one, I'd be a beautician. I just think it must be so satisfying to help people feel better about themselves through something as straightforward as waxed legs or a different arch in their eyebrows. Number two, I'd be a teacher. I don't know for what subject because, to be honest, I wasn't hugely academic at school myself. Maybe home economics? Do they even still teach that? Or, number three, if I didn't own Bridges, I would . . .'

'Run away and join the circus,' Francesco supplied.

'Noooooo.'

'Become a nun, for the habit?'

'Tempting, but no.'

'Stunt double?'

'Not that, either. Counsellor, I think. For cancer survivors. Pay it forward and all that.'

Francesco absorbed this information. 'You'd be a great counsellor,' he said. 'I'd trust you.'

'Cheers,' she replied.

'Was it horrible?' he asked. 'Is it still horrible? You said about being tired . . .'

'My joints seize, sometimes,' Penny explained. 'I don't sleep through the night well – even by myself, let alone when I'm sharing a bed. And I'm not very good at sharing a bed, even though I love waking up with someone. I sweat. From every pore. Sometimes I forget people's names. My libido is pretty up and down. I feel bloated for seemingly no reason, and sometimes just . . . weird. Empty. Anyone going through treatment right now would kill to be on the other side. When you're in it, all you want is for it to be over. But nobody told me about this bit. The aftermath.' She was determined not to be emotional, to not give cancer another tear. She gathered herself. 'I was declared cancer-free four years ago now, but I have hormones injected every month because it was a hormonally-driven strain that I might always be in battle with, so I'm effectively in early menopause. Which I'm sure is very erotic to know.' There it was – more of her truth.

Francesco nodded. He didn't offer her advice or solutions, or insist she look on the bright side: *she was here! She was alive!* He just kept rubbing her feet and letting her talk. It felt good. Not the foot rub – though that was wonderful. But to give air to all of her feelings: sometimes she worried that saying all this out loud would make it grow. That shedding sunlight on her anxieties would encourage them. But as she spoke it felt like a relief. She did more pretending than she gave herself credit for.

'I'm lucky to be here. I know that. And I do my best to get on. I'm in a fortunate situation, and I had Uncle David, and my sister, and Eric all rallying around me. I'd never felt

64

so looked after. Protected. Loved. But I'm also human. And I still find this hard. Harder than I make it look, sometimes. And, well, you may as well know that it was as soon as I got diagnosed that my ex ended things with me. Kind of like how my dad left my mum, weirdly. I was always the strong one, the cheerleader in our relationship, but then he couldn't do the same for me. Not that I'd have wanted him to stay out of pity, but it was pretty devastating. And embarrassing. I haven't really had a relationship since.'

Francesco shook his head gently in disbelief. 'Wow. That's . . . a lot.'

'Yeah. I think Mo had wanted to end it for a while and then had to do it as soon as I got diagnosed or else he'd be the monster who dumped me halfway through treatment. So. Now you know all the skeletons in my closet.'

'You're a strong woman, though. Not in spite of it all. Because of it.'

Penny shrugged.

'You're a strong woman who knows it's okay to be vulnerable. Not a lot of people understand that. I think it's a very special trait.'

'I don't know about that. I feel like a spikey hedgehog most of the time – balled up, not letting anyone really help.'

'Thanks for telling me. Thanks for letting me ask.'

'Thanks for caring,' she replied, gently.

Francesco nodded. 'Is this pressure still okay?' He motioned to her foot.

'Yeah, that's good. I might need you here every night.'

'Easy tiger.'

Penny leaned her head against the side of the sofa, closing her eyes, breathing deeply and smiling just slightly. Francesco studied her, and Penny caught him doing so as she opened one eye.

'It's rude to stare.' She smiled as she said it.

Francesco didn't smile back. He thought about something, and then decided to say it: 'I think I could fall in friendship with you, you know.'

Friendship? Penny thought, alarmed. Her whole body tensed.

'Oh, you mean this isn't . . .' Penny opened her eyes properly and watched him rub her foot, which had tensed up in horror. Was he telling her this wasn't romantic? That he just wanted to be her friend?

'No,' he said. 'It is. Sorry. I didn't mean . . .' he trailed off. 'Okay, you told me some stuff, so now I'll tell you some stuff, okay?'

'. . . Okay.'

'I've never had a proper teammate before, you know? Somebody who I fancied and wanted to rip their clothes off and who I laughed with, yeah, but never somebody who was also just my mate. Because the passion and stuff fades, doesn't it – or at least, it changes – and I have this theory that before I fall in love with somebody – my person – I'd like to fall in friendship with them first. As the basis of it.'

'So you . . . don't wanna sleep with me.' She said it as a statement.

Francesco laughed. 'I do not have words for the extent to which I want to sleep with you, Penny Bridge,' he replied, and relief washed over her. 'But also, I just want you to know that it's easy to be with you. And I just think you're the coolest. I really respect you. Which sounds like the corniest thing in the world to say because of course I've respected anyone I've gone out with but, I mean . . . I feel like my best version of myself with you. Not like I need you to be better, to be my life coach, but . . . even after knowing you this short amount of time, I suppose you make me play my best game. Because you're a good player too.'

'Francesco. It would be my honour and privilege to fall in friendship with you right back.' She reached out to one of his lotion-covered hands and laced her fingers with his. 'I'm very pleased to be spending time with you.'

'Is that the stupidest thing you've ever heard? Falling in friendship?' He held his free palm up in question. 'Wait, don't answer that. It's lame city, I know.'

Penny closed her eyes again and smiled. 'No,' she said. 'It's not.'

Francesco didn't say anything in response, he simply absorbed what she'd said. Penny moved so that instead of sitting at the opposite end of the sofa she was curled up beside him, her head on his chest. He wiped his hands on the cloth he'd thought to leave on the coffee table and then tenderly played with her hair. He watched the flame from the candles dance as they burned down. On the speaker the notes of an old Italian song he recognized from his childhood played – his parents had owned it on CD in the car. It was from a film called *Senza Sapere Niente Di Lei* – 'Without Knowing Much About Her'. His parents had always been very happily married, and he'd always had the sense they loved each other, but that they worked to like each other, too. That's what he wanted for himself.

He noticed Penny's breathing had deepened. She was asleep. Francesco listened to the inhale and exhale noises she made. He let the rhythm of her breathing wash over him, becoming a meditation.

Him.

Her.

He felt peaceful, and protective.

Eventually, seeing the time on the big clock by her TV, Francesco moved Penny's head over to a cushion and slipped away, covering her with the blanket. Tip-toeing, he cleared away their empty water glasses and put them in the sink, blew out the candles, and checked the back door to the small terrace was locked. He took out the key and put it soundlessly on the sideboard. Then he let himself out – but before he headed down the stairs he looked back to where she slept, committing the moment to memory.

'Hey sis,' Clementine's voice came through the phone. 'That was a superb voice note you sent – you continue to sound . . . I don't know? Really dreamy? But like, in a good way. In a *I'm not worried* way. He just sounds like a real stand-up guy, and I know we don't know many of those – well, many straight ones – but if you think he might be one of them, I am totally on board. Everything here is great, but I'm ready to come home for a bit. I'll be back for two whole weeks on Saturday! Can you imagine? I don't think I've had two weeks in my own bed all year yet. I'm excited for us all to get together for Eric's birthday, too. Why don't we go up there? We never go up there. And, when I'm back, I'd like to talk to you. I've got an idea. No – a suggestion. Just something I want to run by you. Also I am desperate to come and see the café and eat your food and be on your sofa and have you over for dinner. I've really missed you lately! More than usual. I just want my big sister. Okay, that's all from me. Keep me up to date with this handsome Italian situation, please. Does he take bookings for the foot massages? Love you. Bye!'

*

Penny listened to the message right before the first breakfast order came through, and spent the next few hours wondering what Clementine's 'suggestion' might be. Penny was the older sister but it was Clementine who acted like it. It hadn't always been that way. As with almost everything in her life, most things changed with the cancer. Penny had been so full of life up until then. Ambitious, but without taking anything too seriously – she'd loved working in kitchens and learning about food and then playing hard, too, taking impromptu trips to new cities and staying up all night. She'd been a textbook twenty-something until she wasn't. Life was divided into 'Before I Got Ill' and 'After I Got Ill', and in the after bit, Clementine definitely became the protector, and Penny had had no choice but to let her.

'Pen, there's a bloke out there who says he has to compliment the chef,' Stuart said from the doorway of the kitchen, a tea towel in his hands, interrupting her last dishes of the day. 'Says your heirloom carrots are the best he's ever had, for a little café.'

'You what?' Penny replied. 'He said that? For a little café?'

'He's a handsome bastard. Italian, I think.'

Penny smiled in understanding. 'There's ten minutes left of service. Let me just get this Panzanella out and then tell Francesco I'll be right up.'

Stuart started to leave. He turned around and said, 'Pen?'

Penny looked up.

'I like him.'

She grinned. 'Me too.'

Penny pulled a baking sheet lined with kale from the oven and put it on the counter, arranging it on a plate with radicchio leaves and beetroot before sprinkling croutons over the top and spooning smoked ricotta on the side. She lost herself in the music of her art, drizzling over olive oil and saba, finishing the plate with flaked salt.

'Service!' she called out, and Estelle, a petite blonde with half her head shaved, appeared to whisk it away.

Penny looked around the kitchen. It had been a busier service than normal, and her section was a mess.

'Bobby?' she said in the direction of the pot-wash. 'I'm just running upstairs for a sec. Do what you can over there and then I'll sweep and mop. I know you need to leave by half past.'

'Cheers, boss,' said the kitchen-hand from behind a mound of sudsy water. 'I promise I wouldn't have asked if it wasn't important.'

'I know,' Penny said. 'It's cool. Thank you.'

Penny headed up the six or so stairs from the lower ground level kitchen at the back to the main part of the café out front. Stuart saw her as she turned the corner and from behind the counter tipped his head in the direction of the window where, at a table meant for four, sat Francesco on his own. She walked over, smiling.

'Can I buy you a coffee?'

'Hello, you,' Penny replied. 'What are you doing here?'

'I told you I needed to eat here,' he said, as way of explanation. 'And now I have. Penny, you're brilliant. I didn't want you to know it was me you were feeding. I wanted to be treated like any other regular guy.'

'Yes, I would have been rather distracted to know I was cooking for the world's best foot masseuse.'

'You understand my logic, then,' retorted Francesco. He hadn't shaved that day and his five o'clock shadow made him look rugged and outdoorsy. He dabbed at his lips with his napkin delicately, the gesture at odds with his appearance. It was – *oh god,* Penny cringed, *I need to come up with another bloody word for him* – disarmingly sexy.

'You left without saying goodbye last night,' Penny said. She pulled up the chair opposite. Francesco looked like a framed picture with the street in early bloom behind him, the light hazy as evening threatened to arrive soon, his jacket in a pile beside him.

'Like I said in my text, I didn't want to wake you.'

'I'm a terrible host,' Penny said. 'Falling asleep on you like that.'

'Nah,' Francesco replied. 'I'm glad you felt comfortable enough to do so.'

They stared at each other, beaming.

'It's good here,' Francesco said. 'It's really, really good. The food, the vibe, the service. You deserve all the hype.'

'Did you hear that, Stu?' Penny said, turning around. 'Great service, he said!'

Stuart raised a hand to say he'd heard.

'What's it really like, having your own place? I know we talked about it a bit last night but honestly, chef-to-chef, are you satisfied?'

'Chef to chef?'

Francesco nodded.

'It's the fucking best.'

Bobby interrupted them then, rounding the corner of the stairs and lingering at the table on his way out of the door. 'Thanks again, boss. It's pretty decent down there, but it's not perfect.'

'Give your mother my love,' Penny said. 'And tell her I'm determined to get that chowder recipe out of her sooner or later!'

'Will do, boss. Cheers.'

'Well,' Penny sighed. 'That's my cue. I'm a kitchen porter

71

down and I get too tired if I linger, so I'm sorry that I can't stay and drink coffee with you.'

'Oh, well – let me help,' Francesco said, standing. 'I don't have anywhere to be. I'm not going in until five thirty. I can play kitchen porter with you.'

Penny raised her eyebrows and lowered her chin. 'You want to help clean the kitchen?'

'Sure!'

'On an afternoon when you are not working at your job, which is in a kitchen?'

'Come on,' he said, already walking away. 'Many hands make light work and all that.'

Penny shrugged. 'As long as it isn't a pity hand,' she said after him, meaning: don't feel sorry for me because I told you I used to have cancer.

He turned around and caught Stu's eye as he did so, winking at him and so bringing him into the joke. 'Have you ever been told you complicate things too much? I just wanna hang out with you! I don't care what we do!'

Penny felt weirdly suspicious, but conceded. 'Okay,' she said, knowing Stuart was looking at her and deliberately ignoring his smugness. She knew he felt proud of the hand he'd had in her current contentedness. 'If you're sure.'

'I'm so sure.'

'You could just stand and keep me company as I finish off,' Penny said, after they'd assessed what needed doing and she'd pulled her apron back on.

'Pass me an apron, too,' Francesco replied. 'Like I said: many hands make light work. And maybe being behind the scenes of the famous Bridges Café means I'll get some insider info on how the magic is made.'

'I guard my secrets with my life,' Penny warned, wiggling her eyebrows.

'I have my ways of seduction,' said Francesco, taking a step closer to her.

'I don't doubt it,' Penny laughed, and she didn't. She leaned forward and kissed him deeply, pulling back before she got carried away. He tasted like coffee and promise.

'Mmmmm,' Francesco smiled. He added, 'One more please.'

She leaned in and kissed him again, the length of her body pressed up against his. He put one hand behind her neck and held her to him.

'I find your payment terms very favourable,' he joked in hushed tones when she pulled away again, his hand lingering on her waist. His touch made the top of Penny's thighs ache.

Sex-y.

Francesco set about with the last of the pans in the dishwash area as Penny sprayed and wiped down all the surfaces, and he'd been right: working together meant they got done in super quick time.

'What are we listening to?' he asked across the kitchen, after about ten minutes of companionable effort.

'The High Low podcast,' Penny replied.

'They're funny,' he said, resuming his work.

Penny snuck glances of him from the other side of the workspace. She watched him crumple his face, concentrating on the two women coming from the speaker talking about the high maternal death rate in black mothers. He nodded slightly, as if agreeing with the point at hand, and Penny saw the way it made the muscle of his shoulders ripple under his t-shirt, how his neck moved.

'It's rude to stare,' he said, not looking up from the sink. 'You taught me that.'

'Caught red-handed,' Penny said.

He flashed her a smile, elbow deep in the bubbles from the washing up.

Francesco loaded the last few pieces into the dishwasher, pulled the plug on the sink, and then rinsed everything down with the shower head attached to the plug.

'Let's go outside for your smoke,' he said, after Estelle and Stuart had come down to say goodbye for the day.

'I'll mop us out and we can share a San Pellegrino from my stash out there,' Penny replied.

'How illicit.'

'Just go,' she said, laughing and pointing to the exit.

He stood outside the open door, against the walk-in fridge. It was his turn to watch her now, and it had turned into an unspoken game: she'd watched him and not been bothered at being caught, so now he watched her without hiding it, refusing to shy from doing exactly the same.

'Listen,' Penny said, as she crouched down to the bottom step, her 4 p.m. ritual, passing him a can of her fizzy drink and preparing to roll a cigarette. 'Can I be totally upfront with you?'

'You can,' Francesco encouraged, moving towards her. He stood in front of her and she forgot what she was going to say. She swore she could feel the heat radiating from his trousers, and her breath got shallow at his proximity.

'I, um . . .' she began, and then BOOM. Somehow the pair of them went from two separate entities to enmeshed together, mouth to mouth, breathlessly consuming each other. Penny stumbled so that her back was against the outside wall, and she could feel Francesco through his jeans. They moved up against one another, the friction getting more and more urgent, the kissing deeper and deeper. Penny melted into Francesco's every movement, furious with passion. He moved to her jawline, her neck, he pulled at Penny's apron, pawed at her chef's whites to find his way to bare skin. Whatever she'd been about to say was forgotten.

'Mmmm,' she moaned, electrified by him. And then: 'Wait – wait!'

Francesco pulled away. 'Stop?' he said.

'No,' Penny intoned. 'Not stop. Upstairs.'

'Upstairs,' Francesco repeated. 'Good.'

Penny pulled him by the wrist so that he was inside, locking the back door behind him. She led the way through the sparklingly clean kitchen and up to the café so they could get to the flat, Francesco pushed up against her back, kissing her neck and behind her ears, stopping every few steps so that she could turn around and have their mouths meet.

In her front room she said, 'Can I shower? I don't want our first time to be when I smell like a kitchen.'

'I don't care what you smell of,' Francesco told her, coming in for another kiss, but she put a finger to his lips and insisted.

'I do. Wait here.' As she left, she said to her Amazon speaker: 'Alexa, play some Frank Ocean. Thank you.' She lit a sandalwood incense stick on the table.

'You're very polite to your voice-activated technology,' Francesco said, loosening his belt.

'When the A.I. revolution comes, it is I who shall be spared,' Penny smirked, noting the way he was making himself more comfortable. She added: 'Okay, hold on.'

Penny returned only after she'd taken the day off her, standing naked in front of him, hair damp and loose around her shoulders, her eyes wide and lips parted.

Francesco took in the sight of her.

'Come here,' he growled, standing and walking towards her, taking her hand. 'This is going to be a lot of fun.'

5

'Okay, mmmm. Yeah,' Penny lightly sighed.

'Yeah?' Francesco asked.

'Yeah,' Penny said. 'Yeah. That feels good.'

'Okay. Good. Could you just . . .'

'Oh. Sure. Like this?'

'Or maybe—'

'Ouch! Watch my hair, it's caught—'

'Oh, shit, yeah. Sorry.'

'It's okay.'

Francesco and Penny had initiated incredibly bad sex.

He had kissed her – kissed her everywhere. Penny had let his tongue roam her body, her cheeks, her chin, her breasts, her thighs, between her legs. She had undressed him, and pushed him onto the sofa, rolling a condom onto him and straddling his lap. She'd braced herself for the feeling of being filled, of handing herself over to him, of their two bodies becoming one . . . but it wasn't working.

'What if I go on top?' Francesco said.

'Yeah, okay,' Penny murmured, moving off him and lying back.

He loomed over her, and she grumbled, 'I just – these cushions. I'll just move these . . .' She picked up a throw pillow and dropped it to the floor.

Silently, and with increasing half-heartedness, Francesco pumped away. His eyes were scrunched closed in intense concentration. Penny coughed a little. She'd been hugely turned on but now things felt significantly less . . . *lubricated.*

Francesco stopped for a second to wipe hair from his clammy brow.

They made eye contact and smiled, Francesco going to speak but seeing that Penny was about to, and Penny going to speak but seeing Francesco was about to, and so both nervously giggling and neither saying anything until Francesco uttered, gingerly: 'Should we stop?'

Penny said, 'Yeah. It's okay. Let's stop.'

The relief was palpable to them both.

6

Penny couldn't believe it. Hadn't she and Sharon joked about this exact outcome – that a man as handsome as Francesco would be rubbish in bed?

'Clemmie!' Penny said in a panicked Personal Podcast. 'What the hell! I knew it was too good to be true!' Clementine had replied telling her not to be so bloody precious.

'Bad sex happens to good people,' Clementine said in response. 'Remember when you were sleeping with that anonymous sex blogger you refused to introduce anyone to, but he was the best sex you'd had since Mo? You know why he was the best sex you'd had, don't you? Because it was the only time you felt close to him. It's easy to have good sex without any emotions because in bed is the only time you truly connected. But if you and this handsome Italian are all, *go! go! go! connection central!* outside of the bedroom, maybe there's a bit more riding on what happens when the lights go out. It's not like you don't fancy him, is it? You do fancy him. So I'm afraid the only thing to do is chill out and try again, sis. Also, can you book train tickets for Eric's birthday weekend? And is your Italian stallion coming too?'

Penny had texted her back as soon as she'd listened to what Clementine had to say.

It's irritating that you have such perspective on my life, Penny typed. *I would say 'screw you', but obviously the person I've got to screw, again, is Francesco.*

Clementine replied: *That's my girl! Let me know how it goes. And please acknowledge my request about the trains! xxx*

Penny couldn't help but feel embarrassed, though. She knew she fancied Francesco, but did having bad sex mean that actually he didn't quite fancy her?

'He fancies you!' Sharon said, over a 6 p.m. after-work tea.

'Come here, you,' Penny said to Mia, scooping up Sharon's daughter to make her squeal in delighted giggles.

'Auntie Penny! Again!' pleaded Mia, as Penny tried to put her down. Penny reached for her once more, blowing a raspberry on her tummy that meant before she'd even stopped, Mia was begging for 'again!' once more. It made Penny's heart grow twelve sizes, having a pudgy hand wrapped around her own in glee and being the one who made that noise of joy happen. She loved kids, and she loved her friend's kids.

'Let Auntie Penny drink her tea,' Sharon instructed. 'Can you draw her a picture of a unicorn, or a queen?'

'Yeah,' shrieked Mia, padding to her tiny table and chair in the corner of the kitchen. 'I can draw.'

'Good girl,' whispered Sharon, bending to kiss her daughter on the head.

'So, a rubbish shag.' Sharon returned to the breakfast stools and Penny, who watched Mia bend over a blank sheet of A4 with her crayons. Sharon lowered her voice to say it, so Mia didn't hear.

'Yeah,' sighed Penny. 'I'm gutted.'

'Can I ask you something?'

'You can . . .' said Penny.

'Where are you at with having a family right now? Finding a surrogate? I thought all this was a bit of fun but you're actually falling for him properly, aren't you?'

Penny had spoken to Sharon at great length about her desire to become a mother, and how she wanted that almost more than anything in the world. She'd explained to Sharon almost right after they'd met that before the radiotherapy and ensuing hormone therapy, Penny's eggs had been retrieved and then fertilized with German donor sperm, so that the resulting embryos could be checked for the BRCA mutation. That way, Penny could prevent passing on the risk of breast cancer to her children, and feel a bit more in control about her future. The embryos were currently in a storage unit for the princely sum of three hundred pounds a year, and on-and-off Penny talked about using them, via IVF and with a surrogate. She'd not had a boyfriend since Mo, so it had been about finding the courage to do it alone – she didn't necessarily believe that first comes love, then comes marriage, then comes the baby in the baby carriage, especially when the baby already half-existed as an embryo. She went through increasingly determined phases of feeling incredibly empowered about using them and then finding love later – especially since up until last month it had seemed like love was going to elude her forever – and then getting cold feet and deciding to wait another six months, just in case.

'Well,' said Penny. 'I just don't know. It's all been going so well with him, so to be honest I haven't really been thinking about IVF or surrogacy or motherhood. Which is weird because I was definitely getting to "at least ninety per cent ready" territory. But then he walked into the café, and it's just been lovely. I mean, it's a bit different now, though, because . . .'

'Crap sex.'

'Crap. Sex. And so maybe he'll run a mile embarrassed, or maybe I want to run a mile embarrassed. And I mean, it's too early to tell him about the whole can't-carry-kids-myself thing, or even that if in some crazy world where we end up together we actually couldn't have *his* kids. I'd be stupid to bring that up two weeks in. But yeah. It feels different with him, worth pausing the constant shall-I-or-shan't-I "do it now" question I keep asking myself. I've got nothing to lose by seeing where this goes . . .'

'Have you heard from him today?'

'He texted this morning to say he hoped I had a good day, but to be honest we'd normally have called one another as we prepped at work, so something is already different.'

'Text him right now,' Sharon instructed. 'Don't sit and wonder. If you think your ego is bruised then honestly, try being a man. A disappointing lay to you is upsetting, but to a man who needs his testosterone to validate his masculinity? Devastating.'

Penny shook her head. 'Francesco isn't like that,' she contended, picking up her phone and unlocking it anyway. 'He's not a caveman.'

'Darling,' Sharon insisted, wandering over to check on her daughter. 'When it comes to s-e-x, they're all cavemen.'

Penny opened the text thread between her and Francesco right as a new message appeared on her screen from him. It said: *So, last night was . . .*

Penny smiled. *Yeah,* she replied, instantly, adding, *(So weird! Just picked up my phone to message you as you messaged me!)*

It makes no sense, Francesco texted back. *We should be on fire! Like so, so hot. (Great minds think alike!)*

'Do you want to stay for dinner?' Sharon asked. 'It's shepherd's pie.'

'Sure,' said Penny. 'Sorry to be rude – he's texting me right now.'

'Oh, what's he saying?'

'He's a bit confused as well, I think.'

Penny typed: *Maybe we'd put too much pressure on it?*

His reply came: *Well it's not like we planned it to happen then, did we? I mean, you weren't expecting me, and I was genuinely only stopping by for the food . . .*

True. Penny responded. *Although I'd definitely been thinking about it . . .*

Oh really???

She smiled. She had thought about it. She kept a small vibrator in her bedside table and had used it more than once before bed as she thought about it. Penny had wanted him since they met. Since she'd watched him unload bread from the van. She replied provocatively with three dots.

Okay, I'd thought about it too, Francesco texted. *A lot. I'd even . . . you know . . . THOUGHT ABOUT IT.*

Well, at least they'd both had good sex in their minds, Penny reasoned. She responded: ☺ ☺ ☺

So we should try it again, he replied. *Right?*

'He's asking if we should try again,' Penny called over to Sharon. 'And that's what I want, right? A second go-around?'

'You tell me,' said Sharon, fishing about in the freezer.

For sure! Yes! OMG yes. I would like that very much, Penny typed back. She wanted to sound enthusiastic in case what Sharon had said about the male ego thing was true, even for him.

'Yes,' Penny said out loud.

Okay, well, good talk, came the reply.

GREAT talk, said Penny.

I've got service now, but I'll speak to you later?

Yes, said Penny. *Speak to you later xxxxx*

'Do you know what?' said Sharon, reappearing from her freezer. 'I don't actually fancy the pie. Shall I order pizza instead?'

'You've got something wholesome and good for you right within reach, and you want what isn't?' Penny said.

Sharon shrugged, smiling.

'Okay, pizza,' said Penny.

Penny and Francesco took more afternoon walks around the reservoir, fitting them in after her service but before his, and kissing at what Penny thought of as 'their' gate. They talked on the phone. They texted when they woke up, and before they went to sleep. They made plans, starting sentences with 'We should . . .' or 'We could . . .' or 'Shall we . . .' Penny wasn't used to being a 'we'. It was seductive. The 'us' thing . . . well, 'us' felt okay with Francesco. She didn't feel the usual fear and she didn't feel like she had to hold him away from her, close enough to know him but far enough away so that he'd never truly know her. She liked him. And what was more, she was starting to trust him. *Maybe I will tell him about the kids thing,* she reflected. *Sooner rather than later.*

'Wow,' said Clementine, as they sat together on a bench in Clissold Park. 'Big feelings are happening.'

'Maybe?' Penny replied. 'I daren't believe it, but I think . . . yes?'

'Well you've got to figure out the bedroom thing then. Without a doubt.'

Francesco and Penny had tried again to find their sexual groove, but it still wasn't right. It was like there was something else in the room with them, some third entity that distracted them and made them too self-conscious to enjoy the moment. It was maddening. They'd started to laugh about it, which eased the mood, but they were yet to manage a ten-out-of-ten romp. They were stalling at about a three-and-a-half. A C-minus. Passable at a push.

'Everything goes where it should, and the theory is all there,' explained Penny. 'But in practice it's not exactly on fire, you know?'

'Well,' said Clementine, 'that kind of fits in to what I wanted to talk to you about.'

'Okay . . .' said Penny, searching her sister's face for clues but coming up short. Clementine wanted to talk about Penny's lacklustre sex life?

'I wanted to tell you that I've given this a lot of thought, and – just so you know, and in case you wanted me to – when you're ready, I would absolutely love to be your surrogate.'

'My surrogate?' said Penny, stunned.

'Your surrogate,' repeated back Clementine, nodding. Smiling. She did a little 'ta-da!' motion with one hand, but Penny didn't smile back.

'You want to be my surrogate.'

'I really, really do, Pen.'

They were clutching hot chocolates from the café in the middle of the park, where Clementine went every morning when she was in London to ensure she hit her daily 10,000 steps.

'Can we sit down?' Penny said. 'Just for a minute. This is . . . a lot.'

'We are sitting down,' said Clementine, her voice quiet. 'Are you okay? I figured you knew this was coming . . .'

'Yes, I'm okay,' Penny said. 'No. I wasn't expecting this.'

They sat overlooking the water feature. The second 'fake spring' of the season was doing a great job of acting like actual spring, with a cloudless sky and neither of them in coats. Uncle David had said on the family WhatsApp group this morning that they should both enjoy it, because snow was forecast at the weekend. He'd sent a gif of the two sisters from *Frozen*, for emphasis. He often joked that they looked like those sisters: Clementine with her long blonde hair and Penny the bright redhead.

'I mean this in the most grateful possible way, Clementine, but please don't mess with me.'

Clementine turned and put her hand on her sister's knee. She fixed her features to sit encouragingly and kindly. 'Let me speak,' she said, slowly. 'I don't want to screw this up.' She took a breath. 'Rima and I have really thought this through, and we want to do it. We want a part in continuing our – yours and mine – bloodline. Because, without family, what else is there? We support this decision one thousand per cent, and if you want to use me as your oven, well, you absolutely can.'

Penny shook her head. Could finding someone to help her start her family really be this simple? 'This is . . . I don't know. I can do what I said. I can go to Russia for it. People do.'

'That worries me,' Clementine mused. 'Who knows if those girls are doing it willingly, or for the money, or . . .' She paused. 'Is it selfish of me to say I want to be a part of this process? Rima and I will truly never start a family of our own – we don't want that, really, really. But we know how much you want it.' Clementine bumped her shoulder against Penny's, smiling. 'I hereby volunteer as tribute.'

Penny twisted the cardboard sleeve around her takeaway cup, staring at it going around and around. It felt dangerous to be hopeful, to think this was something her sister really would do. It wasn't offering to share her chips or pick up the tab for lunch. This was everything.

'I can't get my head around this. It's too much.'

Penny had very first dared talk about motherhood after Bridges had celebrated its second birthday. She had overcome the darkest period of her life, made a total success of her dream business, and gone upstairs to her flat and cried and cried and cried, because somehow it wasn't enough. It felt anti-feminist, in a weird way, to say she needed something beyond work. She'd sent Clementine a voice note that said, 'I want to come upstairs after my shift and for my child to be there. To be doing all this for a reason. I want kids, Clementine. Like . . . now. I just feel so sad! I don't want it to be just me! I want a family!' It was with unending gratitude that Clementine had been so kind in her response, and never once made Penny feel ridiculous for thinking about doing it alone.

But all of that was before Francesco. It was too soon to know if he changed things, but Penny felt a small notion that it might. She *wanted* to ask him, just in theory, but what exactly would she say? *Hey, Francesco? I know I met you twenty minutes ago but just trying to get a read on how you'd feel about being a daddy, except I've already fertilized my eggs so it wouldn't really be 'yours', and it's too dangerous to come off my hormone medication so I wouldn't actually be the one getting pregnant. What's your timeframe on that? Maybe within the year? Is this a do-able scenario for you? No pressure.*

'I didn't mean to blindside you,' Clementine said. 'I honestly thought you knew this is what I'd been thinking about for ages. I wanted to tell you now, today, because then I'm gone again and it's not exactly the kind of thing you say over a Personal Podcast, is it? But I've honestly been thinking about this ever since you said you wanted to be a mum. Rima and me, we've discussed this at least once a month for a year. I couldn't take away the cancer for you, but I can help with this.'

Neither spoke. The fountain sprayed and the sun shone and they sat and sat.

'They're my embryos,' Penny said, eventually.

'They're your embryos,' said Clementine, before shaking her head. 'Sorry. I keep repeating everything that you say. I'm just trying to let you know that I hear you.'

The pair observed a pregnant mother pushing a toddler in a pram, talking to him about the ducks he could see and laughing as he mispronounced the word 'walking': *They wokking, mama! They wokking!*

'I know I'm still only thirty, so there's my whole life ahead of me for kids,' Penny said. 'Except, every day feels like this perfect, beautiful gift, and I don't want to throw that away. My business is secure, I work really sensible hours, I can afford childcare . . . the only thing I don't have is the ability to carry the kid myself. And, well, a father-figure.'

'That's where I come in – not as a father-figure, obvs, but I can carry it. At least let me do the tests, see if I'm viable to help. Because I want to.'

'I can't ask you to do this,' Penny said.

'You're not,' Clementine replied. 'I offered. My womb, your

baby, made from some lovely German sperm. You said it's German, didn't you? And I'm bringing this up now as I'm going to be in London for at least six months this autumn, because we're doing a concession stand in Selfridges as well as the new White City store. I'll be around, like *actually* around, and I've also got a *lot* of holiday to take as well. Logistically, now is the time I can help, plus I'm young and I'm healthy, and I think you've sat on the idea long enough to hold your head high in saying you've given it real thought. Not that I'm judge and jury on a woman knowing her own mind. Just, I see what this means to you.'

Penny moved to rest her head on her sister's arm. 'I keep thinking of that yoga retreat. The stories of all those women. What are the chances that on my very first retreat I'd end up with nine women who all had different motherhood stories? There was a forty-three-year-old there who had used a donor and was already seven months pregnant. A lesbian who'd done a turkey baster with her best gay mate, and because they were doctors they got it sorted literally the second time they tried. And that was more than twenty years ago! Their son just graduated from Cambridge!'

Clementine nodded, making her shoulder jiggle and Penny's head move up and down with it.

'I know you worry about getting Uncle David on side, but I think he just worries that you'd be alone, and that having a baby on your own is a lot of work. He's still old school that way.'

'Well, I am seeing somebody now . . .'

'You are . . .'

'And I'm not saying I'm going to marry him, but . . . I have to admit that it feels weird to be discussing this now. Even a month ago if we'd have talked about this I'd have said, "Okay, sod it, great, shall we start next week?" But now . . . not that I want to change my plans for a man, but . . . this feels different. Worth the pause.' She issued a funny noise from the back of her throat. 'Bloody hell, I felt like a bad feminist for wanting a bloody kid in the first place, and now I feel like a bad feminist for waiting. I can't win with myself.'

'Hey,' said Clementine. 'I'm not going anywhere. The offer isn't going anywhere. I'm here in the autumn but we can always figure it out for whenever you're ready. This autumn, next year, in five years. I just really wanted to tell you.'

'What did I do to deserve a sister like you?' Penny asked.

'Well, you were basically my mother growing up, so there's that.'

'Talking about becoming a mum makes me miss her even more, you know. Maybe that's why it feels so pressing to me. Bringing a new life into the world, being a parent . . . I could know what she felt like when she had us.'

'I think that's why I want to help, too. It's a way for her to live on a bit, isn't it?'

'Yeah,' said Penny. 'It is.'

7

When Penny got home there was a bouquet in her hallway. 'For no other reason than you make me want to be the kind of man who sends flowers,' the note said, and it was signed 'F' with a kiss after.

Penny knew that life was too short not to think about a baby when that was a burning desire for her, but also that the baby really could wait if love – or something like it - was on the table. Maybe Francesco *could* stomach a conversation about it. Maybe this is what she had been looking for every time she'd stalled: the 'us'. And as for the sex – they'd figure it out. Maybe they could go to a class, or a therapist. Maybe they just needed to watch some porn together.

Penny texted him: *They're gorgeous, and you're wonderful. Thank you x.* She felt genuinely fond of him. He was just so nice. Why did that feel so radical? A man! Being nice! To her!!!

Francesco replied: *I can't get you out of my head.*

Penny smelled the roses. She couldn't get him out of her

head either. It made her want to tell Uncle David about him.

'Davvy?' Penny said over FaceTime, seeing her uncle's ear and shouting to the screen. 'Davvy! It's video! Show me your face!'

She heard muffling and then his face came into view. 'Oh! I see!' he tittered. 'I thought it was a phone call!'

'How are you?' said Penny. 'I miss you!'

'I miss you too, sunshine. I'm okay. Bit of heartburn today though.'

'Have you had a glass of milk?' Penny said.

'Good idea,' he replied. 'See, this is why I need you. You know which way is up.'

Penny smiled at him.

'I've met somebody,' she said.

Uncle David raised an eyebrow. 'Oh?'

'Another chef. Francesco. It's been a few weeks.'

Penny could see her uncle's face light up at the mention of another chef. It was written all over his expression.

'Stop it,' said Penny, in playful warning. 'He's very much a London-based chef, Davvy.'

'I didn't say anything!' he said. 'What!'

Penny rolled her eyes. She was bored of this subtle pressure he frequently put on her. Before the cancer, her career trajectory naturally pointed to her one day becoming the next *chef de patron* of The Red Panda. But then, when her ambition changed and she set up a smaller, much more manageable place, Uncle David's retirement plan suddenly looked different. He was still sure he could change her mind, though – even last time she'd visited Uncle David and Eric, he'd said over dessert: 'But people should know who you are, Penny! That small café, twenty-five covers – you're so much better than that! You could really be somebody with your own restaurant – you could be somebody here. Bigger really is better!'

Penny had reminded him that her small café with twenty-five covers turned over almost a quarter of a million and employed six different people. 'I wish you could keep your eyes on your own mat,' she'd said. Uncle David had shaken his head, not understanding. 'It's a yoga thing. You can't do crow, or tree – or anything really – if you're too busy looking at what everyone else can do. Yoga only works if you focus on your breathing, and your own mat.'

'How did I raise such a hippie?'

'You know, the most common misconception about Frankenstein is that it's the name of the monster. The monster actually belongs to Frankenstein – it's actually "Frankenstein's Monster".'

'I'm Doctor Frankenstein in this analogy, I presume?'

Penny had smirked.

Across FaceTime, Uncle David sighed.

'I love you so, so much, you know,' he said. 'I'd take a bullet for you. I just want you to be happy. I know I tease about you coming up here, but it's only because I think you really would thrive . . .'

'I am happy here!' Penny yelled. Why did it always have to descend into a campaign to have her run his pub? It was exhausting.

'How's Eric?' she said, changing tack.

'He misses you too,' David said. 'He's out in the garden just now but has found the perfect place for his birthday next week. Come hungry! Offft – sorry Pen. This heartburn is chronic.'

'Maybe you should go and lie down,' Penny said. 'I can call later this week if you don't feel well now.'

'Okay. Yes. Sorry poppet.'

'It's okay. I just wanted you to know that everything down here is good. I'm good.'

'And his name is Francesco?'

'Yup,' Penny said, smiling. 'And I think I might actually quite like him.'

'Hey, you,' Penny said, picking up the phone to Francesco as she prepared the vegetables for that day's service. 'Hold on, let me find my ears.'

'Find my ears' was their shorthand for 'find my earbuds' – it had become a habit of theirs to call one another during morning prep, both talking to the other from their respective kitchens via hands-free Bluetooth headphones.

'How are you today?'

'I've just been online shopping,' Francesco said down the phone.

'Uh-huh,' Penny replied.

'For some fun things . . .'

'Fun like party poppers fun? Or fun like a new ACNE handbag fun? I'm devastated I still don't own one of their bags. It's just so much money! And I never even use a handbag, which I cannot discount totally from the argument . . .'

Francesco dropped his voice. 'More fun than both of those things . . .' he said.

'More fun than both of those things. Okay, well then I am all out of ideas. You'll just have to tell me.'

'Well,' he replied, and Penny couldn't place his tone. 'I'd rather show you.'

Penny stopped what she was doing. 'Are you . . . using a sexy-time voice?' she suddenly realized.

'Well picked-up on,' Francesco replied. 'I am.'

'You got me a sexy-time surprise . . .' Penny ruminated,

aware that pot-wash Bobby had slowed down his movements, probably because he was trying not to make too much noise as he eavesdropped.

'Uh-huh,' Francesco said.

'I can't talk about that right now then,' Penny said, immediately a bit more prim and proper. 'Perhaps we can address the . . . *matter at hand* . . . um, tomorrow?'

Francesco laughed. 'I certainly hope so,' he replied. 'Because I am very, very excited for it.'

Penny was under instruction to meet Francesco at the bar of The Standard in Kings Cross.

'This place is phenomenal,' she said, approaching him where he was perched on a stool towards the right-hand side. It was a hotel primarily, with signs in the lobby pointing to various bars and restaurants. It was incredibly plush, and Penny was relieved she'd worn the same red dress she'd worn the night of Dofi's restaurant opening. It made her feel confident and sexy. 'Also: hi,' she added, leaning in for a kiss.

'Hi,' he said into her mouth, and then, 'You smell amazing. Mmmm.'

'Thank you,' she replied. She hopped up beside him and took in the atmosphere of the bar. She hadn't been to The Standard since it opened, and she liked it. 'What are you drinking?' she asked, nodding towards his glass. 'I'm gagging for something cold.'

'Old Fashioned, because I am a millennial male cliché,' he replied. 'It's good. This guy knows what he is doing.'

'I'll do that too,' decided Penny.

Francesco ordered two more drinks with the barperson and turned his chair so that he could rest his feet on the bottom bar of hers, so he was closer to her.

'You're quite the man of mystery,' Penny said. 'Do I get to find out what the evening entails yet? You've been very secretive.'

Francesco grinned. 'Convince me,' he challenged.

'Okay . . .' Penny reached out an arm and rested a hand on the back of Francesco's neck, where she idly stroked the space just below his hairline. 'You're looking very handsome tonight.' She flicked her hair from her shoulder as she said it, letting the neck of her dress fall slightly to bare her shoulder. 'And, um . . .?'

Francesco started to smile.

'Ah!' he said. 'You were doing so well!'

'Seduction isn't my forte!' Penny laughed. 'It's too much pressure!'

'Okay, okay, that's fair,' he replied. 'But you do have me laughing, which is the same result but just with a different technique.'

'Phew!'

'You're adorable,' he said, though Penny scrunched up her face at the word. 'And I will tell you why we are here.'

Francesco picked up his phone from where it lay on the bar, revealing a white keycard underneath that said, in small emboldened font: SUITE TERRACE.

'No . . .' marvelled Penny.

'Yup!' said Francesco. 'I know a guy. Eighth floor. All night. And *this*,' he said, reaching down for a sleek golden shopping bag, 'is full of play toys. If I may be so bold.'

The barperson set down their drinks, and Francesco said, 'Are we good to take these up to our room?'

'Sure thing, man. Have a great night.'

'Oh, we will,' said Francesco. 'We will,' he whispered again, for emphasis, into Penny's ear.

The pair stood in the lift grinning, in cahoots together.

'I'm excited,' Penny said, bashfully.

'Me too,' said Francesco, equally as shy. 'I hope you like it.'

'Francesco,' Penny replied, looking earnestly into his eyes. 'I already do.'

Upstairs, they both gasped as they entered the room. They could see out over the whole city, all the twinkly lights of a million other lives, St Pancras station in all its glory opposite.

'This is beautiful,' Penny said, the awe in her voice clear. 'Thank you.'

'You are very welcome,' Francesco murmured. 'I figured this might be just what we needed: neutral territory, a nice cocktail, high thread-count sheets . . .'

'And fluffy bathrobes?'

'Shall we take a bath?'

Penny grinned. 'Let's.'

In the bath they soaked in bubbles that left their skin silky soft, the lights turned down low, sipping on their drinks as they talked about what they liked in bed, and what they didn't. The bath was big enough for Penny to sit between Francesco's legs, with her back to him, so that they could touch without looking at each other. It felt easier that way, rather than having to hold eye contact. Less pressurized. The talk came easier.

'I like it when you kiss me slowly,' Penny told him, her hand gently floating on the surface of the water.

'I like it when you move your hips,' Francesco said, his hand running up and down the top of her arm.

'I like when you're deep inside me,' Penny said. 'When you forget to be gentle and get . . .' she started to laugh. 'When you're a bit animalistic.'

Francesco laughed too. 'I don't think I would have worded it that way, but that's what I like too. When I can be that way, and so you can be that way. It makes me feel like . . .' He didn't finish his sentence.

'You can tell me,' Penny urged. 'There isn't a wrong thing you can say. That's why we're doing this, isn't it? To be . . .' Now it was her turn to not finish a sentence.

'Yeah,' said Francesco. 'You're right.'

'So . . .?'

'I think what I mean is, you know. I respect you, obviously.'

'Obviously,' Penny said.

'And I'm not saying I want to, I don't know, give you a golden shower or anything.'

'No judgement,' said Penny, straight-faced.

'But I like it when it's like . . . losing control. Really going hard. I don't know. I don't want it to sound like I've been watching crap porn and I want you with a gag in your mouth and tied up to a bondage table. I just mean . . .'

'That you want to fuck me like a dirty little side piece?'

'If I say yes, is that bad?'

Penny turned around so that water sloshed over the side of the bath and she could face him.

'Francesco, that's exactly what I want too. Go for it like you don't care about being polite.'

She felt him press against her stomach.

'Oh,' she said, searching for him under the bubbles. 'Is that a hint?'

They started slowly, the room lit by candles, music softly playing. Francesco talked her through the bag of toys he'd had delivered, and the practicality of it – explaining speed settings and the mechanics and the angles of each thing – was so at odds with them sitting across from each other, naked, that it was the foreplay before the foreplay. By the time they finally touched Penny was practically quivering with desire, and within minutes was panting Francesco's name, climaxing and whimpering, 'Oh. My. God.'

Francesco came to her and kissed her deeply.

'That was so hot to watch,' he said.

'Give me a second to recover,' Penny replied, catching her breath. 'And I will return the favour.'

'To be honest,' Francesco said, 'watching you writhe around like that felt like the favour.'

Penny chuckled and jokingly smacked his arm. 'Save it for your wank bank,' she giggled, before letting out another satisfied sigh.

As the spring sun started to peek through the curtains, the pair lay entwined in each other, the music having stopped, the candles burnt down, just the two of them and the dawn silence.

'Five times. I can't believe . . .'

'I know,' said Francesco. 'I was really starting to freak out about it. Everything else was so great but I thought, what if we don't get the hang of it? Would we have had to break up?'

'Well, five times certainly makes up for a few false starts.'

'I'll say,' said Francesco, slipping his hand further down her body and forcing Penny to pull away.

'Mister, you're going to have to feed me before I have the energy to go again. I think we've proved our point.'

Francesco retreated. 'Fair play,' he said. 'I'll poke about for a breakfast menu in a minute. I'm sure they'll do room service.'

'Oh, for sure,' said Penny. 'But don't get up. Don't move yet. I like you right here.'

Penny closed her eyes, her face nuzzled into Francesco's neck from behind, the big spoon to his little spoon. She was her normal hot-water-bottle self, but it made her feel womanly and powerful, pushed up against him this way.

'Are you real?' she said, quietly.

'If you're real, I'm real,' Francesco whispered.

'Falling in friendship,' Penny said, and Francesco moved so that they were nose-to-nose.

'Falling in friendship,' he repeated.

Penny traced the outline of his face with her fingertip.

'I like to be the one who makes you laugh,' she said. 'That's my favourite thing. The first morning you came to the café somebody on the phone made you laugh, and I saw through the window, and I thought – I wonder what it would take to make a man that handsome laugh so much.'

'Somebody probably told me a fart joke,' Francesco said. Then he added, 'I knew you were watching me you know. I could feel it. You barely said hello to me after you let me in. You just carried on talking to Stu. And I thought, who is this woman who doesn't even care who is delivering her bread? But then I felt you staring.'

'Mr Ego.'

'No, not Mr Ego. I just . . . I wanted you to notice me.'

'Job done.'

'Making me wait weeks before you texted me, though . . . Totally outrageous.'

'No! Don't!' Penny said. 'I still don't know what I was thinking. I was intimidated.'

'Intimidated.' He arched his eyebrow, disbelievingly.

'Nobody ever fancies me. I didn't actually think you did.

I dunno. This is cringey, but sometimes I feel . . . unloveable. Like everyone is going to have their turn except me.'

'You're very loveable, Penny Bridge. I promise you that.'

Penny pulled a face.

'Hey,' Francesco said urgently. 'Listen to me. I know what came before me, but I'm here now, okay? And I'm not going anywhere.'

Penny shook her head as if trying to shake off her thoughts. 'Urgh,' she said. 'I'm sorry.'

'Don't be sorry. It's okay. I get it.'

'I don't think you do,' she said. 'I think you've never had to be alone.'

Francesco didn't say anything.

'My ex,' she said. 'Mo. I honestly thought . . . you know. I'm still so, so mad at him for leaving. He left me when I had nobody and nothing. Right after I got diagnosed. Why would somebody do that to a person they say they love, Francesco?'

'I honestly don't know,' he said. Then he changed his tone. 'If I ever met him . . .' he said, in a silly voice.

Penny chuckled sadly.

'I think I'm mad at myself for dating a coward,' she continued. 'We'd been together five years and the second my life didn't revolve around him, he bailed. He couldn't even wait until I'd had my radiotherapy. And it makes me so mad that I wasn't even surprised. It was so common on the ward. There was one woman I met in treatment who'd hired a private investigator to prove that her husband was cheating on her. Isn't that horrible? All these women with breast cancer married to men who can't cope when somebody they say they love gets sick.'

'Have you seen him since?'

'Clemmie has. She bumped into him getting off a bus on Oxford Street and slapped him, and apparently he burst into tears.'

'Ouch.'

'That's so not Clemmie, slapping somebody. I mean, it's basically assault. But apparently he just cried and cried, and she called him pathetic, and not long after his mum called me to apologize. She said she was disgusted by him.'

It didn't hurt her anymore – not really. It was weird how somebody she'd known for half a decade would disappear, not even in a cloud of smoke, simply . . . there one day, gone the next. Just like her dad.

Francesco stroked her arm. Eventually he said: 'You know, if you were married to some bloke called Mo right now I wouldn't have a hard-on pressed up against your leg in the fanciest hotel I've ever stayed in. And not to minimize your pain or anything but bloody hell I feel like the luckiest bastard in London.'

Instantly the mood was changed, and Penny was relieved. She didn't want to think about the bad men in her life when such a good one was beside her in bed.

'How can you be ready to go again?' Penny exclaimed. 'It's a physical impossibility. You've got the libido of a teenager!'

'There's just something about you, Penny Bridge, that really turns me on.'

'Who was your last girlfriend? You haven't told me about her.'

'Well . . .' said Francesco. 'She took my heart out of my chest, and held it in her hand, and clenched her fist until it was pulp. She cheated on me. If there is one thing I don't get it is cheating – it's the most disrespectful thing anyone can do. Let the record show that she regrets it, though. It was a year ago and she still sometimes calls. I'm glad she feels bad. So, when you talk about what a happy guy I am, know that there is a woman out there who I hope never forgives herself.'

'Oh, Francesco. I'm so sorry.'

'People hurt other people, don't they?'

'I promise never to hurt you, okay? Not if I can help it.'

'I promise never to hurt you either,' Francesco said. 'Not if I can help it.'

'And I know it's not polite to brag,' Penny said in a Personal Podcast to Clementine, 'but Jesus. It's a wonder I haven't got a water infection we've been doing it that much. He's stayed at mine every night for a week now, and to be honest we don't even use the toys most of the time. It's like – well, sorry, I know you're my sister and everything, and this is probably too much information but . . . now we know we don't have to be so bloody well-mannered with each other we can just let it rip, you know? Which is amazing, and also interesting because now I'm thinking that if before there was a reason he wasn't Mr Perfect, but now it's great sex . . . does that mean there's nothing wrong with him? Surely there is. I just can't figure it out. I'll bet he forgets my birthday. Or loses all of his hair. Or . . . oh I don't know. Somebody comes out of the woodwork and says he's her Me Too man. I know you're going to tell me to stop looking for faults, because that's exactly what I'd say to you, but if only I could find one I would! I promise I would! Anyway. Shall we do dinner tomorrow? All four of us? I want you to meet him.'

Clementine and Rima loved him.

'He's wonderful,' Clementine said as Penny deposited their

dirty dessert plates into the sink. 'The way he looks at you makes me very happy. He worships you.'

Penny looked over her shoulder to where Francesco was sitting with Rima, talking about something that made Rima cry, 'No! That can't be true! I don't believe you!' but she was laughing, signalling that whatever he was saying, she absolutely did.

'I don't need to be worshipped . . .' Penny started, but her sister patted her arm and said: 'Yes Penny, you do. And you deserve to be.'

Penny might not have needed it, but she certainly did love it.

'I liked being there tonight,' Francesco said later, as they lay in bed, sweaty and happy.

'I liked you being there too,' said Penny. 'Isn't Rima wonderful? I can't believe the good fortune of being raised with one sister and now having two.'

'That's a beautiful thing to say,' Francesco said, kissing the top of her head. 'And I'm excited to see the whole family in action tomorrow.'

'Me too. Clementine, Rima, Uncle David and Eric – we all hold each other close,' Penny said. 'There's a weird bond when you decide to choose to love your family. Everyone knows they *should* love their family, but when you make a decision to love them, I mean to *like* them, as people, and to keep showing up even when things are hard and uncomfortable and everyone knows exactly how to push your buttons . . . I feel really lucky. I mean, my sister and her wife, my uncle and his husband, me and everything I went through, all banding together to be this unit, even though we're all over the country – well, with Clem travelling like she does, all over the world! – it's special. And now you're here.'

'I am,' Francesco said. 'So I passed the test?'

'The practical element,' said Penny. 'Tomorrow morning you have the written portion of the exam.'

'What happens after that?'

'You finally get to meet Uncle David, I suppose.'

'Crikey.'

'I know. The honour will be all yours.'

'We should go to sleep so we're ready for it.'

'We should,' said Penny.

'But you're so warm,' said Francesco, 'and so naked . . .'

He disappeared under the duvet to kiss Penny's collarbone, her chest, her breasts. He kept kissing, lower and lower, and Penny closed her eyes and sighed contentedly.

'Francesco?' Penny said, when they finally tried to go to sleep.

'Mmmmm?' he said, drowsy.

'Don't freak out, but – do you want kids?'

She could feel Francesco open his eyes in the dark, even though she couldn't see him.

'Now?' he said, immediately wider awake and cheeky with it.

'One day. In theory. You know.'

He thought about it. 'I do,' he said. 'When the time is right, and the woman is right, yeah. It's what life is all about, isn't it?'

'Yeah, I think so.' She paused, thinking of how to phrase the next part of her question. 'What do you think about adoption?'

'Adoption?'

'You know, like, having children that aren't biologically yours but still being their dad.'

He took a moment before he answered. 'Do you want to adopt?'

'I'm just asking in theory, really. Do you think you could do it?'

Francesco stroked her arm and nuzzled into her neck. 'I think there's a million ways to make a family, and I'm open to them all,' he said.

Penny closed her eyes, smiling. 'I think the same,' she replied. 'Night.'

8

'Oh my god,' said Penny, her phone screen lighting up her face in the darkness. 'Francesco, wake up. Francesco!'

Francesco stirred and looked at the clock on the bedside table – it was 5 a.m.

'It's Uncle David. Something happened.'

He propped himself up on one elbow. 'What? What happened?'

'I'm not sure. Something to do with his heart? He's at the hospital. I've got to . . .'

Francesco reached out a hand. 'Hey,' he said, his touch warm and his voice calm. 'I'm here. It's okay. Get dressed. I'll take you.'

Penny could barely hear him. It felt like she'd been hit in the stomach with a plank of wood. All Eric's text said, after a string of missed calls, was: *We're at the Derby Royal. He's asking for you. It started with chest pains, waiting to find out more. Call me!!*

The next few hours were a blur. Francesco borrowed Safiya's bread delivery van and drove at one hundred miles per hour up the M1. It got lighter outside. Penny remembered realizing, sat in the hospital waiting room, that she was wearing her pyjama shorts under her jeans instead of underwear. She remembered how pale Eric had looked – she might remember that forever – and how little there was of him when they'd hugged, as if he'd shrunk from the worry. She remembered walking into the emergency room and wanting to walk back out, because Uncle David did not look like Uncle David.

'Eric . . .' Penny said. And then she burst into tears.

Francesco stayed with her through all of it, feeding her sugared tea when she refused to eat and calling Clementine to establish when she'd arrive with Rima. He'd gone down to the hospital shop to get a flannel, toothbrush and toothpaste so that Penny could freshen up, and let her rest her head in his lap, stroking her hair, as they waited for David to come out of surgery. He'd stayed, even in the scariest bits – especially because they were scary – and Penny had let herself need him throughout all of it. She held his hand, and didn't let go.

'You had me so fucking worried, Davvy.'

Penny all but launched herself at her uncle's bed, where he was sat up, feebly eating a hospital dinner. He was the colour of the pillowcase.

'He had us all worried,' Eric said, shaking his head. 'Fuck is about right.'

'The language in this room!' Uncle David croaked. 'Can we just tone it down!' He didn't sound like himself. He sounded paper thin, as though if Penny blew on him hard enough, he would crumple under the weight of her breath.

'You sound like hell,' she told him.

'Darling, I feel like hell,' he replied, feebly.

The three of them sat in silence for a moment, exhaling in the relief that he was alive, all of them acknowledging that it was a very close call.

'He works too hard,' Eric said. 'If you didn't work so hard . . .'

'Eric. Come on. Now's not the time.'

'You were at the pub when it happened?' Penny asked. Details were arriving piecemeal and she was trying to thread it all together.

'I found him surrounded by petit fours on the floor of the pastry section after service,' Eric said. 'I thought he'd slipped, but then he wasn't getting up.' He turned to David. 'You and me, we're going to have a talk. If you'd have died . . .'

Uncle David looked at Penny in a way that would have been pointed if he wasn't so sallow and grey. Penny gave him half a smile, happy to be his teammate against Eric's stern words. She'd made every promise she could think of to a god she wasn't even sure she believed in as they'd waited for him outside the operating room. *I'll visit him more,* she'd promised whoever was able to listen to the thoughts in her head. *I'll be a better niece. I'll buy him nicer presents for his birthday and call every day instead of once a week and if he gets through this I'll stop giving him a hard time about taking over the pub. I'll understand that he only wants the best for me. I'll be kinder to him, I will tell him I love him more . . .*

'Can I tell her?' Eric said to his husband.

'Tell me what?' Penny looked between them.

Uncle David nodded once, curtly. Eric turned to Penny and said, 'This is his second one.'

'Second what?'

109

'Second heart attack. He had one at New Year's. We didn't tell you, because . . .' Eric trailed off, as if he wasn't sure why.

Uncle David supplied, 'It was barely even a heart attack. It was . . . we just didn't want you to worry.'

Penny's jaw dropped. Why wouldn't they tell her Uncle David had been ill? Had had a heart attack?

'Does Clemmie know?' she said, trying to keep her voice level.

'No, darling.'

'And you've been working since then? Who has been running the pub?'

Eric and David looked at each other. To their testament they at least had the decency to look guilty. 'We've been doing our best,' Eric said slowly. 'I've done what I can. I don't know numbers very well and it's been a bit of a muddle, but Charlie has been brilliant behind the bar and all the staff have stepped up and done their best as well.'

Penny started to shake. 'I can't believe you didn't tell me,' she began. 'I need to know these things. What if something worse had happened? What if you'd died and I didn't know and I could have helped and . . .' The last two words came out in powerful sobs, and she stood back up from her plastic visitor's chair to go to her uncle, holding his arm and bending down to hug him, crying onto his shoulder. He let her.

'I'm sorry, Pen,' he said, trying to move his body so he could rub her back, a move that he'd done to her her whole life whenever she was upset.

'You can't be sorry for being ill!' she cried into his bedsheets.

'I'm getting old, these things happen . . .'

'You shouldn't be working if your health is bad! Bloody

hell!' She realized, then, in an instant, why the pressure to take over had become stronger and stronger lately. He couldn't run his own business – the business he'd spent his entire adult life building. He'd had a heart attack. And now another. The understanding of it all was dizzying. Penny felt sick. He'd been trying to tell her, in his own way, and every time Penny had accused him of trying to boss her around in her own life out of – what? Malice? His own interest? She'd been willingly deaf to the hints he'd tried to give her.

'Well,' Eric said. 'He won't be working now. The doctor says his heart muscle is very weak. He's been lucky, but apparently it's going to take several months for him to get better. The decision has been made for him.'

'Okay,' Penny nodded. 'That's good. Rest is good. You can do that, can't you Davvy? You can rest?'

'I've got no choice,' said Uncle David.

'Knock, knock,' a gentle voice came at the door. 'I don't mean to intrude, but Penny – I brought you a hot chocolate.' Penny had been lightly dozing and stirred slowly, taking it from Francesco with gratitude. 'I thought you could use the sugar.'

'Clever bean,' said Eric, standing. 'David, this is the Italian we've been hearing about. He was the one who got Penny up here, and in record time.'

'Hi,' said Francesco, extending a hand. 'I'm so sorry for what happened.'

'David,' Uncle David said, limply giving a handshake.

'I'm so pleased you're okay.'

'Thank you.' Uncle David's voice was still hollow. 'Thank you for getting my girl here, too. I appreciate it.'

Francesco nodded in response and then read the mood of

the room. 'Okay,' he said, 'I'll leave you all to it. Penny – do you want me to call someone at the café? Stuart knows what's going on and is just going to do coffee and cake service, but is there anything else I can tell him?'

Penny shook her head. 'Whatever you think is best,' she said, unable to even think about work. 'I trust you.'

'Sure. Okay. Well, feel better,' Francesco said to David. Uncle David smiled.

When he'd gone, Uncle David said, 'Nice man.'

'Yeah,' said Penny, sipping delicately at the drink he'd brought her. 'He is.'

Later, waiting in the hall because Uncle David had nurses in his room running checks and fussing with blankets, Eric hugged Penny and told her, 'I was so scared, Pen. I'm going to do whatever it takes to get him back to full health. I promise you.' Eric and Uncle David had been together for eleven years now. He was as much a part of the family as they all were. Penny felt a stab of shame that she hadn't thought to pick up the mantle and look after him in the same way Francesco had looked after her. All she could think about was her uncle – in her worry she forgot that Eric must have been beside himself, too. Uncle David and Eric lived for each other – she couldn't imagine one without the other.

'I'll do anything to help,' she said. 'I can't lose him, either. He's all we have . . .' She started to cry again, and Eric hugged her closer, crying too.

'Sssssssh,' he said, in between his own tears. 'Sssssssssh. It's okay. He's going to be okay.'

They stood for a long time, gaining strength from each other as they cried it out. Uncle David had Eric. And, thankfully,

Penny still had Uncle David. Whoever Penny had prayed to had spared her uncle and for that she was endlessly thankful. Without him, she'd be lost. It was unthinkable.

'I want to take him to the coast for a bit,' Eric explained, as they wandered the ward aimlessly, sitting feeling like too little action, even though there was nothing they could be doing. 'To my sister's holiday place. Rest. Sea air. No work.'

Penny nodded. 'I think that's a good idea,' she replied. 'The doctors made it very clear he needs to be kept away from that kitchen and I think the more miles between him and work, so much the better.'

'The thing is . . .' Eric started, and Penny understood. The thing was, was that somebody else needed to run The Red Panda.

'You need me up here,' Penny supplied.

'I can't think how else we might manage. We can't sell it. Not right now. It would kill him. That place is his life's work.'

'I know,' nodded Penny. She had tears in her eyes again. When would she stop crying?

'And to be honest, after the start to the year we've had, business hasn't been easy. So even if I could convince him to sell it, the books don't look as good as usual. We just need a year or so to get all that lined up. Looking strong. Maybe then we could sell.'

Penny tried to think of another way to do it. Hiring somebody else, maybe, or . . . Well. Maybe those were the options: they hired somebody else, or they hired Penny, who had grown up there, and knew the village and the people and the kitchen and what her uncle had been trying to achieve all along.

She had the edges of a truth at the forefront of her mind, and the faintest notion that it was time for her to step up for her family – the way her family had stepped up for her – lingering on the outer parts of her consciousness. She wasn't ready to agree to it yet, though. There was Bridges, and Francesco, and her life. But then, as they looped back to David's room, she got it implicitly: *what is all that for if I don't have my uncle?* she thought. And then: *Oh, shit.*

'I'm just glad he's going to be okay,' Clementine said, sat beside Rima, and opposite Penny and Francesco. She was pale and the circles under her eyes looked like bruises. Penny assumed she looked no better. 'I need to see him more. I've been a bad niece. Daughter. Person. I don't see him enough.'

'Hey,' said Rima, her arm around her wife. 'Don't be so hard on yourself. You do your best. You call him when you're away, you visit when you can.'

'It's not enough though, is it? I should love him harder.'

'I should love him harder too,' Penny cried, wrapping her arms around herself. 'Oh, Clem, I just don't know what to do. Like, it's supposed to be a no-brainer: I go and take over the pub. If I loved him that's what I would do, isn't it?'

Clementine shrugged, dabbing at her eyes with a tissue. 'I can't tell you what to do on that one,' she stuttered. Her voice was kind, like she really felt sorry for Penny. 'Nobody would expect you to uproot your life that way . . .'

'Except they would. And if you were the sister who cooked, I'd expect you to do it.'

Clementine didn't say anything to that.

'I know I can do it. It's a huge place, and I'd have to work twice as hard as I do. I just . . . I changed my mind about wanting that life. I know you understand that. I love Stoke Newington, now, and I love Bridges and my life there. I'd feel this way even if The Red Panda was next door. It's a lot. A whole pub. A restaurant pub. I don't want that anymore.'

She was letting it all out, now, this stream of consciousness.

'But he was there through everything, Clementine. He's a dad and a mum and an uncle and a friend and a cheerleader. And I am so, so mad he's putting me in this position, and what's worse is that he hasn't even asked me yet. Eric basically did, but I get a sense that they're waiting for me to offer. I wonder if I can give it a year, or agree to do it for two. Until he is stronger and can decide if he wants to sell. Huh. Like that isn't what Eric has wanted for years. Eric has wanted to sell and Uncle David has waited it out to see if he can convince me to take over, and now here we are . . . literally life or death. I can't tell him I'm mad but I am. I am so, so mad he'd ask me to do this. Even though he isn't asking. I'm so mad that I have to offer.'

The tears came harder, every atom of worry from the past twelve hours leaking from her eyes.

'I'm so mad. But I'm so relieved.'

'I'm going to go and find some tissues,' Francesco soothed, understanding he was encroaching on a deeply personal family discussion. 'Can I get anybody anything else?' He knew Penny needed her sister right now, and it was better to excuse himself for a moment. The women all watched him head towards the hospital shop for fake supplies.

'And then there's Francesco,' Penny hissed, her voice lowered. 'It started to feel like something, and I know it still can be, in theory, but also he is there and I will be here and he works shifts and I'm going to be in charge and probably

115

never get a day off and it's just asking for heartbreak, isn't it? I'd be heartbroken to leave him in London – but I don't want to limp on with him until Christmas and then be heartbroken all over again.'

Clementine slid across to Penny's side of the table and started to stroke her hair, like their mother used to do when they were small.

'No,' she insisted. 'You could make it work. People do.' Rima leaned across the table with both hands, each one grabbing a sister and doing the only thing she could: holding on tightly.

'I'm just not strong enough, Clemmie. I don't feel strong enough for any of it.' Penny looked to the ceiling, the tiles of it blurring as she blinked away her misgivings. 'But for Uncle David I have to pull myself together, don't I? What is the point of love if your family is falling apart? Family first, right? Look at all he has done for us.'

'It's alright,' Clementine whispered. 'You don't have to decide this now. It's okay. Come on.'

But Penny did have to decide now. She had to decide so much in an instant, and yet, really, truly, the choice had already been made: of course she'd go and run The Red Panda. Of course she would.

'And the surrogacy . . .' Penny said, trailing off. She couldn't stand to finish the sentence. Whatever trepidation she'd had around it, it was another choice made for her: it would have to wait.

'I know,' said Clementine. 'But the offer isn't going anywhere. Everything is figureoutable.'

Penny closed her eyes in Clementine's lap. The tears dried up and she felt an eerie sense of numbness. Her uncle was alive – but there was so much more she would now be losing.

She counted to five as she inhaled, and counted the same as she exhaled. It felt like the only thing she had any say over was that. Five in, five out. Five in, five out. She counted until she fell asleep in her sister's lap.

9

'You're sure this is what you want?'

'Yes.'

'You want to stop seeing each other?'

'Yes.'

'Even though we already fell in friendship?'

Penny smiled. She was doing her best to do her best. Trying hard to do the right thing. It hurt, but she couldn't see any other way.

'But that's just it, isn't it?' she said. 'Wasn't that always the point? We *can* be friends.'

Francesco sat for a moment on Penny's sofa, chewing his bottom lip and staring at the coffee table. 'But,' he said, plainly. 'I don't want to be friends. I want to be with you properly.'

Penny had paced up and down the flat, around and around, as she'd waited for him to arrive that evening. He'd stayed with her all day at the hospital and then driven her back that night, once they knew David would be okay. She'd told him in the car on the way down that she was thinking of going up to Havingley, in Derbyshire, to help out as her uncle recovered, but Francesco hadn't fully understood that she meant that she would move there for the foreseeable future and have Stuart run Bridges. By the time she'd woken up that morning, what needed to happen next was crystal clear to her.

'This makes no sense to me,' Francesco said. He didn't move to be beside her, or kiss her, or try to change her mind with his touch. All he had were his words, and already he knew they weren't enough. Her body language had changed, she'd made something about herself harder already.

'I promised I would never knowingly hurt you,' Penny consoled. 'And you promised to never knowingly hurt me. If we don't end this now, one of us will get hurt. I just know it. I can't . . .' She refused to cry. Crying wouldn't be fair on Francesco because then he'd want to reassure her, and she couldn't make him do that. 'I just don't have it in me. This is all too much. I owe it to Uncle David to do this.'

She straightened up, and Francesco could see her literally pull herself together.

'My mind is made up,' she said. 'This is the way it has to be. Let's be friends. I want that desperately.'

Francesco was blindsided but what else was there to say?

'Okay,' was all he could manage, trying to be strong for her, not understanding that what Penny needed was for him to crumble and say he couldn't live without her and that he'd come as well. She knew, of course, that that would never happen. They'd only been together three weeks. Not even a month. That would be crazy, to go with her. She couldn't ask him to, and he couldn't offer.

And so he didn't say anything except *okay.*

Okay, even though it was anything but.

*

Things moved fast. Arrangements were made for Penny's occasional stand-in chef Billy to take over the cooking at Bridges, and for Stu to run the day-to-day handling of the place. Penny would just about break even in what it would cost to pay everyone more to cover her time, but at least she wasn't losing anything and the business could truck on without her. She told herself it was for a year – eighteen months, max. It took her a day and a half to decide what to take with her and what to leave behind, and Francesco organized a small hire car for her so she could drive up there herself, and then that was it. She would be leaving.

The day came. Francesco helped her move her things from the flat, and she thought, maybe naively, that he really was going to ask to come with her. It had been the best three weeks of her life before Uncle David's heart attack, and then in the blink of an eye it had become a sort of waking nightmare in which the man who'd parented her was sick, her sister was unavoidably heading to the other side of the world again, Eric had missed his own birthday party and a man she really bloody fancied was a man she couldn't now be with. If they'd been together only the tiniest bit longer – six weeks, say, or three months – then she'd have asked him. She would have said, 'This is crazy, and I know it is, but: do you want an adventure?'

After they'd packed the car together, she opened the driver's door and climbed in. Slamming it shut and starting the engine she could see Francesco and how sad he looked, and part of her thought he was going to do it. That he was going to say, 'Penny, let me come with you.'

He didn't though. He didn't say anything. She wound the window down and croaked, 'Everything is going to be fine.'

She wiped at her eyes. She hadn't noticed when she'd started to cry. 'Tell me it's all going to be fine.'

'It's all going to be fine,' Francesco said, smiling.

Her phone beeped. It was Sharon. *I love you, brave friend,* it said. Penny didn't reply.

Stuart blew a kiss to her from beside Francesco and said, 'Drive safe, and text when you get there, okay?'

'I will,' she said. 'I promise.'

Her gaze shifted to Francesco. 'See you,' she said.

Francesco raised a hand. 'See you,' he replied.

Penny pulled away from the kerb, heading slowly up the high street. She turned the corner and waited with her blinker on to pull out onto the main road. The traffic felt endless. She sat with tears now flowing freely only realizing she'd stopped the bravado of being strong when one dropped from her chin onto her hand, which she then saw was shaking. Moving this way, leaving everything behind – she'd had no choice. That's what she told herself. Uncle David was her world, he was the only family she had left besides her sister, and if this is what he needed from her then this is what she had to do.

But at the same time, visions of Francesco doing it alongside her flashed through her mind.

The realization came. She didn't know the details, but she needed to go back. It wasn't like he was happy at his job, anyway – right?

'Gah!' she screamed, understanding that she really did have to ask him. He'd once told her he wanted to stay in London forever if he could, that he couldn't bear the thought of moving again, but it didn't matter what he said in response – life was too short not to ask. She knew that all too well, and she knew better than to think a connection like this could happen more than a handful of times in a person's life. She bet that there were people out there for whom a connection like this had *never* happened and what? She wasn't going to trust enough in it to turn around and at least *enquire*?

A car behind her honked and she made her choice. She pulled out onto the road in a right-hand swing that meant she had enough room to U-turn back down the road she'd just come from. Penny was only driving at fifteen miles per hour but she felt like she was hitting a hundred for all the adrenaline coursing through her.

'This is crazy . . .' she rehearsed under her breath. 'Francesco! Come with me!' she practised.

The car made the last corner turn back to Bridges and she could see him still out on the street in front. 'I'm coming!' she said under her breath. But then she could see that there was another person with him – a woman. She had long, wild, curly hair and skin the colour of a polished walnut. The woman was gesticulating with her hands and Francesco was gesticulating back, and in the middle of the road, far enough from them not to be able to hear but close enough to be able to see, Penny watched as the woman pushed her face against Francesco's. Penny slowed to a halt. She waited for Francesco to pull away, for this to have been a mistake, for him to turn around and see her and understand that she'd done it – she'd come back for him. But that's not what happened. Their faces stayed pressed together, and Francesco moved to push the woman up against the wall beside the café – Penny's café – and before Penny could unpick the who or the what or the why or the how, she'd put the gear stick into reverse, checked her mirrors, and edged back around the corner to speed, as fast as she could, towards the M1 north. By the time she'd reached Toddington Services she'd convinced herself that she'd known all along Francesco would break her heart, and she was relieved she'd found out the truth about him sooner rather than later.

Deciding to hate him was the only thing that finally stopped her crying.

10

'Service!' Penny called out from behind the pass, where four plates were lined up, ready to be delivered to the table they called Bar Four.

'Yes chef!' replied Agnieszka, a Polish waitress with alabaster white skin and feline, blue eyes.

Penny spoke quickly but firmly. She had two more tables to plate up. 'We've got the Sri Lankan King Prawn and Cod Curry,' she said, using a cloth from her shoulder to wipe a small dollop of liquid from the side of the bowl. 'This is Derbyshire Lamb Rump, that one is the Club Sandwich, and that one,' she said, pointing to the final dish, 'is the Pork Chop with Apples. Sides are seasonal veg, creamed savoy cabbage, and two portions of parmesan truffle fries. Thank you.' She turned to her sous chef, Manuela. 'How long on the sauce for the braised beef, chef?'

'Thirty seconds, chef,' Manuela replied, not looking up from the pan she was vigorously stirring.

Manuela was a small fifty-something-year-old Filipino woman who Uncle David had hired seven years ago for her quiet demeanour and steady work ethic. Penny had met her in passing over the years as she'd come to visit, but hadn't truly understood Manuela's capabilities until she took over from her uncle. It turned out Manuela had been running the kitchen more or less herself since last Christmas, when Uncle David started to slow down, so she thought like a head chef – making her the best sous Penny could have asked for.

Penny plated up another curry and pork chop, called service, and then started in on the last dishes of the day.

'Bar One say that was delicious, chef,' Agnieszka trilled, as she sailed by the pass carrying dirty plates she'd just cleared.

'Ahhh, thank you!' Penny replied, wiping sweat from her brow.

Hair stuck to the side of her face. She'd cut it all off just after moving, so that it was shoulder length, and now she had the last remnants of a fringe that – it turned out – hadn't suited her. How many women would have to suffer the ill-fated 'fringe after a romantic devastation' before a less strident expression of malaise was found?

Penny added: 'How many covers tonight?'

'I'll check with Charlie,' Agnieszka said, her accent thick and delivery efficient. Penny adored her – she never complained, the customers loved her, and she didn't take any shit.

Penny flicked off the lights opposite the cookers, instantly feeling relief from the heat.

'That must have been more than seventy people we served tonight,' Manuela instructed. 'Maybe seventy-five.'

'It felt like a hundred and seventy-five,' replied Penny,

slipping her foot out of her Croc so she could stretch out her ankle. 'I still can't get used to the leap from thirty or forty plates a day to *this*. This is kicking my ass.'

'They're all coming for you, Pen,' Manuela grinned. 'I've never seen anything like it. You're putting this place on the map.'

The Red Panda was going from strength to strength under Penny's command, and her impact on staff morale, the kitchen, the décor – all of it was immediate. Profit was up, overheads were down, but more than that: she was good at running a bigger place. There'd been a few early issues – she'd not known how to work the till, and screwed up the rota the first three weeks she'd been there, not to mention sleeping in one Sunday and almost missing service because she was used to Bridges being closed on a Sunday and having the day off – but mostly, she'd hit her stride. Maybe it was because there wasn't much else to focus on – no men to distract her, no big city to seduce her and occupy her time – but Uncle David had been right that she'd thrive under a different sort of pressure. Penny had updated the menu and streamlined how service was run, as well as laying out training days and enforcing 'Family Dinners' so that staff got fed together between lunch and evening service.

She missed Sharon, and Stuart, and the tiny kitchen at the back of Bridges. She missed her routine, and the rhythm of her days. She missed so much of her old life, but took comfort in being surrounded by lush green hills and the almost obscene friendliness of everyone in the village. It was lovely to go for a walk and see people who knew her name and asked after her uncle. There weren't many people she'd gone to school with left – loads had moved to Nottingham, or

Leicester – making the median age of the immediate demographic closer to sixty than thirty. But Havingley was where her mother was buried and being there made Penny feel close to her. She was enjoying the change of scenery, too, and the physical space around her meant she felt physical space in her mind as well.

Especially from *him*.

Penny had been steadfast in her promise to herself: she'd never cried over him, and hadn't spoken to him since she'd left, either.

That prick, is how Sharon referred to him. She'd been even more furious than Penny. *That. Prick.* Penny tried not to think of him by name, either.

That prick is all he got.

That prick had tried to text and tried to call over and over again for weeks after Penny had left. He'd even sent a letter to the pub. He'd started out hopeful, wondering how she was, if they were allowed to talk – they'd not discussed any 'rules' around communication, but friends stayed in touch so this was him staying in touch, he'd said.

Stay in touch with that woman you were kissing, Penny had thought, darkly.

She'd examined that whole situation from every perspective, trying to make sense of what had happened. It could have been his ex, but after what he'd said Penny was sure he'd never get back with her. Had he been dating somebody else at the same time he'd been dating her? Clementine said she just couldn't believe it. Sharon said at least they'd found out he was an arse sooner rather than later. Stuart said he'd seen nothing, but he did have a vague recollection of a woman with big curly hair asking after Francesco once, which he'd thought was odd because how had she known Francesco had been spending time at Bridges? Not that it mattered anymore. Penny had a job to do: get The Red Panda in tip-top shape, and in only six more months, once Uncle David was fully better, she could be back at home. She didn't hate having to be there, but she knew it wasn't the place for her. London was her heart and soul's true home.

Uncle David had come to visit once, but otherwise he'd stayed at Eric's sister's second home on the Cornish coast to convalesce. He was still mildly grey in complexion, even months after his heart attack, and Penny had tried to suggest to Eric that maybe he was depressed. Penny had experienced it herself – the feeling of total helplessness when the body betrays, when it feels so out of your control to do anything other than rest, and go slow, and accept the help of everyone around you. Penny knew there was no way he could have continued to work. There was no way this could have played out any differently. She was always going to end up here, so she just had to make the best of it. She kept her head down, all of her attentions on the pub, and pressed on.

Penny's favourite person at The Red Panda, even considering the strong contenders of second-in-command Manuela and efficient Agnieszka, was her old friend Charlie.

After Penny and Clementine had moved from a village ten miles away to be with their uncle in Havingley, they'd often walk to school with Charlie or hang out after homework club eating jam sandwiches and watching TV. Charlie's mother was a cleaner at the pub, and had taken Penny and Clementine under her wing, never asking questions about their mother or talking ill of their father, but simply being there as a routine, a benign figure in the background who never overstepped the maternal mark but provided reassurance through continuity. As an adult, Penny recognized that was half the battle of feeling okay on any sort of day-to-day basis: continuity. She'd spent so long in her twenties trying to eschew any kind of banality in routine, and yet it was inevitable as she got older that banality was often the sweetest kind of refuge.

'You stay here,' Charlie said to Penny from where they waded through old bottles and kegs in the cellar, in between lunch and dinner service. A voice had infiltrated where they were hanging out whilst also working, and immediately Charlie had identified it as belonging to Priyesh, their wine merchant. Penny rolled her eyes.

'I'll deal with him,' Charlie insisted. 'I know how. We don't want him lingering for a whole hour like he did last time he held you hostage.'

Penny fixed her mouth in a traumatized straight line at the memory – Priyesh was a man who liked a monologue, and an audience for it. Not long after she'd taken over, Penny had been cornered by him out by the recycling bins and returned back to the kitchen with visible sunburn she'd been out there that long. She'd avoided him ever since, under the excuse that she didn't need to interfere with the bar when Charlie was so capable. Really, she simply didn't like him.

Charlie was gender non-binary and recently had explained – patiently, Penny had thought – that they didn't want to be referred to as 'she' or 'her'. Charlie was 'they' or 'them', and had clarified that they didn't need Penny to understand them in order to respect them, which Penny understood implicitly.

Penny pulled bottles from the wine-rack on the furthest wall as Charlie clamoured up to the bar. She blew dust off of a 2016 bottle of Tignanello Antinori Toscana and admired her find. 'I might keep this,' she thought, *that prick*'s face elbowing its way into her head. She had a sudden image of them by the fire, drinking it together, him taking in the surroundings and admiring this new place she called home. There are a lot of things she would have liked to have told him about the past six months – if they were speaking.

'Well, I was rather hoping to see the proprietress,' Penny could hear from up in the bar. His voice was booming and commanding, and it was Penny's default response to roll her eyes. She couldn't help it. 'It seems rather improper that I don't deal with the person in charge.'

Penny stepped a few inches closer to the ladder up to the bar where he was talking with Charlie. She knew she *should* see the wine merchant, but she couldn't be bothered to paint on a smile and be charming today. Not when her perfectly capable front of house manager was there and was much better at getting rid of him quickly. What was it about men who liked their own voices and could never take a hint? He should respect Charlie's authority, Penny thought.

Charlie said, 'Unless you want to scramble down those steps through the cobwebs and into the underground cellar in your three-piece suit, I don't think today's your day.'

Good on ya, thought Penny. *You tell him.*

'David always gave me the time,' the man continued. 'This is the second time I've been by and she's busy. I'd hate to take it personally.'

'Priyesh, are you after a free lunch? Is that what this is all about?'

'Hardly,' Priyesh replied. 'I can buy my own lunch, and you know that. Although David did often try out his dishes on me. I've got a very attuned palate, you know.'

'I am sure you do,' Charlie said. 'Listen. We need a minute before we figure out the last seasonal order, if that's okay. I just found out we're closing after December twenty-fifth and Penny has discovered whole crates of stuff we didn't know we had, so we're getting the lay of the land.'

'Perhaps I could assist . . .' Priyesh began.

'We'll let you know if we need anything. Penny is pretty au fait with wine. David taught her a lot.'

'Well, we know who schooled David.'

Penny made a gagging noise from the floor below him. He truly was the most boring person to have ever crossed The Red Panda's threshold. She had no idea how Uncle David managed him – she'd have to ask next time they spoke.

'Thanks so much for understanding, and for dropping by unannounced personally. That's quite the service,' Charlie smiled, and Penny could tell from their voice it was through gritted teeth.

'Well, as I said. I was rather hoping to see Penelope.'

'She just goes by Penny,' Charlie sighed. 'I don't think we're supposed to rename people without their permission.'

'I see,' Priyesh said. 'Penny. Very well. Please do pass along my calling card to her and tell her I look forward to an audience just as soon as we might find a time of mutual convenience. I'm doing my best not to take offence, and yet here we are.'

'I'll pass the message along.'

'What a twat,' said Penny, as Charlie re-entered the cellar.

'I've never wanted to colour your opinion,' they said. 'But yeah.'

'Tell you what,' grinned Penny, pulling out another bottle of the Tignanello. 'Make sure he gets an invite to the staff Christmas party, so I can give him a bit of attention, but also have a get-out clause. If I have to relive our summer interaction

132

again I'll die. Actually cease to exist on this mortal coil through sheer boredom of interacting. And Penelope? Urgh. Nobody has called me that since my mother.'

The mention of her mother made her heart beat in double time. *Tug, tug, tug* – never would she be able to refer to her mother without feeling the loss all over again. Grief was like that. There was no end point.

'Priyesh at a party,' marvelled Charlie. 'I can't picture it.'

'He really is that bad, isn't he? Even that first time I met him I thought so. I can't believe we haven't talked about this!'

'He's just . . . buttoned up. He's all business and doesn't really laugh a lot and there's a distance he keeps you at. You can ask him how his weekend was or whatever and he always just says, "Fine, thank you," and never returns the question or gives you any details. I've known him maybe seven years now and I couldn't even tell you anything beyond his name. And he doesn't seem interested in anything other than *my* name. I just find it a bit odd.'

'How old do you reckon he is?'

'Forty-five, maybe fifty?'

'Yeah, I think so too. The thing is, he's actually quite fit. But boring. But also . . . fit! Do you think he's married?'

'Oh, that's something I do know about, actually. Not from him. I think he was married a while ago – before I started working here full time – and she left him. He has this huge estate and lives there alone and sells wine. Let the record show that I've never seen the estate, and all of this is pure rumour. But yeah, jilted appaz.'

'I would say something cutting about small minds gossiping, but here I am, getting the gossip myself.'

'I'll make sure he gets an invite to the party, anyway,' Charlie said. 'I can't believe it's nearly Christmas already.'

'And we've hit our financial target for the year already too,' Penny said. 'Which means only one sitting on Christmas Day. I can't wait to close right through to the second week of the new year. I need a proper break.'

'Yeah, all this change has been a lot,' Charlie agreed.

'Hasn't it just?' said Penny, flopping down on a beer barrel to take a breath. 'I'm so thankful you're here, though. Have I told you that lately?'

'Well, you haven't told me in at least forty-five minutes.'

Penny laughed. 'How would you feel about this bottle of red tonight? They've just put *The Notebook* on Netflix again if you want to cry like a baby with me. It's one of my favourite pastimes. Lights out by midnight, though, otherwise I'll be no good to anyone.'

'I'll bring the Minstrels,' said Charlie.

'Oooooh, maybe some sweet and salty popcorn too?'

'Perfect.'

Penny ended up with a hangover from the bottle of red she'd shared with Charlie, and a margarita they'd had beforehand, too, as an *aperitif*. That was all it took – one cocktail and half a bottle of wine – to feel murderous the next day.

'Well darling,' Uncle David said. 'That's not exactly a small amount, is it?'

'Oh piss off,' Penny shot back, to which Uncle David looked hugely shocked across FaceTime, making Penny promptly burst into tears. 'I'm sorry,' she sniffled, pathetically. 'I'm sorry Davvy.'

'It's okay darling. Are these hangover tears? Or something else?'

Penny shook her head. Uncle David looked unwell still, and it upset her. She could tell just by looking he was still weak, still not himself. She just wanted him to be better already.

'Hangover tears,' Penny said, hoping that that was true. She'd woken up feeling like something was sat on her chest, suffocating her. Not literally – emotionally. Maybe it was because she'd been drinking the night before, but she felt anxious about everything as she made her morning coffee and switched on the news. Anxious about Uncle David, anxious about her life, and weirdly anxious about *that prick*. Surely it wasn't normal to obsess over a fling for this long, she worried. Surely she was over-dramatizing the whole thing. She hated how he could barrel into her imagination and demand her attention. She probably didn't even cross his mind. *Penny who?* he'd say, if somebody asked about her.

Uncle David smiled down the camera. 'Nice big glass of water and five minutes in the sun before service, alright jelly-belly?'

'Yeah,' she said.

'And maybe get out of Havingley for a bit, if you can. I know it's busy, but it's important to take some time out for yourself, too, even if it's just for an afternoon.'

'Okay,' acknowledged Penny. 'Sorry to cry. I think my hormones are doing something crazy is all. I'll ask the doctor next time I see him.'

'I love you,' Uncle David soothed. 'You're making me so, so proud. I'd be proud anyway, but. Well. You know. Thank you. I know you never really wanted to be up there, but I'm grateful you are.'

'It's okay. I love you too,' Penny said. 'Tell Eric I love him as well.'

'Will do darling. Have a good day, okay?'

*

135

The water and five minutes in the sun helped, and fortunately Penny was ahead of herself in terms of kitchen prep so, as long as it was a quiet service, she knew she'd have time to nap before dinner. She definitely felt delicate, though, and so it was with a wince that she heard the gravel of the car park being flung into the air as somebody spun around and into a parking bay at a speed about twenty times higher than they should. Two more cars followed behind.

'What the hell . . .?' she said, under her breath, glancing out the window. 'Who the hell are these guys, Manuela? Have you seen them? All the sports cars in the car park?'

'The boys,' said Manuela, rolling her eyes. 'A big group of them – maybe every three or four months. They come, they drink, and then they drive home.'

'They drink and drive?'

Manuela nodded.

'But they also spend a lot.'

'Figures,' said Penny, craning her neck to try and see them better. 'I should say something. They can't drive that fast! They could honest-to-god kill somebody! Urgh!'

'Idiots,' said Manuela.

Later, Charlie said a table out front wanted to meet the chef. It had happened a few times since her arrival, though it still surprised Penny that guests could be so kind as to tell her they'd enjoyed her food face to face.

When the kitchen ran well it was like a ballet – her and Manuela working in harmony to create the dishes, Paul on the pastry section and Ollie in the pot-wash. It was true teamwork, and those shifts, where Penny truly occupied herself in the moment, were her happiest, and it was often reflected in the food. Those were the shifts where people requested to shake her hand, asking after her uncle and her future plans for the place. Those were the days she felt like she belonged. Today, though, had not been one of those days. Her hangover meant Penny had felt agitated and irritable. She'd snapped at Manuela *and* at Paul. Everything felt like too much work, and on those days the veneer of positivity she'd adopted – that she was okay being there, that she didn't miss Bridges that much, that it was only for a year anyway – came crashing down. She'd tried to get out of going out front and speaking to the customers who'd requested her but Charlie said the group were insistent, and it was then Penny understood it was the group of men who drove their fancy cars and drank too much for a lunch and were stupid enough to drive home afterwards.

'Oh god,' she said to Charlie. 'Let the record show I tried to fight you on this, so if I now end up fighting one of these fools that's my get-out-of-jail-free card, okay?'

'You're too charming to be rude,' said Charlie. 'But just so you know: I'm hungover too and I've managed them okay, so no excuses.' They shot a placating smile and went to unload the glasswasher.

Penny pushed through the doors and arranged the features of her face into the closest approximation of friendly that she could muster. The kitchen led on to what they called 'Bottom Bar', with five tables that were all now empty. The group of men were sat through the archway in 'Top Bar', meaning Penny could hear them before she saw them.

She turned the corner and they all looked up.

'Whaaayyyyy!' shouted one of them, like he was at a football match. 'Chef!'

The other men around the table – six of them, all about

Penny's age, if not a tiny bit older, used their fingers to drum on the wood with increasing volume before a head of blonde curls yelled above the din, 'Alright chaps, she gets it! She gets the point!'

Penny stood, bemused, wondering if that was it. Their drumming had made her head throb. The men resumed talking amongst themselves, arguing over who was going to pay the bill that sat in the middle of their table. They were all waving their credit cards about like swords, vying to be the one to show off by settling up what was indelibly in the high hundreds.

'Thank you, gentlemen,' Penny said, turning back around. 'I'm glad you enjoyed it.' She would normally have added *please come again* but she wasn't sure if she actually did want them to come again. They were bloody noisy.

'Sorry about us all,' the blonde curls bellowed after her. 'We've had a great time!'

Penny didn't turn back around. She wanted a cigarette. And she wanted the men to go home.

It was a dry day for winter, and so Penny flopped down on the back step down to the car park to smoke her roll-up. She typically didn't like customers seeing her staff smoking or loitering, and for anybody else she would have stood and moved out of sight – but, hangover considered, she stayed where she was when she saw the lingering group from lunch leaving.

'Oh hey!' said one of them, clocking where she was sat. It was the blonde, curly-haired one. He wore Gucci silk joggers, boisterously shouting about their designer status with looping 'G's' all over them. His collared t-shirt was similarly patterned but Louis Vuitton, and he'd pushed up the sleeves of his

Burberry coat to reveal a huge Omega Seamaster weighing down his wrist – Penny spotted it because she knew Uncle David had once bought a similar one for Eric, who had made him take it back because, he said, 'Nobody needs five grand to tell the time, you big twat.'

Playboy, was her assessment. *He's a total playboy.* She could just about wager that if she looked him up on Instagram there'd be photo after photo of him in varying states of undress and in a smorgasbord of exotic locales around the country, if not the world. She bet none of them would feature a smile – only a pout – and that if he hadn't applied for *Love Island* directly he had at least imagined that if he did, he'd get on it. He was *that* kind of man. That kind of playboy.

'I don't get to come home too often,' the playboy said to her, reaching out a hand, inviting her to shake it, 'and truly, I'll miss it all the more now I know what my local has become. My compliments,' he added. 'This was the best meal I've had in a long time. And sorry we were so loud. There's no excuse. We're just a bit twattish after a drink.'

Penny didn't stand, but extended a hand in return.

'You're very kind,' she said, primly. 'Thank you.'

He waited for her to say something else, but Penny refused. She was knackered, emotional, and didn't have time for men who acted like louts and drunk drove.

'Did you grow up here?' the playboy pressed. 'The barperson – they said something about you being related to Dave?'

'David,' Penny responded, taking the last drag of her cigarette.

'Oh, yes. David. I called him Dave – it was a bit of a joke between us.'

Penny stood to go back inside and take that nap she'd promised herself.

'Not very talkative today?'

Penny raised her eyebrows. 'I'm just tired, and have a lot to do.' She knew she was being overtly stand-offish, so also added: 'Thank you so much for telling me you enjoyed it. Have a good afternoon.'

He wouldn't let her go.

'You weren't at Havingley School, were you?' he said to her back. 'I feel like I recognize you.' She turned around again to face him. 'How old are you?'

Penny audibly exhaled. 'I just had my birthday. I'm thirty-one. And yes, I was.'

'I knew I knew your face! I'm Thomas. Thomas Eddlington. I was in the year above you.'

Penny narrowed her eyes, trying to place him. 'Did you used to go out with Veronica Meadows?'

The playboy – Thomas – let out a hoot. 'Yes! Verny! She's married now, to her university boyfriend. Got two kids and a big house in Sheffield.'

'Good for her,' Penny said. 'I mean, unless she left you for the man she's married to now. In which case, sucks to be you.' The playboy laughed.

'No, no, we were long over. I think I might have snogged her mate, actually. All very immature.'

'How shocking.'

'Hey, don't judge me on one loud lunch. I said sorry!'

'Well. Anyway. I really do have to go. And you guys should call cabs.'

Thomas nodded. 'Listen, um. I'm around for a couple of weeks,' he continued. 'I'm in the music business and it can all get a bit crazy, so I keep the house out here to remind me to calm down a bit. You know, when I get a bit carried away and all that.'

'Party boy,' Penny said, but it wasn't a question. She'd seen how many empty bottles there were – although, to his credit, talking to him didn't feel like talking to a drunk. His eyes weren't glazed or anything.

'I don't really drink, actually. I'm designated driver. Definitely don't do drugs. I think I'd get addicted – I've got an addictive personality. Workaholic, more like,' he replied. 'I just love what I do.'

Penny smiled. 'That, I understand,' she admitted.

'You can tell. Your food – you're really good.'

'Cheers,' Penny said. They stood. Out of politeness more than a real desire to talk to him she commented, 'The music industry sounds cool, though.'

'It is. It's as cool as you'd expect. I've been working with Lizzo for years and years – do you know her? – and then two years ago she got massive and it's just been the wildest time since then. We've been everywhere.'

'Lizzo?' said Penny, her interest piqued. 'What do you do for Lizzo? I love her! I literally had her album on when I was cooking your food.'

'Oh, no way, really? I can get you tickets to one of the UK shows soon if you want. I'm her tour manager,' he said with a boyish enthusiasm.

'Her album is brilliant,' Penny said. 'That song "Jerome" – urgh. That's my shower song. In my imagination when I am in the shower I *am* Lizzo.'

Thomas chuckled.

'No, actually, more than that – I am Lizzo *at Glastonbury*,' Penny continued. 'Bottle of tequila in one hand, microphone in the other . . .'

'Yeah, she killed it that afternoon,' he agreed. 'We were all on cloud nine after that.'

'You were there?'

'I was. And I'm not even going to pretend I'm not smug about it. Like I said, I love what I do.'

'It's written all over your face,' Penny acknowledged.

Thomas sensed the change in Penny's tone, then, and changed tack with her. 'Do you get much time away from here?' he said, hopefully. 'I like to go walking, try to stay out in the fresh air a lot when I'm back. I'm sure you're very busy but, in case, you know, you aren't. If you want to hang out.'

'That's a kind offer,' said Penny. She wanted to tell him she had plenty of friends, and not a lot of time off, but in that split second she realized the only friend she really had in Havingley was Charlie – and they were an employee, too. Everybody else was a phone call or FaceTime or voice note away, and whilst she was loved and heard and seen, very little of that was actually done in person. The realization of just how starved she was of physical human connection hit her then. She needed more friends. And she certainly needed more time away from the pub, which was hard when she was the one in charge. She'd only really even left Havingley a handful of times since arriving.

'I would love to go out for a walk with you, actually.' She meant it. She didn't realize until he'd asked that she was longing for fresh air, and the outdoors, and, basically, time away from The Red Panda. No wonder she was feeling exhausted lately: she lived and breathed the place. Uncle David had been right.

'Excellent. I'll stop by sometime? We'll walk?'

Penny nodded. It would do her good, she figured. 'Yeah,' she said. 'Awesome.'

'Okay, awesome.'

He went to say something else but then didn't.

'Awesome,' he repeated, before one of his mates stuck his head around the corner and said,

'Come on, Eddlington. I'm gagging for a piss.'

11

'Hey sis,' said Clementine over a voice note. 'I know you've been feeling rotten, and I'm just so sorry. Your new walking buddy sounds great, though! Like a good distraction. We can't wait to see you on Boxing Day! I miss you. I know it's only a small consolation but Uncle David said how happy he is the place is in good hands. I think it really does bring him comfort, you know. Everything is good here. I mean, we're dangerously close to budget and I'm still trying to talk Stella out of the more expensive decisions but that's project management! It never stops! Love you, sis. You're doing so, so well. I . . . I wish I was there. I know me feeling guilty doesn't help anything, but I think of you all the time.'

How's it going, friend? Stoke Newington misses you! a text from Sharon read.

*

What about that for a view? said Uncle David in the family WhatsApp, attaching a photo of the sea meeting the horizon, as taken from a bench in his new garden.

Hiya! a text from Stuart said. *We got sorted with the electrician and he's coming out this afternoon, just to keep you in the loop 👍 Also, I know you said you didn't want to know if Francesco came by again, but he just did. And he asked if I would tell you. He said he won't bother you again after this. I don't want to be piggy in the middle but I think he really wants to sort out whatever happened. I won't mention him again. But yeah. Now you know.*

'Gah!' said Penny, out loud and to nobody.

She wasn't an idiot. She was smart enough and had enough counselling during 'The Cancer Years' to know how her brain tried to protect her from herself. Her dad left when he knew her mum was dying. Mo had been a coward about her own treatment – he knew what had happened to her mother and, it seemed to Penny, got out whilst he could. It was heartless and weird and it made Penny question her own judgement. And as soon as she'd seen *that prick* kissing another woman, it was like confirmation in her brain that she was right – men weren't to be trusted. It was a waste to have faith. She'd used the absolute last of hers on *that prick* and he'd ruined it, with whoever that woman had been, so that was that. It didn't matter if that was the truth or if it was a convenient way to emotionally distance herself from him and what they'd had, she was out. Would never let him into her heart again.

She did miss him as her mate, though.

'Well,' said Charlie, when Penny explained her psychological theory. 'Maybe that means you can have him back as your friend. Obviously only you know if that's possible, and if it's what you really want. But, maybe if he hurt you romantically but you still miss talking to him, you really could just be friends.'

'Does that make me an idiot?' sighed Penny. She felt like an idiot. Stuart's text about him stopping by had really got under her skin. She wished it could be water off a duck's back.

'I don't think so,' said Charlie. 'You've got to do what works for you, haven't you?'

'Right,' said Penny. 'I just . . . don't have that many friends. Not in a weird way, it's just after I got sick, and having already moved around so much like chefs do . . . There was something he said to me that I think of all the time. That before anything else, we were buddies.'

'Oh honey, you don't have to justify yourself to me. All these movies and TV shows where everyone has this gang of mates that do everything together – it's not real. That's not how real life works. I have two BFFs, my mum and dad, my brother when he's not being a dick and, well, I guess you, now you're back.'

'Ahhhh, are you being soppy with me, Charlie?'

'Bugger off,' they said, rolling their eyes playfully. 'You could text him, you know. It wouldn't make you weak or anything. It's obviously unfinished business, and friendship would be a nice olive branch to get closure.'

'Maybe,' said Penny.

'More than maybe,' said Charlie.

Penny scrunched up her face. 'I hate that I still think of him. It makes me feel like I'm failing at being a strong, independent woman.'

'If you think of him and wish he'd stand on an upturned plug, or that his boiler would break on Christmas Day, I think that's "Upset You" talking. But if he made you laugh and you want a giggle and he adds something to your life rather than takes away, you're in the safe zone. It's not a failure to forgive somebody. It's actually quite gracious.'

Penny nodded. 'You give okay advice, you know.'

'What a compliment,' Charlie replied, smirking. 'I can hardly stand how effusive your admiration for me is.'

* * *

Penny had no plan to where she was headed, but she knew she needed some fresh air before the day began. Ever since meeting that guy from school last week – Thomas – she'd been craving time away from work. She hadn't realized how Red-Panda-centric she'd become. She'd slid into it consuming all her waking hours, and she knew it wasn't healthy. She wondered if that's why she obsessed over Francesco – she literally had nothing else to occupy her thoughts.

Penny made a left out of the car park, and took the first left after that. The air was cold but the sky was bright – her favourite kind of weather. If she couldn't be on a sun-lounger by an infinity pool, England when it was like this was a close second. It made her consider if she should book a sun holiday for over New Year's. Perhaps she would – Clemmie and Rima could even come, too. She passed a few dog-walkers and waved through the door of the butcher to her supplier, Freddie, and then made a right turn at the end of the lane. She hadn't realized she was heading for where she'd used to loiter after school, where the village reached the fields that stretched for miles, but of course she was. It was an empty vast space that her bones just *knew*. She hopped over the stile and stood in front of the wide open fields, marvelling at the thawing frost and how the

148

light bounced off the grass. They didn't have endless green like this in London. It felt peaceful and freeing. She closed her eyes and let herself feel the brightness of the sun.

'Beautiful, isn't it?' came a voice.

Penny opened her eyes and turned to see Thomas wrapped in a chunky knit scarf, a scrappy little dog at his feet.

'Hello,' said Penny, startled at his appearance. 'I didn't know you had a dog.'

'Well you wouldn't, would you?'

'No, I suppose not,' Penny nodded. Thomas never had stopped by the pub about that walk. She bent down to the puppy. 'Hello, you! Aren't you beautiful? You're so beautiful!'

'Are you heading up that way? That's where we normally go. We can go together?'

Penny's gaze followed the direction he was motioning in. She checked her watch. 'You know what, I've got a staff meeting in a minute,' she said, and it was the truth. How long had she been stood there, just being? 'It's a good job you interrupted my little reverie, actually – I didn't realize the time. I only meant to pop out for a minute.'

'Pleased to be of service,' Thomas clowned, doing a small bow. 'We should take that walk together we talked about, though. If you still want to.'

'Yes,' Penny replied. 'I do.'

'There's just one thing,' he added. 'Something I'd like to make clear.'

Penny waited for him to clarify what he meant. 'Yes?'

'Well, I made out like I wanted to be your mate, but when I said let's go for a walk what I meant was let's spend time together and tell each other our secrets and maybe we could end up . . .'

Penny raised an eyebrow, taken aback by his candour.

'. . . in a heated game of Scrabble.'

She burst out laughing. 'What an offer!' she chuckled. 'What an incredibly audacious offer! Is this how you seduced Veronica back in the day?'

'I'm only half kidding,' he said. '*Obviously* I don't play Scrabble on the first date.'

'And there it is,' Penny said.

'What?'

'The d-word.'

'Do you object to my offer?' he asked. 'I just wanted to put it out there because I don't want there to be any confusion. I like to shoot straight. Best way.'

Penny pulled her hat down further over her ears and glanced out to the view, as if that would have her answer. She'd not really thought about dating – Havingley had evoked a lot of emotions in her, but aside from the odd *self-partnered* session, her sexuality had definitely been lying dormant. Really, she'd thought of this year as something she just had to survive. Thriving hadn't occurred to her. But, she didn't see why she couldn't date. Didn't she deserve a bit of flirting? Plus Thomas was away a lot, he'd said. He was basically asking her if she'd consider a fling, which fit in with her own Havingley aims and objectives, really: low-commitment, make the most of it, don't get too attached.

'Go on then,' she said, deciding in the moment that she was open to being flung. 'Since it's nearly Christmas.'

'Cool,' Thomas replied. 'Well. Put your number in here,' he said, handing her his phone, 'and I'll call you later.'

'Okay,' Penny said, pleased, and she didn't so much walk home as float. It felt good to have a date. To have something else to daydream about beyond till systems and food orders and *that prick*.

I might even wage war with this hair growing down my thighs, she mused.

A date!

When she got back to the pub she said to Charlie, 'That guy from school – the one with the Gucci joggers who had that loud lunch – do you remember?'

'Thomas Eddlington. The one you called a playboy?' Charlie said.

'Yeah.'

'Uh-huh.'

'I just saw him, and he asked me out.'

'What?! You went out for air and came back with a boyfriend? Go, you!'

'Do you think he's a playboy?'

Charlie shrugged. 'Maybe he's a playboy with hidden depths,' they said, to which they both burst out laughing. Funnily enough, though, his being a playboy felt like a perfect fling-worthy fit.

'I suppose I'll find out.'

'Well, be sure to report back,' Charlie sniggered, before shaking their head and saying, 'Thomas Eddlington. Okay, then . . .'

Penny shrugged. 'Nobody is more surprised than me,' she said, and then, 'Oh crap – the staff meeting. Can you find me a chair to stand on?'

'And I just want to say,' Penny intoned to her staff, 'that I am beyond thrilled with how these past six months have run. Teething problems aside,' she paused here, letting everyone know that they could issue a giggle, 'we're now having more good days than bad ones,' – more giggles – 'And I just wanted to get everyone in the same place to say we will, of course, be celebrating with a very big pre-Christmas party . . .' she paused again, to allow for the small cheer, '. . . And I look forward to sharing with you our Continuing Training programmes. It is my commitment to you that this is more than just a job that you clock in and out of. We're a family here, and look after each other. My pledge is that I will invest in skills that are useful at The Red Panda, and also in real life, or any other job you might go on to have. I use the skills and knowledge from the kitchens I've worked in over the years every single day, and my most sincere wish is that what you learn here – as well as what you contribute – will be something you look back on for the rest of your lives as being a formative, important part of who you are, no matter what stage of your catering and hospitality career you're at. If that doesn't sound too intense, ha. Anyway. Cheers, one and all!'

'You said all that?' Thomas would later ask on the phone as they whispered to each other before bed. He'd called her when she was still in the dinner shift, and followed through on his promise to call her later, then, when she was done. Penny wondered if this is what she'd misunderstood in all the years of dating: men who aren't really that bothered text, men who actually want you, call. A simple way to establish who was wheat and who was chaff.

'Something like that, yes,' Penny said. 'And the cringiest thing is – I meant it. I'm really proud of it all.'

'Bib Gourmand proud . . .?' He was referring to the Michelin Guide award – an award not as prestigious as a Michelin star, but still a nod to consumers in an annual guide of noteworthy places for good food. Penny knew of customers who used it as their bible. If a place wasn't featured, they didn't risk eating there.

'Who sent you?' Penny laughed. 'Did Uncle David put you up to this? He always thought if I came on board that we could chase the Bib.'

'I've been around enough to know that a country pub like The Red Panda should be striving for certain things. Did I guess right?'

'I don't want to talk about it,' said Penny. 'Maybe. Probably. I don't know. Why does everyone always expect bigger and better and more? What's wrong with the way things are?'

She could hear Thomas smiling down the phone. 'Well. We can pick this up another time. I can better prepare my argument then. You said you're off on Monday?'

'That's the best day, yeah. I don't like to ask Manuela to cover for me. It feels like an imposition.'

'We can talk about that on Monday too. I'll look forward to it.'

'Same,' said Penny, realizing she really meant it.

She suddenly thought of *that prick*. She'd been furious at him for so long but, almost in an instant, she wasn't mad anymore. What Charlie said had helped. It's not that she thought she was going to marry Thomas and live happily ever after – for one thing, she would never marry a man who wore silk Gucci jogging bottoms – but in making a friend from outside the pub, and knowing how happy her team were about the Christmas party, and that she'd see her sister soon – she felt lighter. Not happy, exactly, but like she had everything a bit more under control. She was going to hang out with a cute guy and it's not like she and *that prick* had been girlfriend or boyfriend or anything. Maybe she'd over-reacted? Or at the very least reacted exactly right and now was simply over it? That could happen, couldn't it – that's how anger worked. You could be mad for ages and then one day, the thing you were mad about just doesn't make you feel mad anymore.

And anyway, it remained exactly as she'd always said: she lived here and he lived there, and he'd probably already be seeing somebody else – maybe the woman he'd been snogging – and so, whatever. If he'd been into Bridges to ask her to get in touch, she'd get in touch. She'd punished him enough. She was moving on. It was time.

She texted him: *Long time no speak.* And then she put her phone in a drawer.

12

'I can't believe you've convinced me to do this,' Penny panted, halfway up a small hill just off the A6 outside of Bakewell.

'Yes you can,' Thomas bellowed from up ahead. 'Of course you can! I'm the man who can!'

Penny stopped walking. 'I'm the chick who can't.'

'No!' pleaded Thomas. 'Don't stop! Just get at least two thirds of the way up, then I have a surprise for you.'

The pair of them were fifteen minutes into a four-hour hike through the Peak District, Thomas's 'Favourite Ever Walk.' He'd told her the day before, as they'd arranged it, 'It's the walk I do every time I come back off tour. It tells my brain: okay, work over, relax time now. It's my reset button.'

'How many women have you roped into helping you press your reset button?' Penny had asked provocatively.

'Down girl,' he'd replied, grinning. They'd been like that every time they'd spoken. They both knew what it was all a prelude to.

Penny squinted in the low autumn light. 'Urggghhh,' she said, beginning to walk, very slowly, towards where he stood. He was wearing head-to-toe North Face in an orange camouflage print and his breath made clouds in front of him as he exhaled. 'Urgh, urgh, urgh! I've been tricked! You said this would be fun.'

'Yes! You're doing it! Good girl! Come on!'

'Oh wow,' said Penny. 'Okay, dude, let me just fill you in: one, I'm not a girl, I am a woman. I wouldn't call you boy, because you're not nine. Well, physically, anyway. Mentally, the jury is out.'

'Toilet humour is still humour,' said Thomas, mock-defensively.

'And two,' she was closer to him now. 'I am also not a dog. Do not cheer me on like I am a Labrador that just brought you the paper.'

As she reached him he put out a hand and patted her head. 'Good girl,' he said in a silly voice, and Penny rolled her eyes. 'Now turn around.'

Penny turned around from the way she'd come, and across the small valley she could see a huge manor house, surrounded by manicured gardens and pathways.

'Oh gosh,' she said, genuinely impressed. 'That's beautiful.'

'It's Haddon Hall,' Thomas said. 'It's a Tudor hall, but the gardens are Elizabethan. Stunning, huh?'

'I wonder who lives there now,' Penny admired.

'Oh, actually. I know that.'

'Of course you do,' Penny said. '*Of course.* By the way, what's my surprise?'

Thomas rolled his eyes. 'This view isn't surprise enough?' he asked.

Penny blinked at him, her face unimpressed.

'Well, not that you are a Labrador bringing me the paper but I have treats, too.'

He rummaged in his backpack and handed her a bottle

of water and opened a cereal bar, taking half and passing her the rest. Penny plopped down onto the cold, dry grass, thankful for the break.

'So who lives there?' she said, relishing the sweetness of the snack and feeling revived almost instantly.

'The brother of the Duke of Rutland,' he said, 'whose daughter I met on a boat in the Greek islands and with whom I may have had a small liaison, resulting in an invitation to spend the weekend there a few years ago. Very cold. Impossible to heat such a big place.'

'I can imagine,' Penny said. 'It didn't work out with the daughter?'

'Well,' admitted Thomas. 'I was a bit of a cad. I shagged a producer for some BBC series shooting there. I mean, not the weekend I was a guest – obviously, I'm not a complete arsehole, only a partial arsehole – but yes, she didn't quite understand that when I said I don't do monogamy that what I meant was with anybody. Ever. Not even with her. I suppose on some level I thought I'd explained my situation enough, but I knew I hadn't really.'

Penny screwed the lid to her water bottle back on and handed it to him. She stood and brushed off her bum. 'And where do you stand on monogamy now?' she asked.

'Are you ready to carry on?' he said, ignoring her question. 'Because this is nothing compared to the views we'll get further along.'

'And there's a pub? With chips and mayonnaise?'

'You don't eat like a chef, you know.'

'I bloody do. I hardly think cod roe and whipped foam of watercress is going to cut it after a walk like this though, is it? All chefs love pie, and sandwiches, and cake. We muck about enough for our customers.'

'Fair point,' said Thomas. 'Well made. Yes, there are chips.'

'Then I am ready,' Penny declared. 'Onwards!'

They climbed over a gate that wouldn't open properly, walking through several fields where the only sound was of the wind whipping through the trees and their own conversation.

'I just,' Thomas said, finally addressing the question. 'I don't think monogamy is truly very realistic. I mean, for some people, maybe it is. And I respect that. If two people want to commit their lives to each other exclusively, and it makes both of them happy, it's not my place to judge that. But also, it's nobody's place to judge if that isn't for me.'

'Uh-huh, okay. I get that. Love is an individual choice.'

'Or maybe not even a choice. Maybe I am *built* to love more than one person.'

They descended a hill towards a gravel path that wound down into a picturesque village.

'Civilization? Pub?' Penny said, hopefully.

Thomas shook his head. 'We've got about the same distance to go again,' he said. 'Do you want another snack break?'

'Maybe just some more water?'

They found part of a dry stone wall to lean against and Thomas rummaged through his backpack again.

'So, lay it all out for me then,' Penny said. 'A woman who dates you – what can she expect?' In another life she would have felt bold asking that, but there was something about the dynamic with Thomas that meant she didn't feel as shy as normal. It was expiration-dating: it came with an end-point already established, so the rules felt different. She didn't have to play games when the match was so short.

Thomas took a long gulp of water and then used the back of his hand to wipe his mouth.

'Charming banter,' he settled on. 'Long walks in the country.

Snacks. Gig tickets. My sexual prowess. Compliments on how good their arse looks in yoga pants.' He shifted his gaze to her rear and Penny smirked.

'Sounds very tempting,' she sniggered.

'Does it, now?'

'And the non-monogamy?'

'Look, I tour for months at a time. I wouldn't expect anybody I was with to live their life waiting for the moment I walk through the door again because I don't "come home" as such. I love being out on the road. In so many ways that's how I feel *most* at home. The tour bus, the planes, the people. I love the buzz of it all. I love fixing problems and clearing paths and everyone thinks the person on stage is the star but anyone I've ever worked with has known they can't do what they do in front of an audience night after night without what happens behind the scenes. And I am so, so hooked on managing all that. It sounds silly but it makes me feel like a rock star, too, a bit. I just don't do it in front of stadiums of people.'

'Work is the real love of your life?'

'No. I don't mean it like that. That would feel like a sad thing to say because work can't wipe your arse for you when you're old, or suck your dick when you're young.'

'Ah yes, the two hallmarks of everlasting companionship,' observed Penny. 'Bodily fluid management.'

'I'm just being realistic. Isn't that what people want from each other?'

'What, to know they won't die alone and that there will always be somebody to hump?'

'Basically.'

Penny considered it. 'Oh, I don't know about that. Isn't it about a witness to your life? Somebody who is on your team, who is there for the big moments, yeah. But a lot of people will be there for those. Holidays and birthdays and babies and illnesses. We're normally surrounded by people for those things. But I think a partnership is about a witness to everything that happens in between. It's the smaller moments, isn't it?'

Thomas drank from the water bottle as they continued to hike. 'You're proving my point,' he said. 'I travel so much. Most of the year, in fact. So my person – they deserve other people in their lives to be that witness. And out on the road, so do I.'

'Do you have a woman in every port?'

'Hardly. But I meet new people all the time, and the team is so big, and there's a freedom in possibility. I think that's the thing for me – non-monogamy means there's always possibility around the corner. I like that.'

'And everyone you date knows this?'

'I learned my lesson from the duke's niece, yes. I don't think I've ever even kissed somebody in the past decade who didn't know I am ethically non-monogamous.'

'Ethically?'

'Yup. I totally respect anyone I get involved with, even if it's just for one night. I always wear a condom, the other person knows my situation, and I expect to know theirs, too. Everyone has feelings, right?'

Penny nodded.

'So it's not about mindless sex or whatever. I love connection. Connection is key.' He made deliberate eye contact when he said that, and it made her stomach flip excitedly. His eyes were bright blue, like Frank Sinatra's. 'I just think it's possible to have a connection to more than one person.'

'I see.'

'Am I making sense?'

'I think so. I've never really met anyone who . . . does it. Non-monogamy. I suppose I always thought it was just called cheating.'

'That's the ethical part.'

Penny stood to catch her breath. 'How much further?'

'Okay, so at the end of this path there's a very steep hill, and then another incredible view – more incredible than Haddon Hall – and then the Latkill Hotel.'

'That I can do,' Penny said. 'There's a pint of cider with my name on it.'

'Oh, how kind of you to offer to get in the first round,' Thomas winked, cheekily, jogging up ahead of her to show off his stamina.

After walking along the road and across a small bridge over the river, Penny paused and pulled out her phone. She captured a picture of some ducks paddling upstream, and then said to Thomas, 'Come here, let's get a photo.' She turned on the selfie camera and caught them, heads tilted towards each other, the Peak District framing them in the background.

'Let me see it,' he said, lingering close to her.

Penny fiddled with her phone and pulled the picture up, aware of his lips close to her ear and the way he put his arm around her to take the phone, holding her in a sort of hug from behind and looking over her shoulder.

'I think we look very good together,' he said, his voice low.

'We do, don't we?' Penny agreed, speaking just as softly. She could feel his breath on her neck, the heat of his skin.

'How do you feel about what I've told you today?' Thomas

asked, not shifting. It was a power move: he was holding her in place so she couldn't dodge the question.

She thought about it. 'I don't . . . feel anything about it. I always knew you'd be here, and then you wouldn't.'

'Uh-huh,' he said.

'I appreciate the information.'

'My pleasure.' He was still close. The phone screen faded to black and automatically locked itself. They lingered. Penny knew if she looked to her right his mouth would be level with hers and that they would kiss.

It took her half a second to decide.

She looked to her right.

Her mouth was level with his.

They kissed.

'Do you have any idea how gorgeous you are?' he said to her, as they pulled apart. 'I wanted this even before I met you. Do you think that's possible? Your food, it made me feel things.'

'I think a table leg could make you feel things.'

'Hey!' said Thomas. 'Come on.'

Penny took a step back. 'I'm sorry,' she said. 'That came out wrong. I should have just said thank you. I'm trying to be more gracious. I can be . . . prickly.'

'I'd noticed.'

'Sorry.'

'Can I kiss you again?'

'Yes, please.'

Penny followed him up the road and over two more gates, culminating in the steepest part of their walk so far. She didn't complain out loud, but she was very tired, now, and ready for a rest. It was almost too much. They must have done almost six miles.

162

'Okay, make it as far as that post there, and then look out over the valley,' Thomas instructed.

Penny plodded on. 'Gotcha,' she said, breathlessly.

Penny put one foot in front of the other through the sheep-poo-dotted field. She thought about Francesco – Thomas was the first man she'd kissed since him. She didn't need it to be 'everything' – if she thought about it, she was just glad to be moving on. She wasn't holding her breath for Francesco to text her back, but she was half-aware that it had been twenty-four hours and he hadn't. But, Thomas was here, and he felt exciting, and needed. She deserved a little light-heartedness, a little romance. Thomas was amusing, and carefree, and she enjoyed spending time with him. She'd heard the phrase 'monoga-normative' before, about how it was wrong to assume the right way to be in love was with just one person. She hoped she wasn't being monoga-normative about Thomas and his choices. Anyway, he went back out on the road at the beginning of December, which was only two more weeks. For two more weeks he could continue to make her laugh, and show her the area, and that was enjoyable for both of them. As long as they were both having a good time, who cared?

'Now look,' Thomas instructed, and Penny stood alongside him and looked out to where he was pointing.

'Holy shit,' she said, genuinely marvelling at the sprawling valley below them. To one side the river wound over several small drops, covered by trees in every colour of copper and gold and bronze either side. Further down was hill after hill and tree after tree, stretching as far as she could see until the earth hit the sky. 'This is remarkable. I've never seen anything like this,' she said in awe.

'Feel reset?' Thomas said.

She smiled up at him. 'I get it now,' she said. She pulled

out her phone again to snap a photo. She sent it to the family WhatsApp with the note *I can give your views a run for their money!* and then sent it to Sharon, too, with the message, *I may have just snogged a guy I went to school with, with this as the backdrop . . .*

'And that white building there,' Thomas said, pointing towards the village up ahead. 'That's where the chips are.'

'Chips!' Penny exclaimed, high on endorphins and the view and the promise of proper fuel. She threw her arms up as she said it and, as she brought them back down, she aimed them for Thomas's shoulders. 'But before that,' she said, melting into him again. 'Another incentive, please, if you don't mind . . .'

13

'I did it. I texted Francesco.'

Charlie issued a whistle. 'He's got his name back,' they observed, as they closed down the bar for the night.

'And I snogged Thomas yesterday.' Penny acted shy about saying it, but she didn't truly feel it. It had been a nice day with him, and she felt more like her old self today than she had done in ages.

'Shocker,' replied Charlie.

'What?!' said Penny. 'How can you think you knew that was going to happen when I didn't even know it was going to happen?'

Charlie pulled a face. 'You knew it was going to happen,' they said.

Penny pretended to think about it, her eyes moving shiftily to one side. 'Yeah,' she admitted. 'I did.'

They grinned at each other. 'You'll see him again?'

She nodded. 'I will,' Penny replied. 'He's good company. Good chat. And it gets me out and about, doesn't it?'

'I suspect the next out and about you have will actually be more in and out, if you get what I mean . . .'

'Gross!' said Penny, laughing in spite of herself. 'Why would you say that!'

Charlie laughed too. 'I'm not wrong though, am I?'

Penny didn't answer. 'I guess I'm ready to move on,' she settled on, knowing she really was ready to talk to Francesco, too. Her phone buzzed.

Update at my end, a text from Sharon said: *My love life is very boring because: married, so I miss hearing about yours! Tell me everything about this man you used to go to school with . . . ! Xxx*

'By the by, I meant to say: Priyesh came by again today. The wine merchant. He said it was to confirm that he is coming to the party, but he seemed quite annoyed you weren't here.'

'I suppose that's what we get for inviting him,' Penny groaned.

'What exactly happened that day in the summer? It's like he can't wait to see you again. Did you flirt with him? Because he might even fancy you.'

Penny guffawed. 'Impossible,' she said. 'He didn't ask me a single question, and I remember because I complained to Clementine about it on a voice note right after. He basically performed a one-man play for me and then I came inside. I think he just likes to feel important, is all.'

'Hmmm,' replied Charlie. 'I just have a feeling, though.'

'A feeling? That's very helpful, thank you.'

'Welcome.'

'Okay,' Penny continued. 'I'm going upstairs to reconcile the accounts from the comfort of my sofa. You're okay to lock up?'

'You betcha,' responded Charlie. 'And Penny?'

Penny spun to look at her friend.

'I'm glad you're feeling perkier. It's really nice to see.'

Penny!!!!! came his reply, popping up in the corner of her computer screen after she'd linked her MacBook to her iPhone apps. Penny looked at the clock. Seven minutes past eleven. Francesco would be getting out of service around about now.

Nothing else came, so Penny took the hint that it was her turn to say something. *I just wanted to say hi,* she typed back. *Stuart said you'd been in Bridges.*

Yeah, Francesco replied. *I've been thinking about you is all. I didn't know why you'd disappeared . . .*

I've been thinking about you too, Penny said. She yawned. *I'm going to bed now,* she added, *but talk soon, maybe?*

For sure, said Francesco. *I'll call you?*

Yeah, said Penny. *If you do, I'll pick up.*

I'm really pleased you've made contact.

Yeah. Can we just . . . not even talk about why? I just wanna move forward. I don't want to rehash everything.

Moving forward sounds like a great plan, he typed back. *I think I know why, anyway. It's okay. I'm glad you're back.*

Okay . . . . she typed back. *Well. Talk properly soon. Night xxx*

Yeah! And sleep tight. I'm really pumped to hear from you Penny x

She closed her laptop and lay on the sofa, staring at the wall. He was going to call her. She was excited about that. And he'd seemed cool and breezy, happy to agree to simply move forward. That probably meant he thought he was off the hook, Penny reasoned, but exactly like Charlie had said, that didn't matter. Penny didn't need some big long conversation about what had happened, with a big grovelling apology that threatened to make her cry, she just wanted his dumb jokes back in her life. She tried not to read too much into his response. *I think I know why,* he'd said. That was almost an apology without anyone having to actually raise their issues. Close enough. Anyway. It didn't matter now. Penny forgave him, because to do anything else just felt too heavy.

14

After not speaking for six months, getting a daily phone call from Francesco Cipolla was like being able to breathe again. She really had missed him. She didn't care about the other woman, about the kissing – *she*'d left *him* by moving, and she didn't need him to be in love with her. She just needed her friend back. What was it he'd said, really early on in their relationship? Something about falling in friendship together. Well. It had happened, and quickly, and since that first text the other night their phone calls had resumed daily, both as they prepped for lunch service, just like they'd begun doing after they'd met.

'What's on the menu today?' he asked, and she could hear his knife hitting the chopping board with speed on the other end of the line. She loved that. It was like they were cooking together.

'Nice bit of chicken liver,' Penny said. 'Burgers that I'm going to dare serve medium rare, for all my sins. What are you making?'

'Pistachio tart,' Francesco said. 'With fresh mango sorbet.'

'Oh god,' Penny said. 'I'd kill for that. Send some up here will you? We're in sticky toffee pudding purgatory.'

'Nothing wrong with a bit of S-T-P,' Francesco said. 'It's a British staple!'

'Oh I know,' sighed Penny. 'I just wish we could push the boundaries a bit. Put some twists on the classics, maybe, or run a series of specials to see what people respond to before deciding what to add to the menu properly. Paul is great, but . . . not exactly passionate, you know? He does what he does well enough, but it's what he's always done.'

Penny looked up to make sure Paul wasn't in yet. He wasn't. Of course he wasn't. Paul never came before he had to – that was part of his personal brand, exerting the minimum amount of effort for the closest to passable result as possible. If it wasn't her kitchen he was in, Penny would be impressed. Why work harder than you had to? And yet, she wished Paul could even muster a 50 per cent. *Half.* Half effort wasn't too much to ask, was it?

'Hey, did you read that article I sent you?' Penny asked.

'About the miniature support horse on the flight from Chicago? Yes ma'am I did. He was cute. Nice outfit.'

'I wonder how big his poop is though. Can't feel very thrilling to be the one picking up after him, can it?'

'No,' reflected Francesco. 'I suppose not. Do support animals come with support staff for that kind of stuff?'

'We should investigate that before we get you your support gorilla.'

'I don't think you have to pick up after gorillas though.'

Penny laughed. 'Mate, if your support gorilla relieves itself on the flight from Heathrow to my imaginary holiday home on the isle of Mustique, I'm afraid I'm going to have to ask you to deal with that.'

Francesco conceded. 'Okay. On the occasion of us flying to your imaginary holiday home on Mustique I hereby declare I will pick up after my imaginary support gorilla.'

'Excellent,' said Penny. 'Thank you for being so understanding.' Penny could hear something happening in Francesco's kitchen – shouting, with some quite liberal swearing.

'I've gotta go,' he said, suddenly, in a hushed voice. 'But have a great day, Penny.'

It was easier to enjoy a shift after she'd spoken with him. It really would be a great day now.

'You too,' she replied, smiling.

Penny decided to come right out and say it.

'Francesco, are you dating anyone right now?'

She asked it because she wanted to tell him about Thomas, because not telling him was like a lie by omission, and if they were friends there was no need to lie to him, deliberately or not. Also, Sharon had called her once Penny revealed they were back in contact and made her swear she'd actually *only* be his friend, because, 'He's a prick, Penny! When somebody shows you who they are, believe them!' Sharon insisted Penny know up front who he was seeing and how long it had been happening for. Information was power, she declared.

At the other end of the line Francesco's voice faltered.

'Why are you asking me that?' he said, with trepidation.

It was almost midnight, and they were both lying in bed; Penny in her flat above the pub in Havingley, and Francesco in his flat in London.

'Because we're friends, and friends know who each other is sleeping with.'

'I see,' Francesco said. 'Are you sleeping with somebody?'

Penny couldn't get a read on his tone of voice.

171

'Perhaps.'

'Perhaps . . .'

'Perhaps!'

'I see. Well, thank you for your honesty.'

'Not telling you felt like a secret, and I don't want us to have secrets.'

Francesco didn't say anything.

'Well?' Penny said. 'Are you?'

He took a breath. 'I hang out with one of the waitresses here, sometimes. It's been on and off for a while now.'

Penny nodded, and then realized he couldn't see her nodding. She couldn't help herself from asking, 'Does she have curly hair?'

Francesco snorted, taken aback by the strangeness of the question. 'Um, it's normally tied back in a ponytail,' he said. 'But it's pretty straight. It gets a sort of kink in it if it's been off her face, I guess.'

Penny felt sick that she'd even asked. 'Okay, well,' she said. 'What a great bedtime story.'

'You sound mad. I thought you wanted to know?'

'No, I did! I asked! That's cool! I'm pleased that you're . . . happy. Or whatever.'

'Yeah,' Francesco replied. 'I'm pleased that you're happy – or whatever – too.'

'Night then.'

'Night.'

Penny was furious at herself for having asked, and furious at herself for being upset by the answer. But, at least it made things clear in her mind: she definitely wouldn't go back there with him. In a way, it was a relief to have that clarified with herself. He'd moved on, exactly as she was doing. Her phone lit up.

Last night was amazing, it said.

Penny's stomach did a tiny somersault at the memory of it. *I think so too,* she replied. *I'm really enjoying spending time with you, Thomas.*

She could see the three dots on screen that meant he was typing a response. After a moment, another message came through.

Me too, Penny. You've certainly added some exhilaration to Havingley! ☺

Ha, she said. *I feel exactly the same.*

'Well, you know they say you can fall in love with thirty questions,' Penny remarked.

She was with Thomas in the pub, after service. They'd seen each other every night for the whole week since their first date in the Peaks. He'd taken her for drives, on two more early morning walks, and shown her the cinema room at his house, which was beautiful. Their dynamic was light. Pure. Honest. Penny had made a friend who distracted her from being too *work work work,* and she also happened to like kissing him. The sex wasn't half bad either. Since she'd established that she and Francesco were squarely in the friend zone, it felt very sincere to savour Thomas's company. He might have terrible dress sense, but he was also curious and authentic and his boyish enthusiasm for, well, everything, was infectious.

'Thirty questions?'

'Or maybe it's thirty-five. I saw something on Twitter about it. You ask each other the questions that are supposed to get more and more intimate and then at the end you look into each other's eyes for five minutes and hey presto! It's love!'

'Oh my god!' Thomas trilled, in a silly high-pitched voice.

'Let's fall in love!' He went to pull out his phone. 'I'm googling it now.' He stabbed at his phone with his thumbs. 'Questions . . . to . . . fall . . .' he said, under his breath. 'In . . . love. Oh you're right – there's loads of stuff about it here. It's thirty-six questions, though. Okay.'

Penny leaned over his shoulder, looking at his screen with him. He turned and gave her a peck on the cheek. He wasn't shy about his physical affection. He was always pawing at her waist or smoothing her hair or kissing her. Penny liked it. Using her body with him put her firmly back into her physical self, instead of where she had been living: in her head.

'Okay, I'll just pick a link. Surely they all say the same thing.'

'Surely,' said Penny, 'They all say, *you fancy Penny Bridge.*'

'I think we've established that,' remarked Thomas, humorously. 'The question is, could I *love* Penny Bridge?'

Penny fell quiet. *Love?* She hadn't thought that was on the table. He was heading back on tour in a few days. She'd only been messing around.

'Okay,' he said, as if he hadn't just raised the issue of the 'L' word. 'I've got the questions. Are you comfortable? Shall I get more wine?'

They were snuggled in front of the log fire in the lower bar of the pub, after hours. Penny was excited by the novelty of it – a real fire felt very country, and incredibly festive. Thomas had shown her how to lay it – old newspaper balled up but not too tightly, kindling on top in a tee-pee shape, and a big log to finish it off.

'It's kind of how I feel about relationships,' he'd explained. 'There needs to be enough room to breathe, but also enough going on to get the spark going.'

'Cute,' said Penny, rolling her eyes playfully at his cheesiness.

'I try my best,' he'd replied, winking.

She got up to get a jug of water and some glasses for them, and to top up their snack of homemade roasted almonds – something the local drinkers had gone wild for, and Penny was glad. It was important to her that they felt included in the restaurant's growing reputation. It was a pub that did food, but locals were as welcome as ever to simply come and drink in the top part of the bar. She wanted them to know that.

'Question one,' Thomas said, starting to speak before Penny had even returned to her spot.

'Oh, you're starting, are you?' she questioned, shouting from behind the bar.

'I'm using my initiative,' Thomas responded. 'The quicker we do this, the quicker we get to run off into the sunset.'

Penny rolled her eyes. He was impatient, and she tried to be forgiving about it. 'Question one . . .' she repeated, good-naturedly. 'Go on.'

'Who is your top choice of dinner guest, dead or alive?'

Penny didn't even need to think about it. 'My mother,' she settled on, simply, heading back over to him and sitting back down. 'I'd do anything to dine across from her and tell her what I've been doing these past twenty years. Ask her if she's proud of me.'

Thomas looked at her. 'She's proud of you, Pen.'

Penny avoided eye contact. He was so kind to her, Thomas – impatient, yes, but also sweet and gentle when he needed to be. For somebody she'd dismissed as a playboy, his emotional intelligence was very attuned. She smiled at him fondly and pressed on: 'And your answer?'

Thomas leaned towards her and pressed his nose to hers. Another kiss. 'My number one dinner guest choice would be . . .' he said, into her mouth, landing another light kiss. 'AA Gill.'

'Oh really?' Penny questioned, understanding why he'd chosen the famous *Times* journalist right away. 'Let me guess. Is it the Hermès scarves thing?'

Thomas laughed. 'How did you know?'

'He was a man who lined his suits with silk Hermès scarves, and you,' Penny gestured to his designer ensemble of a Mr P woollen polo shirt and Tom Ford mohair trousers, 'seem like you'd love to have a suit lined with silk Hermès scarves. Unless you already do.' Penny detected the slight change to Thomas's face. 'Ohmygod you do, don't you!'

He hid his face behind his hands. 'Am I that unoriginal?' he said. 'Yes! Yes, I do.' He uncovered his face. 'I remember reading about that in *The Times* one Sunday – my parents always get *The Times* – and thinking it was the coolest thing ever. I must've only been about fifteen. My first big bonus from Sony Music went on one. Only one, though. And let the record show I look after it very well.'

'You're a parody of yourself,' Penny giggled and Thomas shrugged.

'My personal brand is strong,' he acknowledged, handing her his phone. 'I'm not ashamed. I worked hard to dress this pretentiously, you know. Now. You pick the next question.'

Penny scanned the screen.

'Would you like to be famous and in what way?'

Thomas didn't miss a beat before he said, 'Absolutely not. Fame is a trap, man. I think I've got the best gig in the world – I get to be around fame enough to understand it is gross, but I also get a lot of the perks. Like a nice fat salary and quite a bit of free shit and loads of time off in between working like the devil.'

'Yeah, I couldn't imagine, like, not being able to go to dinner without being stared at or whatever. I heard Bradley Cooper doesn't even make eye contact when he walks down the street anymore, in case people recognize him.'

'Oh yeah, that's true. It just invites trouble.'

'Bradley told you that himself, did he?'

'Actually,' Thomas said, 'yeah. I did some research stuff with him for *A Star Is Born*.'

'Of course you did,' exclaimed Penny. 'Why am I even surprised?'

'Okay, says the woman who used to bake cookies for Ed Milliband because his podcast is recorded around the corner from her café that incidentally *Time Out* once listed as one of London's most exclusive hidden spots.'

'One,' said Penny, holding up a finger. 'Thank you for the Google deep-dive, you stalker. And two,' she held up another finger here, 'Ed Milliband is hardly Bradley Cooper.'

'Don't led Ed hear you say that.'

'Isn't it weird how famous people all have those kinds of names? Ed, Bradley . . .'

'Don't get personal, now.'

'You're right.'

'My point being, don't take the piss out of my fabulous lifestyle when you, yourself, have personally cooked for Björk.'

'We only knew it was Björk afterwards. She had on jeans and a t-shirt. Another customer pointed it out after she'd gone.'

'Still,' Thomas said. 'If namaste means "the light in me recognizes the light in you", then let it be known that the pretentiousness in me recognizes the pretentiousness in you.'

Penny narrowed her eyes. 'You take too much pleasure in putting me in my place,' she flirted.

'I'm only giving like for like.'

'Tit for tat.'

'My tat for your tits.'

Penny squealed. 'You're terrible! Ewwww!' She pretended to swat him with a pillow and he pushed it away, grabbing her arm so that she had to lower her weapon and once again submit to being kissed.

'Mmmm,' he said, before taking his phone back. Penny drank her wine as he said, 'Oooooh. This is a good question. Name three things you and your partner appear to have in common.'

Penny considered it. 'Well,' she began, looking into the fire as it crackled and popped. 'We both like sitting cosy by the fire with a good glass of red . . .'

Thomas nodded. 'Correct.'

'And, I think we both know what's important to us. All the noise and glamour and flashy stuff is fun, but not the most important bit. Speaking of which, random segue – where do you fall on the kids front?' She'd been dying to ask him. She couldn't help her curiosity.

'Me?' he said. 'I think I'm a better uncle than I could be dad. I don't really think it's in my future.' Penny nodded. She'd assumed as much, but then he often surprised her with the contradictions to his personality, so she was glad she'd checked. His answer was confirmation that he definitely wasn't her forever guy, however cosy their soon-to-be-goodbye felt. She wanted to be with someone who saw themselves as a parent one day, eventually. That was an immoveable truth. 'You?'

'I want it,' she said. 'Yeah.'

Thomas rested the side of his head against the sofa and watched her talk. One side of his face fell into shadow as the other was lit by the flames of the fire. His eyes were soft and he looked totally at ease. He was good-looking, in a youthful, fresh-faced way. He could easily have been in a boyband a few years ago, or a TV presenter.

'And the third thing we have in common then?' he prompted.

'And . . .' Penny said, thinking. 'We both think Lizzo is the tits. Your turn!'

'And here was me thinking you were about to get all deep with me,' he said, softly.

'I'm as deep as a puddle,' Penny said. If he wasn't her forever man she wasn't going to bare her soul to him. This isn't what this was.

'Oh, you've got a message,' Thomas announced, nodding at her phone on the table. She caught sight of Francesco's name and reached to turn it over, screen down.

'Nothing important,' she said. 'Not when I'm here with you.'

Thomas grinned and held eye contact for a beat longer than was comfortable, then looked back down at the question list. He cleared his throat. 'This is a good one,' he said, pressing on.

'They're all pretty good, aren't they?' Penny said. 'I can see how this works.'

He continued: 'If a crystal ball could tell you the truth about yourself, your life, the future or anything else, what would you want to know?'

'Hmmm,' considered Penny. 'I'd want to know if I will be a mother. I want that very, very much. I thought it would have happened by now, but . . . Well. Maybe soon. And . . . I'd want to know if I will be loved.'

'I think you already are,' said Thomas. 'Your uncle, your sister, your friends . . . you're a very loveable person.'

'Thank you,' Penny said. 'I don't . . . feel it, sometimes. I feel like everyone else knows what the deal is with love, and they find it easier than I do. I don't understand how to find it, let alone what to do once I have it.'

'Everyone feels like that.'

'I don't think they do.'

'You're not alone in how you feel alone.'

'Everybody hurts?'

'Something like that.'

Thomas reached out for her hand. 'Don't let anybody ever make you feel like less than you are,' he said. 'Because you are wonderful, and kind, and fun, and beautiful, and very, very loveable.'

Penny felt something prick at her eyes. Love was all she wanted. A family, something outside of work. She was thankful Thomas was here to add something other than the pub to her time in Havingley. In forcing her to remember life outside of the pub, Penny had started to remember the other hopes and dreams she had for herself.

'I'm not fishing,' she said, swallowing hard to release the lump in her throat. 'I promise.'

'I know,' he said. 'But even if you were, I appreciate the excuse to tell you anyway.'

Penny tilted her chin up, just slightly, an invitation. Thomas leaned in. It was deep and sensuous, and Penny felt her whole body respond to him.

'Mmmmm, almond-y,' he said, smiling.

'Are we done with the game?' Penny said. 'I feel like we're done with the game.' She moved up closer to him and they kissed once more – harder this time. More intense. Penny leaned forward to put down her wine glass and moved so that she straddled him on the sofa.

'We're supposed to look into each other's eyes when we're done with the questions,' Thomas said. 'That's the important bit. The instructions said so.'

'I'm looking into your eyes right now,' Penny said.

'This much is true,' conceded Thomas, grinning. 'But . . . can we do it properly? Not that I don't enjoy having your legs wrapped around me – I don't want you to move – but talking to you this way, getting to know you . . . I like it. I like you.' His hands lay proprietorially on her thighs.

'Me too,' said Penny, pulling back her face from his so that she could see his full expression. 'You make me feel differently about being here.'

'I do?'

'Yeah. I know you're going again and everything, but you've shown me a side of Derbyshire that really means something to me. The walking and the landmarks and places to go and stuff. I was in danger of being a London snob all my life.'

'I think we can be both,' Thomas said. 'It's possible to love London, and miss London, but also see the good in everywhere else. For me, it's medicine.'

'I'm glad you shook me out of my bad mood that day,' Penny said. 'I'm glad you didn't let me be a moody-bum with you.'

'Well, I wasn't expecting . . . you.'

Penny furrowed her eyebrows in question.

'I was expecting somebody older, maybe. Or more . . . matronly. Not a hot thirty-something with a spunky attitude.'

'Spunky attitude!' Penny said, mock-outraged.

'You're not exactly Little Miss Sunshine, are you? You're like Little Ms Independent Woman, or something.'

'There's a compliment in there somewhere, I'm sure,' Penny said.

'No, it is. You're not a pushover. I like it. It challenges me. Okay,' he got serious now. 'Time to stare at each other.'

'Set an alarm on your phone,' Penny instructed.

'Yes, Ms Independent Woman,' Thomas replied, leaning to one side to pick it up and program it with one hand. The other, Penny realized, was now on her bum. She liked the feel of him claiming her that way, touching her where other people couldn't.

'Four minutes staring,' Thomas said. 'No laughing, okay?'

'Okay,' said Penny.

'And go.'

In theory, maintaining eye contact with somebody for four minutes shouldn't be hard. Yet Penny found herself wanting to look away after what, ten seconds? Fifteen? Looking at Thomas, Penny became aware of the rise and fall of her chest as she studied his baby blues. She deliberately tried to inhale and exhale more slowly so that she felt more in control of herself. It felt awkward to be seen by him, with nowhere to go and no witty one-liners to detract from herself. She felt sad, too, as the seconds turned over into minutes. How long had it been since she let herself be seen? Did she think she wasn't worthy of it? Why did she always feel she had to hide? She willed herself to push thoughts of Francesco to one side, because here was Thomas. It was safe to explore how she felt for him because she *knew* he was leaving. She didn't have to worry about him going anywhere because she already knew he would, and in a way that was freeing. As she held his gaze and felt him growing harder underneath her she wanted, more than anything, to make love to him there, on the sofa by the fire and with red wine floating through her. And then he was kissing her and peeling off her t-shirt, and pulling a condom from his wallet.

Thomas pushed up inside of her and Penny thrust her hips, forgetting herself, forgetting everything, back and forth, back and forth, pushing and pulling, and then he shuddered, and he'd come, and Penny had not.

'Shit,' he said, and Penny replied, 'It's okay.'

'No, I meant shit like wow,' Thomas clarified, indicating that she should climb off him.

Penny watched him peel off the used condom and throw it into the fire.

'I don't think that should have gone in there,' Penny mused.

'Ah,' he supposed. 'Yeah. You're right.' He turned towards her. 'I had fun tonight,' he said, and Penny replied, 'Me too.'

'Did you come?' he said.

'I mean . . . Thomas . . . if you have to ask . . .' She said it kindly, but it was important to her to say it.

He looked at her. 'Really?'

Penny gave a tiny shrug.

'Oh,' he exclaimed. 'Well. Let me rectify that.'

He pulled a cushion off the sofa and used it to kneel on. 'Let's see what we've got here,' he pondered, as Penny ran her fingers through the back of his hair and closed her eyes.

15

'Let me put my ears in,' said Francesco, bellowing down the phone.

Penny stood at her work bench, chopping celery and onions for a soup.

'I cannot wait to tell you what I did last night.'

Penny scrunched up her face. 'Do I even want to know?' she said, flushed at the memory of what *she* did last night.

'I went to a Nigel party.'

'A what?'

'A Nigel party!'

'Ahhhh, that well-known annual event on everyone's calendar! A Nigel party!'

Francesco issued a deliberate cough. What he meant by that was 'wanker'. He'd once told her a story about being a kid, and having learned about that insult from one of the British girls at school, had employed it on his father. Only, Francesco's father had understood it and when he'd challenged him ('What did you say to me, boy?') Francesco had tried to tell him he'd only coughed. It became a running joke. Nobody needed to actually say the word 'wanker' when they could cough. In Francesco's family – and now for Penny – everyone knew what a meaningful cough meant.

'Tell me about your Nigel party, then . . .' Penny said.

'Well,' said Francesco, and she could hear the hustle and bustle of the road as he walked somewhere. It must have been his day off. 'Did you know the number of Nigels born in this country is in rapid decline?'

'Imagine my surprise,' said Penny.

Francesco coughed again, refusing to resume conversation.

'Sorry,' Penny said. 'I went to bed late last night. I'm being cranky with you because I'm tired.'

'Did you know teenagers practise emotional boundaries with their parents because it is considered safe to? It's the same in relationships – we're only really horrible to the people we know won't leave us.'

Penny smiled. Francesco was forever telling her facts and stories and titbits that way. 'It's like you've eaten "Psychoanalysis Crunch" for breakfast or something,' she said.

'You are proving my point,' he replied.

'Oh, hush,' she said, affably.

'Can I tell you about Nigel now?'

'I'm dying for you to . . .' she said.

'Well, as I said, the rate of Nigels is in decline. So this guy at a pub near work where we go between shifts sometimes is called Nigel, and when he found out they are a dying species he held a Nigel party! I'm not kidding, there must have been six hundred Nigels in that place.'

'Oh,' exclaimed Penny. 'That's actually pretty cool.'

'It was! There were Nigels from the UK and Australia and New Zealand . . .'

'People actually flew in for this?'

'Yup! So many Nigels that Nigel the Pub Owner had to get a marquee in the beer garden. One woman there even proposed to her Nigel!'

'Well, that is an exciting night,' said Penny. Her phone lit up and she was temporarily distracted as she read a message from Thomas: *My place or yours later?* it said.

Yours, she texted back, following up with an aubergine emoji and a love heart.

'One of us should commit to calling our child Nigel, I think,' Francesco carried on. 'As a contribution to the cause. Except, not me, because I have Italian heritage and need a name that ends in a vowel.'

'You want me to call my child Nigel.'

'Maybe just the bump,' Francesco said. 'If you call your bump Nigel I'll throw you a mini Nigel party, and then when he comes out we won't mention it again but we can sleep soundly knowing we've done our part.'

'Great plan, Nigel Superfan, but I won't ever have a bump, so. Your plan is foiled.'

She could hear Francesco's brain whirring down the line. 'You don't want children?' he said. 'I thought you were really excited to one day be a mum. That really surprises me.' He paused. 'You once asked me about adoption, actually. Is that the plan?'

'Well,' said Penny, slowly. 'I do want children, it's just I can't carry them myself. Something-something-cancer, some-thing-something-early-menopause . . . was going to freeze my eggs but then decided to get them fertilized with donor sperm so we could check for the cancer gene and I wouldn't have to spend years wondering what the deal was . . . now I have embryos in storage at a central London fertility clinic

. . . blah blah blah . . . I won't get a bump, but a surrogate will. Maybe Clementine. So. We'd have to ask her how she feels about a bump called Nigel.'

Francesco went quiet. 'I'm sorry,' he said. 'I didn't know.'

'That's because I never told you,' Penny murmured.

'I feel like an idiot now. I was just being stupid.'

'No,' said Penny. 'No, I'm sorry. I didn't mean to make you feel foolish. I would have told you when we first met, but then . . .'

'Everything happened.'

'Everything happened, yeah.'

'Well. It doesn't surprise me that Penny Bridge has a plan.'

'What do you mean?'

'That's what you do, isn't it? You see the problem and then you figure out how to make it work for you. You're cool like that.'

'Thank you for calling my fertility issues "cool".'

Penny could tell Francesco was rolling his eyes. 'That's not what I said, Pen, is it?'

She sighed dramatically. 'No. I was being cranky and unreasonable again. And also, that was a really clumsy way to tell you. I wanted to back when we were dating, weirdly. I felt like I had a secret from you, but there's no good time to drop into conversation with someone you're sleeping with that you've got this whole plan to have a baby that couldn't ever technically involve them. Can you imagine? You'd have run a mile, either because I was bringing up kids so soon or because it's a massive turn-off.'

'I wouldn't have run a mile, Penny,' said Francesco. 'Not for either reason. I really liked you.' Hearing him say that made her heart beat faster, but she didn't have time to register it because he kept talking. 'I'm glad you've told me, okay?'

'Thank you for knowing the right thing to say.'

'Listen, I'm at my appointment so I've got to go. I've got a job interview. I don't know how much longer I can be at Anthony Farrah's. I need something new. He's driving me mad.'

'Okay. It's good that you're being proactive. I know you've been wanting a change for ages. Good luck! And sorry again for being a grumpy grump.'

'Thanks for telling me what you did. I'm honoured you'd trust me with it.'

Penny pulled a face. 'Friends share their secrets, so . . .'

'So,' he finished. 'I'm glad I am a friend who you trust.'

'You are,' she said. 'Call me later to tell me how this interview goes?'

'Will do,' he said. 'Love ya!'

Penny took out her ear buds like they were on fire. Had Francesco just said, *I love you*?

Penny saw Thomas a handful of times before the day arrived for him to leave for the tour. She'd loved his company and she loved, in a funny way, that she had totally misjudged him and every time they'd spent time together there was something else that he revealed about himself that surprised her. She liked being surprised, and he was a kind man with a very good heart. He'd really made a difference to her past couple of weeks with his jokes and adventures.

'We'll text, or do those voice notes you're obsessed with,' he'd said, before he left. 'Or, even better, you can come out and see me.'

Penny had kissed him intensely and replied, 'Let's not

promise each other anything, okay? It's fine. It's more important to me to be surprised by staying in touch than disappointed if we don't. Just let me know when you're back in Havingley.'

'Okay,' Thomas had agreed, 'I'm definitely back in the new year, once these December gigs are done and we've finished the Asia dates. But you really should come to one of Lizzo's London shows.'

'Let me know,' she said, vaguely, because she knew he'd be in bed with somebody else by the end of the week, if not by that night. It was in his nature, and he'd told her as much right from the start. It made her think of Francesco. They were friends who'd been lovers and gone back to friendship, and knowing him was one of the pleasures of her life. She could be friends with this lover, too – only, with Thomas, she'd leave the sexual door open for his return because she'd always known this is how it would end, and that's what made it possible.

'Everyone deserves a bit of fun! And I just like the sound of him!' Sharon had said on a quick FaceTime. 'All I'm saying is, don't cut your nose off to spite your face. I love that he's making you appreciate more about where you're from, and showing you all this stuff you can enjoy that you can't get in London.'

'Me too,' Penny had agreed. 'He's certainly been . . . unexpected.'

'Exactly. You can pick up the phone on his return without pining for him in his absence.'

That had made Penny grin widely. 'I wonder if this is the kind of advice you'll give Mia.'

Sharon looked very serious. 'You bet your ass it will be!' she replied. 'I don't want her staying home waiting for the phone to ring. My girl is gonna be a go-getter! Exactly like her Auntie Penny.'

'Hey,' Penny said, as she headed back from Thomas's house to the pub for service. Francesco's face was on her screen. 'How are you today?'

'I've done something,' Francesco replied.

'Okay . . .' said Penny, wandering down the back lane that connected to the high street, her big winter coat protecting her from the day's frost.

'I've quit my job.'

Penny's mouth fell open. 'You quit? Is that because you got the job you applied for?'

'Not exactly . . .'

'You quit without another job to go to?'

'I did!'

'Oh, damn. That's . . . ballsy. I know you've wanted to leave for a while, so I guess I say congratulations?' She passed the butcher's and lifted a hand to wave in. She was enthusiastically greeted in return.

'Yes, you say congratulations!' Francesco screamed. 'I'm free!'

Penny giggled. 'But what happened?' She passed by two of her regulars and said hello to them, too.

'Life happened, that's what,' Francesco said. 'I just couldn't do it anymore. Ever since we started talking again I was just reminded how you live *properly*. You're so positive and sure of what you want. And it makes me want to be more like that. I don't just want to exist, you know? And Anthony Farrah, the way he runs that kitchen . . . it's not right. The whole atmosphere is full of fear because of his ego. I couldn't bear it even one second longer. Not even half a second longer.

191

I was really bummed when I didn't get that other pastry chef job, but I figure it won't be long before I do find something. I've got some savings. I'll be fine. So I did it! Urgh, I feel GREAT.'

He sounded almost manic.

Penny saw Priyesh, the wine merchant, drive past in his Land Rover, and nodded her head in greeting. *Hot,* was the word that slipped to the front of her mind, before she could remedy her faulty thinking. *Boring,* she corrected herself. 'What's the notice period?'

'Well, that's the incredible thing. He wants me gone. He's paying me for the next month but doesn't, he says, ever want to see my smug Italian face ever again. He was quite shouty, but I didn't mind. I just wanted to be out of there!'

'A paid month off work,' Penny said, sighing. 'And at Christmas, too. Imagine that.'

'And so . . .' Francesco said. 'I was thinking that maybe I could finally come and visit? What do you think?'

'Visit?' Penny said. The pub was in view now.

'Yeah! We talk every day, I know, but that's not the same as actually hanging out, as seeing you. And now I've got all this time . . .'

'I have the Christmas party,' Penny said.

'After that, then?' Francesco replied. 'It's the day after tomorrow, right? I could come at the end of the week. I can even help out a bit if you need it.'

'Well,' Penny said, not sure of how all this was making her feel. 'Sure. Okay then. You could definitely show Paul a thing or two. Bring your knives with you, just in case.'

'Great,' said Francesco. 'I'll figure out what's what and text you. I can crash with you?'

'Of course,' said Penny, thinking to herself: *Don't shag him.*

Don't you dare shag him! He is your friend! Do. Not. Shag. Him! 'There's a spare room.'

'You look like you've seen a ghost,' Charlie said, from where they were hanging bunting in the corner of the bottom bar.

'It's Francesco,' said Penny, taking off her coat. 'He wants to come visit.'

Charlie cackled. '*That prick* wants to come to The Red Panda? Amazing. I literally cannot wait to meet him. The way you talk about him is like he's a mix of Brad Pitt and Colin Firth and maybe a sprinkling of Hugh Grant but also maybe with an edge of . . .' They considered this next bit carefully. 'Severus Snape? In a hot way.'

'He's just my friend, though,' said Penny, quickly. 'God, please make me not want to shag him. He really did me over, Charlie! But I cannot emphasize enough just how handsome he is, and how good his cooking is, and how much just the smell of him makes me want to jump his bones.'

'Well, if you need something to turn you off him, you could just ask about . . . you know.'

'Yeah,' said Penny, reaching up to where Charlie was trying to tack a wreath.

'Oh,' said Charlie. 'Thank you.'

'I don't know why I've never asked him about it,' Penny said. 'When we started talking I just . . . avoided it. Do you think that's weird?'

Charlie hopped down off the chair and started wading through a box of Christmas ornaments.

'Yes and no,' they said. 'If it had all happened last week, okay fine, maybe then you'd ask because it's fresh. But it's been what? Six months? Seven? And you live a hundred miles

193

apart, and – does he know you're just friends? Does he think this is the gateway to something more?'

'No,' said Penny. 'He knows about Thomas, and we'd agreed to just be friends as soon as I knew I was leaving. Even before . . . the other thing.'

'The other thing that he doesn't know you know about.'

'And so, that's all the evidence I need not to go back there, isn't it? My instinct was obviously right all along. He was never as committed to me as I was him.'

Penny picked up a lilac Christmas ornament. 'How did this end up in here?' she said, holding up a stained-glass dome with a snowman set inside it. 'My mum got this for Clementine, I think, at Nottingham Goose Fair. I remember it.'

'This is just what David has every year.'

'I'll take this one,' said Penny, casting her eye over what else was in the box. 'I'll give it to Clem.'

'No worries,' said Charlie. 'And Penny? It's nice that you've got a friend. You light up when you talk with him, and since you've reconnected you've seemed loads happier. Don't overthink it. He really can just be your pal. You're grown-ups.'

'You're right,' said Penny. 'My pal. My pal is coming to visit! You're going to love him, Charlie. Everybody does.'

'As long as you're not secretly *in* love with him,' Charlie said, distracted by the next task of setting up the nativity scene. Penny didn't reply. She was pretty sure she wasn't. It wasn't exactly the kind of thing a person could hide, was it? No. They were in friendship, not love.

On 1st December, Penny had the Christmas party to distract her from Francesco's imminent visit and Thomas's recent departure. It was held at the pub so that they could do what they wanted, but catered and waiter-ed by an external company so she hadn't had to worry about any of that – she could, for the first time in too long, simply enjoy herself alongside everyone else. It was bound to be a crazy festive season, and so this was her last chance to really throw caution to the wind before everybody else's celebrations threatened to overwork her, and her staff.

'No way,' Penny said as she held court with her kitchen crew, waiters from the catering company walking by with mini Yorkshire puddings stuffed with tiny pieces of beef. 'Who in their right mind would put their socks on before their trousers? That makes no sense!'

Manuela clicked her tongue and Ollie, the pot-wash, said, 'What! Of course you do socks before trousers! Think about it: the sock sits *underneath* the trouser, so you want to make sure it's pulled as high up the leg as possible, and to do that you need a bare leg.'

'I'm with him on this one,' Manuela said, like it was the most serious issue she had ever been given the task of weighing up. 'It's crazy to try and put on socks once your trousers are on. What if you've ironed the trousers and then you have to get them all crumpled?'

Penny was gripping her tummy as she laughed: what had started as an innocent observation was scaling up into world war three.

'I cannot believe you are all arguing about this,' uttered Agnieszka. 'Is this what British people really talk about at parties?'

'Hey!' said Manuela. 'I'm Filipino!'

'I'm Dutch,' said Ollie.

'I am so bored,' said Paul, the pastry chef. 'Shall we do tequila shots?'

There was a rousing cheer that Penny took to mean 'yes'.

'Uh-oh,' Charlie said, nudging Penny's shoulder right as Manuela handed her a glass. Liquid spilled over onto her hand and Penny automatically went to lick it off. The strength of the booze made her tongue tingle. Around them, the lights twinkled and the glasses clinked and everyone was scrubbed up and dressed to the nines. Penny was having a really lovely time. 'Your man Priyesh is here.'

Penny watched him as Charlie walked across and kissed him on each cheek. His shoulder-length black hair was thick and silky, teasing his shirt collar. He had a small amount of silver flecked in it, and it shocked Penny all over again that he was so attractive. His snooty voice didn't match up with his face, and the way he carried himself.

She studied him as he approached and Charlie said, 'Penny – you remember Priyesh, our wine merchant.'

Priyesh stuck out a hand. 'Thank you for the invitation this evening,' he said. 'Your hospitality is most appreciated.'

'You're very welcome,' Penny replied. 'Please, eat. Drink. Be merry.' She gestured around the room, almost knocking empty glasses off a tray that passed by them.

'You're very kind. And maybe if we get a moment I can pick your brain about what you found in the cellar recently. I heard you had quite the excavation down there. I'd love to know what bottles you found.'

He was a formal man. Penny was used to Thomas, who filled the space he occupied with both his belongings and his personality. Priyesh, on the other hand, was compact. Though he was tall, and impeccably dressed, he was totally self-contained, like nothing about him was an accident. It was all purposeful and deliberate. Uptight might be another word for it.

196

'Absolutely,' soothed Penny. 'Once I've done the rounds? Hostess duty calls.'

'Of course,' he nodded. 'Lovely to see you, anyway.'

He did a slight bow as he stepped away, which Penny mimicked before turning to Charlie and uttering in hushed tones, 'That truly is a man with a stick up his arse.'

'Bless him,' said Charlie, already tipsy on a Champagne cocktail. 'Let's see if we can't get him shit-faced, loosen him up a bit.' They followed him, calling, 'Priyesh! Where's your drink! Let me top you up!' At least Charlie could see the funny side of him being there. Penny made a mental note to avoid him, and gratefully accepted another shot from the pot-wash.

Penny wasn't far off being drunk as the night wore on. She hadn't lost control of herself by any stretch of the imagination, but she felt loose and free, happy to be amongst these new faces that were strangers at the start of the year and now the people she spent almost every waking minute with.

'I trust you're having a good night,' a voice droned behind her, unexpectedly making the hairs on the back of her neck stand on end. Priyesh. She turned around. Had he got cuter-er? Or was that the French 75's she'd been downing? Either way, inexplicably she wasn't sorry he'd found her.

'Hello, squire,' she said, not quite sure why she was calling him that, except to sort of take the mickey of his formalness. 'Are you having an enjoyable evening?'

'Not as enjoyable as I suspect yours is,' Priyesh replied, acknowledging the empty glass in her hand. 'But pleasant enough, of course.'

'You don't like my party?' Penny asked, in a way that she intended to be sexy and provocative but, well – over the din of her merry staff and the live band, she couldn't be sure she was succeeding.

'Not at all, your party is most convivial,' Priyesh replied. 'Quite like the hostess.'

'I'm not drunk,' said Penny, defensively.

'You must try harder, then,' suggested Priyesh, nodding in that formal way he insisted on and walking off towards the loos. 'I rather thought you'd be a bit more relaxed than you were an hour ago,' he shouted as his parting shot, over his shoulder.

Penny stood and watched him go. Had he just been rude to her? She couldn't tell. What a bastard if he had been, she thought. He was her guest! How dare he! What was it about pompous men that made them bring out the pompousness of everyone they interacted with? She followed him towards the back of the pub.

'Hey!' she said, as he went through the door into the seldom-used front porch. To the right was a locked front door, and to the left two other doors, the toilets.

'Hello there,' said Priyesh, cool as a cucumber. 'Are you okay?'

'Of course I'm okay,' said Penny, primly.

'Well that's good to hear,' Priyesh said. 'Because for a moment there it sounded like you were going to shout at me for something.' He spoke smoothly, unruffled. Penny found it incredibly irritating.

'Shout at you?' Penny said. 'Why would I shout at you?'

'Well,' Priyesh replied. 'Exactly. Hence my confusion.'

He pushed through to go into the loo. Penny opened up the door behind him and followed.

'What's your problem?' she asked, peeved. 'Why are you such a snooty bastard?'

Priyesh smirked. 'A snooty bastard? My apologies if I've come across that way. I appreciate the feedback.'

He simpered sarcastically as he said it, as if Penny's comment didn't bother him at all and was almost a ridiculous suggestion.

'You come in here with your suit, and your hair, and your face,' Penny said. 'Drinking my booze—'

'Well, booze I sold you, technically,' said Priyesh.

'Oh . . . shut up,' Penny said. She stood in the doorway and Priyesh looked as if he was about to say something, thought better of it, and turned around to the urinal. Penny could only assume that he'd unzipped his trousers because in the next second, she could hear a steady stream of liquid hit the plughole.

'Oh, nice,' she said, bizarrely glued to the spot. 'Really nice.'

Priyesh zipped up his trousers, turned to the sink and washed his hands – with soap – and pulled down a paper towel. He gently flung it to the bin, turned to check his hair in the mirror, and walked up to where Penny was frozen in the doorway, in awe at him. The way he moved, the way he looked at her, the way he walked towards her, it was all like he was a big game cat.

'You've made an awful lot of assumptions about a man you've only met a handful of times,' he said, standing close.

'Your reputation precedes you,' Penny said, her breathing uneven. 'I know all about you.'

'Oh really,' Priyesh said, brushing her hair from her neck and letting the very tips of his fingers brush against her collarbone.

Penny swallowed. She couldn't explain it. This man – he repulsed her, and she wanted him, and she hated herself for wanting him but at the same time life was short and why shouldn't she do exactly as she pleased? What did it matter?

She tugged at the top of his trousers, pulling his hips closer to her as she looked up at him, deep into his eyes. Neither of them pulled away.

'Is this okay?' she asked.

'Yes,' he replied, holding still.

She undid the button to his trousers.

'Is this okay?' she said, searching his eyes again, desperate to see if she could get a reaction from him – any reaction.

'Yes,' he said again, still composed. Still unflustered.

Penny reached into his underwear.

'Is this okay?' she said, and he moaned as she touched him, finally revealing himself to be capable of being unnerved.

'Yes,' he sighed.

16

'Oh Sharon,' Penny said, as she nursed a coffee in the low winter sun, hoping to be brought back to life with vitamin D and caffeine. Her head hurt. Her shoulders ached. Her ego was – well. Not quite bruised, but definitely feeling feelings. Why on earth had she carried on that way with the wine merchant? A drunken bathroom encounter was one thing, but with a man she technically worked with was far beyond the limits she'd ever placed on sex and dating for herself. One doesn't shit where one eats, as the old proverb goes. 'Sharon, I totally shat where I eat!' she cringed down the phone via voice note. 'I don't know what I was thinking! Can you call me after drop-off? I need to talk this one out.'

Sharon FaceTimed at 9:01 exactly, from the nursery gates.

'So who's this wine supplier, then? You've got your knickers in a right twist.'

'Seriously,' said Penny. 'It was so stupid of me.'

'Hey – that's my friend you're beating up over there!' Sharon said. 'Go easy on her.'

'I'm an adult woman who runs two businesses and I had a quickie in a bathroom with a man I should have known better than—'

'Oh come off it,' Sharon interrupted. 'That's the prerogative of an adult woman. You can do whatever you want! Bloody own it, Pen.'

'I feel ashamed.'

'Well you should feel ashamed that you feel ashamed. Come on, it's a new decade, not the turn of the last century. Send the man a thank you note and move on. Jeez.'

'A thank you note,' laughed Penny. 'Sure. *Dear Priyesh,*' she said, putting on a funny voice. '*It was incredibly kind of you to join me in the men's bathroom at the staff Christmas party, and I found you incredibly obliging as I tossed you off. What larks!*'

'Well, I mean, you're joking but it's not far off, is it? It's precisely because you're a grown-up you need to acknowledge it happened, but doing so doesn't mean it has to happen again. And I promise you – what you don't want to do is pray it all goes away and then be caught off guard when he's at the pub for your next order, or sat at the table next to you when you go out for dinner somewhere with that Thomas bloke. Oh, hold on.'

Penny felt woozy as she watched the camera on Sharon's phone move from her face to the sky, which, in several jiggly movements then became a ceiling. Penny could hear voices and then the camera moved again and Sharon stood at the counter of Bridges with Stuart beside her.

'I'm just getting a coffee and look what beautiful specimen is behind the counter,' Sharon said.

'Hi, gorgeous!' Stuart waved down the line. 'We miss you!'

On screen Sharon turned to Stuart and said, 'Penny gave

her wine merchant a hand job at the staff Christmas party last night, and is now having an existential crisis about it.'

'I don't miss those,' he said, and he and Sharon laughed.

'Hello, this is my life that you're ripping to shreds and making me feel awful about!' Penny shrilled. 'I wanted actual advice, not teasing.'

'Hangover?' said Stuart.

'Twenty men playing trumpets behind my eyes,' Penny replied.

'Look,' said Sharon. 'Re the wine merchant, if you're as embarrassed as you say you are, the cleverest thing to do is take control of the situation. Then you can mark it off as "resolved" in your imagination and move on to inventing another problem because you're bored.'

'I'm not bored.'

Stuart started to steam milk and Sharon told him off for the noise, stepping away so she could be heard. 'You are, Penny. It's okay. You're a long way from home and being wined and dined is a good way to distract yourself. There are worse things you could do. I approve of it, in fact.'

'Okay Freud, that's enough,' said Penny. 'Thanks for the analysis.'

'I love you,' Sharon said. 'I really will come up and visit in the new year. It's just been a nightmare with the kids, and work, and Luke's mum not being well. But I am coming. Promise.'

'It's okay,' replied Penny. 'I've spent all this time getting settled. In the new year is perfect. It will give me something to look forward to.'

'Excellent,' said Sharon. 'Okay. Go post a note through that man's door!'

'Enjoy your day,' Penny giggled, rolling her eyes.

'Bye, Penny!' Stuart waved, and as soon as she hung up, a voice came from behind her, 'She's right you know.'

Penny spun around to see Charlie leaning in the doorway. 'Jesus!' she said. 'How long have you been stood there?'

'Ages,' said Charlie. 'I kept waiting for you to notice, and then when you didn't it seemed weird to skulk off so I stayed.'

'Right. So you heard—'

'Yup.'

'And so you know—'

'Yup.'

'Right.' Penny stood. 'Ouch,' she said, the sudden movement causing a nausea to run over her. 'My head.'

'Never mind your head – how's your wrist?' Charlie quipped, and Penny laughed in spite of herself.

'Oh bugger off,' she said.

'Sharon is right, you know. You can't just ignore it and hope you never see him again. You can regret it, but you can't be a dick about it.'

Penny nodded. 'Yeah,' she said. 'Urgh. I hate having to have manners!'

Penny went through to the office and pulled out some headed notecards Clementine had gifted her two birthdays ago. With a patterned border of pink and red swirls, at the top it simply said, *from the desk of Penny Bridge*. She'd sent three of these since she got them, not really ever having occasion to send anything 'from her desk', but she realized that the cards were almost explicitly designed for this exact purpose – to politely recognize an event without dragging it out any further, and to a man exactly like Priyesh who most likely had his own embossed stationery that he used daily or weekly, not bi-annually.

Penny sat with the cap of the pen in her mouth, thinking about what to say. Charlie appeared at the door again.

'For crying out loud,' said Penny. 'Are you just going to

follow me around from doorframe to doorframe? What are you even doing here – we're closed today.'

'Well,' said Charlie, 'I left my phone here last night. But then as a bonus I didn't expect to find you all discombobulated and so I'm staying because this is quite entertaining.'

'What should I put in the note?' Penny said. 'If you're going to make fun of me, at least be helpful as you do it.'

Charlie rested their head against the frame and thought about it. 'Say,' they considered, 'that you were so pleased he could make it, and you look forward to continuing to work together in the new year.'

'I can't put a reference to a continued relationship,' said Penny. 'That makes it sound like I'm inviting him to pursue something.'

'Just say, *I'm so pleased you could come at my party. I mean, to my party.*'

'Ha, ha. Thank you.' Penny rolled her eyes. She thought about it some more and wrote:

Dear Priyesh,

It was wonderful to see you at the Christmas party this week. Forgive my over-familiarity – call it the festive spirits, aka gin, vermouth and a tequila shot. I trust our working relationship will overcome any unduly forward interactions.

Happy holidays,
Penny.

Penny slipped it into an envelope, wrote his name across the front and said to Charlie, 'Can you drop this by his house on the way home? Me and my hangover can't quite face it.'

'Sure,' they replied. 'Fix me a coffee first, though.'

Penny's phone vibrated. *Morning sunshine,* a text from Thomas said. *Just wanted to say you're on my mind. Hope that's okay. Have a good day!*

Penny texted back, *Hey! I hope tour is fun! I think about you too. Xxx*

Her phone buzzed again. *Do you need anything bringing up from the big city to the country hills?* it said. *I can get you anything you might be missing.* Francesco.

There suddenly seemed to be more men than she could willingly handle.

'This is not a drill. Your man Priyesh is in the bar,' Charlie said over the food pass in the kitchen a few days later. 'And he comes bearing flowers.'

'What?' said Penny, using a cloth to wipe up sauce from the rim of one of the plates she was dishing up.

Charlie gestured through the door to the bar. 'He's right there.'

Penny followed their finger to see him smoothing down his hair nervously.

'Get him a drink,' she said. 'And tell him I won't be long.' *Who the hell shows up halfway through service?* she thought, not realizing that it was 2 p.m. and service was now officially over. No more new orders would come through.

Penny took her time sending out the last plates and clearing down her section. She tried to tell herself that she didn't know why he was there, but of course she did really: her note. And why had she sent the note? Oh god, if she was truly honest with herself she'd done it for the attention, mostly. Thomas was gone and there was a part of her that worried she'd actually have to focus on herself and her life and her wants and needs, and how she really felt about being at the pub, if she had to go to bed alone. Not to mention stemming any feelings for Francesco, who was a total no-go zone. Priyesh was smart and confident and she'd gotten a thrill from it. She'd gotten a thrill from making a man who was outwardly so sure of himself, putty in her hands. She wasn't proud of it, but that was about the lay of the land. She'd assumed Thomas was a playboy and he'd revealed himself to have hidden depths and true character, but Penny had swindled Priyesh by play-acting as a woman with hidden depth and true character when in actual fact what they'd done together in the bathroom at the party was nothing short of playboy behaviour on her part. Could she blame the booze? Maybe she could have if she hadn't sent the note. She was going to kill Sharon and Charlie for making that seem like a good idea when she was in the compromised state of morning-after-the-night-before. It was cruel, what she'd done, and now he was here, at the pub, and she'd have to face up to her cruelty by telling him he'd misread the situation because she had deliberately distorted it.

Come on now, she coached herself. *Put your big girl pants on.* She wiped her hands on a towel and threw it into the laundry basket, taking a breath as she pushed through the door to the bar.

'Hello there,' she said, fixing her face into a bright smile. 'What's a nice guy like you doing in a place like this?'

Priyesh smiled. 'Penny,' he said, taking her in. 'Am I inconveniencing you? About this time was often when David said to stop by.'

'Service has just finished. I don't have long but no, of course it's fine. Sorry to have kept you waiting.'

It was like a competition to see who could be the most polite. Penny tried not to notice his suit, his shoes, that bloody face, and in trying not to notice the details of him she had a vivid, pornographic flash back to the way he sounded in her ear when she'd had her hand in his trousers.

Oh god, she thought. *Oh god, oh god, oh god.*

'These are for you,' Priyesh said, after what felt like an eternity. He handed over the bouquet of fern, eucalyptus, and a towering head of something exquisite and purple. 'I described you to the florist, and this is what she made.'

Penny took the flowers and made a show of her admiration, a small private performance to demonstrate her gratitude. They really were beautiful. It made her wonder what words he'd used to describe her, but she couldn't bring herself to ask. She put them on the bar. 'They're gorgeous,' she said. 'You really didn't have to.'

'I wanted to,' Priyesh said. 'I learned from my marriage ending that it never hurts to be demonstrable about one's feelings whilst one can. I'm a proud man, but I'm learning not to be so proud as to withhold telling people when I haven't stopped thinking about them.' He took a breath and smiled. 'And, well, my point is, I've not stopped thinking about you.'

Penny was genuinely touched by his admission. 'I didn't know you'd been married . . .' she said. 'Or that you weren't anymore. That sounds very painful.'

He smiled. 'It was,' he said. 'Although neither of us classes it as a failure, I must say. We were very successful at being married until we weren't. Twenty-one years together is nothing to sniff at.'

'Absolutely,' Penny agreed. 'It's really nice to hear a man speak so kindly about his ex-wife.'

'Although I fear,' Priyesh smiled, 'that perhaps I shouldn't pay too much lip service to the past when I am here to place a bet on my future. I merely mean to underline that I am here in earnest.'

Penny could tell by how rigid Charlie was near the glass-washer that they were listening to every word of the exchange. Their back was straight as a board, as if even breathing might impinge on their eavesdropping capabilities.

'Oh,' said Penny, surprised. 'What a disarming thing to say,' she blurted. 'I'm . . . touched.'

Priyesh smiled and said, his voice low, 'There's a joke in there somewhere.'

'Charlie, I'm just stepping outside. Won't be a minute,' Penny said quickly, before saying to Priyesh, 'Come with me.'

She led him to the back porch of the pub, which led out to the steps and the car park.

'Charlie was listening,' she said, as way of explanation.

'I'd imagine so,' Priyesh said. 'I long ago tried to side-step the prying eyes and ears of the village. Sometimes I throw them a bone. A bit of gossip to get their teeth into. I wonder how long it will take for everyone down at The Boot to know I'm here,' he added, referencing the other pub in the village. 'I have to confess I tend to head in there myself when I'm hungry for a bit of village chatter.'

'Listen,' Penny started, not sure what she was going to say next. Maybe: *sorry about that hand-job I gave you, I can see how you might have the wrong impression.* Or, *I hope the stain came out of your suit.* Or, *I am not emotionally mature enough for this conversation, please just cease to exist.* She wasn't, of course, proud of herself.

'The party,' Priyesh said, instead. 'It took me by surprise.'
Penny nodded. 'Me too.'

'And I'm not sure what the etiquette is for that situation—'
'Me neither.'

209

'But, your note was . . .'

'Yeah.'

'So the flowers are to say thank you for your thank you. And as a gateway to ask if, perhaps, should your schedule permit, you'd consider letting me take you out for dinner. I'd very much enjoy getting to know you.'

'Expensive way to get tossed off again,' Penny kidded.

'What?' said Priyesh.

'I was being silly. Sorry. I'm embarrassed, I think.'

'Embarrassed,' repeated Priyesh, colour rising to his cheeks.

'Oh!' said Penny. 'Not because – not because of you. Embarrassed by me. That I . . . you know. Did that. And—'

'Right,' said Priyesh. 'I've misread this, then.' He said it as a statement.

'No!' Penny exclaimed. 'None of this is your fault. I'm just worried, is all, that work and play shouldn't overlap, and that we have a professional relationship. I overstepped a boundary. I think I behaved improperly.'

'That was the thrill,' Priyesh said.

Penny didn't know what to say to that. Before the party she'd thought he was uptight and boring, but now, after getting better acquainted, he was playful and provocative. She felt nervous around him, actually – his grown-up-ness and his manicured beard and the respect he obviously had for himself. And his directness, too – a man who said what he wanted and knew the diplomatic way to go about getting it was *very* attractive.

'Yes,' she settled on, grinning, now. 'I suppose it was.'

'I know every place worth eating at in a fifty-mile radius, and exactly what wine to order when we're there. Plus, maybe there's something in it for me, too . . .'

'And what's that?' Penny asked.

'I love learning about food. If we went out to dinner, maybe you could broaden my culinary horizons somewhat.'

'You're only in this for your taste buds?' Penny said, eyebrows raised.

'Penny, I find you incredibly interesting and largely elusive. I'm in it for you. I've been trying to pin you down for months.'

Penny's jaw fell slack in disbelief at what she'd just heard.

'Really?' she said, incredulous. And then before she could probe him any more she was distracted by a car pulling into the car park whose driver looked very familiar.

'What the hell!' said Francesco, walking towards Penny and Priyesh. 'Look at this place!'

'Francesco!' said Penny. 'You're here!'

'I'm here!' said Francesco, grinning. 'Are you happy to see me?'

Penny went in for a hug, not knowing what else to do. 'Of course I am!' she said. 'Francesco! My old friend! My buddy! My chum-diddly-chum-chum!' She may as well set the boundary early on, she figured.

The pair pulled apart and it seemed to be only then that Francesco noticed Penny had been stood with another guy.

'Sorry, man,' he said to Priyesh. 'Hi. I'm Francesco, an old friend of Penny's.' It wasn't lost on her that he'd used 'friend' to describe himself. That was good. He knew where he stood, then.

'Priyesh,' said Priyesh. 'The wine supplier for The Red Panda. And I was just in the middle of asking your friend out to dinner . . .'

'Oh,' said Francesco, taken aback. Penny grimaced guiltily.

'I'll leave you two to catch up,' Priyesh said. 'Francesco, what a lovely surprise for a friend. Penny?'

211

'Huh?' said Penny, discombobulated by Francesco's arrival and somewhat turned on by Priyesh's charm, and class, and apparent unflappability. Had he really said he's been trying to ask her out for months?

'Perhaps you'll call me. You have my number.'

'Oh, she doesn't call people,' Francesco said. 'It took me a long time to persuade her to get on the phone. She's a texter.'

'Very well,' Priyesh said. 'Either way, Penny, I have a favour to return.' He winked after he said that, and Penny knew exactly what he meant and it made red blotches flare up her cheeks. Such a polite man, suggesting such dirty things!

'Thank you again for the flowers,' she said. 'I'll call,' she promised.

'Nice to meet you,' Priyesh said to Francesco, heading down the steps and towards his car. Francesco looked from Penny to the back of Priyesh's head.

'Is that the guy you've been seeing?' he asked. 'Why are you only going to dinner with him now?'

'None of your business!' Penny replied. 'But also, no. It's not. Priyesh is a . . . different man to the one I told you about. Back off.'

Francesco held his hands up in surrender. 'Backing off, your honour,' he said. 'Boundaries firmly established.'

'Sorry,' Penny said. 'I didn't mean to snap. I'm flustered you caught me flirting. That was mean of me.'

'It was,' Francesco said. 'And you're already forgiven.'

'Thank you. So, you really quit your job?'

Francesco grimaced. 'Not my finest hour. But yes. I took my knives and got out of there before I could piss him off any more,' he said. 'Can I interest you in my pastry skills? I heard a rumour you might be going for the Bib Gourmand and little old Chef Cipolla might be able to help.'

'I can't believe you're here,' Penny said. 'Just like that.' She loved that he was. She loved that a part of her old life was in her new life, and that Priyesh had just asked her out, and that sometimes, when she least expected it, everything could feel do-able and light and fun. Francesco had once told her she over-complicated things, and in that moment she resolved to herself not to do that anymore. Francesco was here, and he was her friend. That was that.

'I should have called on the way here,' he said. 'For a minute it almost looked like you had forgotten I was coming.'

'No!' said Penny. 'I didn't forget! I just, well, Priyesh . . .'

'Handsome man,' said Francesco.

'Is it weird if you know I'm dating somebody else?'

Francesco looked in the direction Priyesh had left in. 'Nah,' he said. 'I'm just happy we're talking again.'

'Well,' Penny said. 'Good.'

'I'm excited to meet everyone properly,' Francesco declared. 'Everyone you've talked about, everyone you've done impressions of down the phone,' he said.

'Don't think I'm getting soft or anything,' Penny said. 'But it might be nice to share it all with somebody, actually – to show somebody who understands how hard all this is, what we've achieved.'

'Excellent!'

'So what's next? Did you really just ask me for a job?'

'Maybe after service we can make a coffee and sit on the back step as you have your fag and talk about it all,' Francesco laughed. 'Because to be honest, I've got no clue myself.'

'Who amongst us does?' Penny laughed. 'That's supposed to be the fun of it, apparently.'

*

Penny left Francesco in the bar chatting with Charlie, who commented as Penny passed back through to the kitchen, 'You left here with one and came back with another!' Penny rolled her eyes. Charlie made it sound as though she was collecting men. She wasn't, obviously.

'Francesco is my friend,' Penny said, as way of explanation. 'F-R-I-E-N-D.'

'The friend you talk to every morning when you're prepping?'

'Yes,' said Penny. 'Exactly that.'

'Uh-huh,' said Charlie, and Penny didn't know what that noise was exactly supposed to mean. Hadn't Charlie been all for Francesco's friendly visit?

After she'd given instructions to the pot-wash, Ollie, on what needed doing to close down the kitchen until evening service, Penny kept Francesco waiting for a minute longer to slip into the kitchen office and look in the supplier's book for Priyesh's number. She flicked through the heavy binder of business cards and price lists, finding his details handwritten in her uncle's cursive at the back. It had a landline number and a mobile, so Penny dialled his mobile. She needed to focus on the idea of somebody other than Francesco. If he understood that she was seeing somebody else, she knew he'd be respectful of that. Not that she was going to *use* Priyesh. She'd been a bit silly with him at the party, but the way he looked at her afterwards, how he came to the pub and brought flowers and didn't get frustrated when Francesco turned up and interrupted them – that was very attractive. He was a proper man, and Penny knew in her heart she deserved to spend time with a proper man like that. What they'd done together had certainly been spontaneous, but she wasn't going to over-think – that's what she'd pledged to herself.

Penny also wasn't going to fall back into Francesco's arms because he was here, either – he'd kissed somebody else, when she'd not even been gone thirty seconds. She didn't even care why, now. Yes, they'd had chemistry, but hadn't she proved she could have chemistry with other men, too? In London it was as if she would never be fancied again until Francesco came along. Maybe she'd talked herself into liking him more because she was afraid she'd be left on the shelf forever. But here, in Derbyshire, it was different. Here, she magically had choices – Thomas had shown her the area and been open-hearted and kind. Priyesh was straight-laced and serious but playful and sexy too. And he wanted to take her out! So out she would go.

Priyesh picked up the phone. 'Hello, Ms Bridge,' he said, his voice brooding.

'Hey,' she replied. 'I'm sorry we got interrupted. It's a yes to dinner. Of course it's a yes. Just let me know where to be and when, and I'll be there.'

'I'm thrilled to hear it,' he said. 'Sunday night. I'll pick you up at 7 p.m. Dress code is smart.'

Penny went back through to Francesco and Charlie in the bar.

'Right then,' she said, clapping her hands together. 'Shall I give you the grand tour?'

17

It was almost maddening how easily Francesco slipped into Derbyshire life. Penny had agreed to give him a job after catching Paul trying to pass off a Waitrose cheesecake as his own. It was all very straightforward: Francesco came to visit and charmed everyone with his easy ways and help-fulness and had sat and rubbed Penny's feet at night after service, telling her over and over what a brilliant job she was doing. Penny had told him she was going to go out with Priyesh, and the foot-rub was merely a friendly one, and Francesco had promised to honour that. The next morning, Penny had caught Paul in the act and asked him how long he'd been doing it – using shop-bought products as his own – hoping he'd say it was a desperate one-off for a reason that would never crop up again. He didn't. It turned out he'd been doing it for years and, as such, Penny fired him on the spot with a one-week grace period in which he would be paid but not required to show up. He didn't put up a fight. Francesco found a house for rent in the village, and started that day.

'I'm Bib Gourmand-level good, you know,' said Francesco, once it was official. 'And I know that you're Bib Gourmand good, too. And the atmosphere here, the décor, the service? It's going to happen, you know.'

'Don't,' said Penny. 'That's not the objective!' She broke into a smirk. 'Well, unless it happens, in which case it was in the plan all along. I wish we got alerted if they were coming, or told in advance. It's so maddening that there's no way to prepare. Apparently you only know they've been if you get a letter after to say they want to give you the award and include you in the guide.'

'Evening pasta date to celebrate always being ready?' Francesco said. 'After service?'

'You're cooking, or I am?' Penny said.

He looked at her. 'My friend,' he said. 'I am, of course.'

'Just checking you still like me enough to feed me.' She grinned at him. 'But . . . could we do tomorrow? I have a date tonight.'

'Oh, I see,' Francesco said, teasing. 'Lining us all up back to back, are you?'

Penny rolled her eyes. 'I can cook my own pasta, you know.'

'No, no,' insisted Francesco. 'I can be your second choice. You. Me. Tagliatelle. Tomorrow after service.'

'It's a date,' she said. 'Well. A non-date.'

Francesco beamed. 'Penny, it's cool. I'm just pushing your buttons,' he said. 'Tomorrow is fine.'

'This is beautiful,' Penny said to Priyesh over the last of their wine at a local country hotel bar. 'I had no idea this was here.'

'Well, cheers to discovering new things then,' said Priyesh, raising his glass to hers. 'And cheers to that beautiful meal, too.' He had a twinkle in his eye, and Penny understood exactly which direction the night was rapidly going to go in. He was a paradox: outwardly buttoned-up but underneath cheeky and provocative. She liked it. 'I'm glad I got a taste of your maple-soy tofu. Never in a million years would I have ordered that myself.'

'Tofu is so hard to get right,' said Penny. 'But I had a feeling they'd smash it here.'

'I think my starter was my favourite, then your tofu, and then the dessert. I'm such a sucker for anything with passion fruit.'

'And yet that is my least favourite fruit,' said Penny.

'Come on,' uttered Priyesh. 'You're leaving that one wide open to some letchy comment about passion and its place in your life. Don't make me do that.'

Penny laughed. 'You're right,' she said. 'That was short-sighted of me. I shouldn't put you in any kind of position that means jokes about tropical fruit are on the table.'

'I appreciate your understanding,' Priyesh said. There was no denying that Penny was charmed by him.

'So,' she said. 'I know all about how you got into wine because of your sister-in-law, and now I know about your affinity for war dramas, occasional show tunes and that you own two rescue cats that make your furniture smell . . .'

'Hey,' he responded. 'You're sworn to secrecy on the show tunes, remember. Nobody else needs to know that I cried at *Billy Eliot*.'

'Got it,' Penny sniggered, a little tipsy. 'Tell me something that I still don't know, though,' she invited. 'You've told me the top-line stuff, but what about your hopes and dreams and fears and loves and losses? You're this enigma to me –

and to everyone at the pub, too. Who is Priyesh . . . wait. What's your last name, even?'

Priyesh smiled. 'Jones.'

'Priyesh Jones.'

'You were expecting me to say Singh or Khan, weren't you? Or Patel?'

Penny looked horrified. 'No!' she said. 'No! Just because you're . . .' she didn't know the right word. She was terrified she seemed racist, or worse – plain ignorant.

'It's okay, I'm just joshing,' said Priyesh. 'My mother is from India, and my father is from Coventry. Hence Jones, but with brown skin.'

'Do you get on with them well, your parents?'

'I do,' said Priyesh. 'I have a lot of respect for them.'

He didn't ask her about her parents in return, and it occurred to Penny that he must know she didn't have any.

'I try to learn from them as much as possible, especially now I'm old enough to appreciate them – which already feels too late, to be honest. I don't know where I get it from, but I can be very competitive. For a long time I thought it was more important to be right than to be kind, but these last few years I've really tried to practise the opposite. It's more important to be kind than right.'

Penny nodded. 'I've never thought about it that way, but yes, I think I agree. Anybody can be stubborn and hold their ground and get others to bend to their will, but the better person will do the kind thing? Is that what you mean?'

'Exactly,' he said, sniffing the Barolo he'd ordered that lurked at the bottom of his fishbowl of a glass.

'And you said this past few years you've learned the difference?'

'Yeah. Since my divorce, really.'

220

Penny nodded. He'd mentioned his marriage ending the other day, as well. It was obviously still painful for him.

'I don't still dwell on it, for the record,' Priyesh added, as if he'd read her mind. 'I'm very removed from the emotion of it, when I talk about how I used to be married. It's fact to me now: I put my ego before my wife too often, and in the end it cost me. So now I try not to do that. In fact, your uncle was quite the clergyman to me when I was struggling.'

Penny brightened at the mention of Uncle David. 'Oh yeah?' she asked. 'You talked to him about it all?'

Priyesh nodded. 'I did. He'd cook for me and listen to me feel ashamed of myself. He really gave me his time – and Eric, too. They're a great couple, aren't they?'

'So great,' grinned Penny. She played with her wine glass as well, mirroring Priyesh without realizing. 'They met when I was twenty years old, and right from the start it was like the clouds had parted and the heavens smiled upon them and—'

'And angels sang?'

Penny laughed. 'Do you know what I mean though? They are so in harmony together, and have so much respect for each other. It never felt that way with my ex, who I met around about the same time. We were together ages but I always knew – had a little niggle in the back of my mind – that it could be better.'

'Don't tell me you didn't get treated like a princess . . .' Priyesh said.

Penny shook her head. 'I don't need to be treated like a princess,' she said. 'I don't need saving, or rescuing. But I do feel like I made room for him in a way that he didn't make room for me. Like, if ever there was a spotlight it was implicitly understood that I'd be the one to step back and let him

221

take it. There was never a suggestion that we could *share* the spotlight.'

'It's hard,' Priyesh acknowledged. 'Real balance in a relationship is tricky.'

'Maybe,' Penny agreed. 'Or maybe it's only tricky if you don't communicate. And I mean constant communication. I think I was a bit guilty of getting mad he wasn't a mind reader. I could have done better in telling him what I expected. But then, I was so young, I didn't know how to do that yet.'

'Ahhhh, the beauty of getting older: knowing thyself.'

'You seem like you know yourself very well,' Penny suggested.

'I think I'm just getting the hang of it at the ripe old age of fifty-one,' Priyesh replied.

'You are twenty years older than me. Did you know that?'

Priyesh shrugged. 'I assumed I was probably closer to David's age than yours.'

Penny finished what was in her glass.

'Here,' Priyesh said. 'You have this last little bit that's left.' He emptied the bottle for her and Penny continued to drink.

'Does a twenty-year age gap bother you?' Priyesh asked.

Penny shook her head. 'No, it doesn't bother me,' she said. 'I mean, this is . . .'

'Fun,' Priyesh supplied.

'Fun,' Penny repeated.

'Is this the point at which we talk about what a great night it's been, but acknowledge it is such a shame to part so early?'

'Oh wow,' Penny giggled. 'You're really good at this! So smooth! Those twenty years you have on me mean you're better at the sexual segue than I am.'

'Sexual segue?'

222

'You're *so* about to kiss me.'

'Am I now?'

Penny batted her eyelashes and didn't say anything, daring him to prove her right. She was bolder with him than she'd ever dared been in her life. Priyesh leaned in and moved her hair from her neck, exactly as he had done the night of the Christmas party.

'If I was about to kiss you,' he whispered, 'where would I start . . .?'

His lips met her neck softly, and Penny closed her eyes, breathing deeply.

'Would I start here?' he asked. 'Or here . . .?' His second kiss landed at the base of her ear. 'Perhaps I'd start here,' he wondered aloud, kissing behind her ear, now.

'That's nice,' sighed Penny.

Priyesh moved his hand to cradle her chin, rubbing his thumb over her lips.

'Can you kiss me properly now, please?' she asked.

Priyesh smiled. 'Only because you asked so politely,' he mumbled, leaning in.

When they finally pulled apart he said to her, 'Penny, would you like to come home with me?'

* * *

'Francesco, there's a Caroline in the bar for you,' said Charlie from the doorway of the kitchen.

Francesco looked up from the pastry section where he was lining a dish with shortcrust.

'Oh,' he said. 'Damn. This needs to go in. Um . . .' He glanced across to Penny. 'Do you mind if she comes in?' he said. 'Sorry. I can't leave this.'

'No, no, not at all,' she answered, thinking: *Caroline? Who the hell is Caroline?*

'Would you show her in?' requested Francesco. 'Thanks Charlie.'

A second later a goddess of a woman stood amongst them.

'Hey,' she said, lingering by the sinks. She waved at everyone and smiled.

Francesco looked up at her. 'Hey,' he said, motioning that she should come down to where he was working. 'How's it going?'

'Good,' said the goddess. 'Hey,' she said to Penny.

'Hey,' said Penny, in a high-pitched voice. Who was this woman?

'I just wanted to drop this by,' she said. 'You left it in my car this morning.'

Francesco's eyes flickered to the leather jacket and scarf in her hand. *His* leather jacket and scarf, Penny noted. 'That's very kind of you,' he said. 'Thank you.' He was covered in flour and he walked towards her with his hands held up in front of him. 'Can you ask Charlie to hang them up for me behind the bar?' he said. He lowered his voice, but Penny could still hear him. 'Thank you,' he said.

Penny tried to focus on what she was doing – prepping a parsley and shallot sauce for the cod option for evening service – but from under her eyelashes she watched Francesco bend at the knees to give the other woman a kiss.

'See you tomorrow?' he whispered.

'See you tomorrow,' the goddess replied, her pearly white smile wide.

As she left Penny said nothing, and Francesco didn't either. He went back to moulding his edges and, in lieu of conversation, started to whistle.

'Bit young, isn't she?' Penny said, eventually, right as he launched into the chorus of an Ed Sheeran song.

'Young?' said Francesco.

'I mean, no judgement or anything,' Penny said.

'I don't think she's too young,' said Francesco, resuming his whistling again. 'She's twenty-four.'

'Uh-huh,' said Penny, a weird feeling forming in her stomach.

Priyesh was outwardly a gentle man, with a purposefulness to him that meant everything he did was deliberate and considered.

'I like to take my time,' he said, as he traced his fingers over Penny's arm from where they lay in his bed. 'And truly appreciate the task at hand.'

Penny giggled. 'I've noticed that,' she said. He'd turned up at the pub the day before and asked to speak with her outside, where, despite the fact that anyone could have walked out to the outdoor fridge at any moment he had pushed aside her apron and put his hand inside her knickers until she came.

Their love-making was erotic and hot and dirty and exactly the kind of sex Penny had held in her mind for years when she thought of what it meant to have 'good' sex. After they'd spent their first night together it became a twice-weekly and then three-or-four-times-weekly event. Christmas came and went, and she slipped away to visit Uncle David and Eric and Clementine and Rima for Boxing Day, but then instead of going anyway to sunnier climes Penny spent the whole of her New Year's break in Priyesh's luxurious house, half-naked with the fire burning. Uncle David had seemed encouraged that she couldn't wait to get back – she didn't have the courage to tell him the real reason for it.

Now, in January, she enjoyed getting away from the pub after service, showering at Priyesh's big fancy house using the oils and shampoos in his shower and padding into his bedroom barefoot, in a big fluffy dressing gown, smelling clean and fresh. He'd turn the corner of the page of his book, gently take off his reading glasses and set them on his bedside table, and then do filthy things to her for an hour until she slept like a baby curled up beside him.

Penny wouldn't have called it dating, since most of their time together was confined to the bedroom, but she was definitely fond of him. He was attentive and respectful, and after welcoming in a new month that marked eight months of her leadership at the pub, Penny held tight to the fact that she was over halfway through her commitment. She wouldn't be here much longer – but in the meantime she was determined to keep finding her pleasure where she could. She felt like she had the best of all worlds – a hot present, and a change in her future. And really, with the age gap, it couldn't really be much else.

'What are you thinking?' he asked her one night, as they lay next to each other, naked and recovering.

Penny lazily inhaled and smiled. 'I was thinking about Uncle David,' she said. 'And what he might make of . . . this.'

'I see,' Priyesh replied. 'Are you intending to tell him?'

'Not especially,' said Penny. 'Unless you think I should?'

Priyesh put a hand out to her thigh. 'Whatever you think,' he said. 'Although, obviously he is my friend, and you are basically his daughter, so there is that to consider. If you are going to tell him, give me a head's up so I can talk to him too.'

'Are we doing something wrong, do you think?' Penny asked.

He shook his head. 'No,' he said. 'We know what we're doing, don't we?'

'We're . . . enjoying ourselves,' Penny said.

'Exactly,' said Priyesh. 'And for what it's worth, the extent to which I am enjoying myself is a lot.'

Penny looked at him. 'Same,' she replied. 'But you're right. There isn't really anything to tell him, is there?'

'Not yet,' agreed Priyesh. 'I think for now this can still be ours.'

'If you could be any mythological creature, what would you be and why?' Francesco asked as he flattened some garlic with the back of his knife. Service had ended an hour ago, and the waitstaff were getting set up for tomorrow's service before closing down for the night. The kitchen was lit by just a single back lamp, and Penny and Francesco had decided on pasta pesto as a midnight snack.

'Well,' Penny mused. 'Aside from the myth and the legend that is Penny Bridge—'

'Obviously.'

'I'd be . . .'

'Don't say a phoenix. You're better than answering phoenix.'

'Why can't I say a phoenix?'

'Because that's so basic. Rising from the ashes and all that. Everyone feels like they've overcome some past hardship to be a new version of themselves. It's boring.'

Penny balked. 'It's boring when people feel like they've overcome obstacles to become who they are?'

'Yes,' said Francesco, grating parmesan. 'Or, it's boring when they think they're special because of it. We're all special. You know?'

'Harsh,' said Penny. 'But I see your point. Tell me more about what you're doing with those walnuts, please.'

'Personal question,' joked Francesco. Penny stood beside him and observed his work, ignoring his comment. 'I prefer the flavour of walnuts, sometimes,' he said, 'instead of pine nuts. It's very simple,' he continued. 'You don't make pesto?'

'Of course I make pesto,' said Penny. 'It's just fascinating, isn't it, to see how someone else does it?'

Francesco fired up the food processor, adding in his own reserve of oil, brought back with him after he saw in the new year with his family in Bologna – it was his uncle's private supply. He poured it in a steady stream until the pesto was mostly smooth, with just a few flecks of green. He peered inside, satisfied, and added in the salt.

'How is Uncle David today?' he said, using his favourite spatula to scrape the mixture out into a bowl. 'I'd love to visit him at some point. There are so many stories I bet he could tell about this place. He wasn't exactly in the best way to share all of his hints and tips when we met last time. Plus, I've never been to Cornwall.'

Penny thought about it. A trip with Francesco to see Uncle David and Eric down on the coast could actually be really fun.

'Oh, that's a great idea!' Penny said. 'Maybe Priyesh could come, too. Although, it's still very casual. Uncle David doesn't actually know about us since they're quite good friends and, well. You know. It needs to be dealt with delicately.' Penny considered it. 'On second thoughts, taking Priyesh would be a terrible idea. Forget I mentioned it.'

'Thank goodness,' said Francesco, emphatically. It took Penny by surprise.

'What's your problem with Priyesh? He likes you a lot,' Penny said. 'I thought you two got on?'

'I don't trust him,' Francesco said. 'I've never seen him in the same suit twice.'

'You don't trust him because he has a varied wardrobe?' Penny questioned.

Francesco shrugged. 'I think linguine for this,' he said, changing the subject.

'Sometimes I think you act a bit jealous, you know,' Penny said. 'Don't be mad at me for saying that, but I think you do.'

'I don't act jealous,' said Francesco, almost reflexively. 'Why would you say that? What do I have to be jealous of?'

Penny didn't know why she'd said it. She wanted him to be jealous, in a way, in the same way she felt jealous that he'd kissed that curly-haired woman, and kept going for drinks with the goddess.

She tried to laugh it off. 'Just checking you're not secretly in love with me or anything,' she said, trying to sound cool. 'Lesser men have fallen harder you know.'

Francesco looked up at her. 'I know they have,' he said, looking at her for a split second too long. Penny's heart beat in double time. She pulled herself up to sit on the countertop.

'Thank you for cooking,' she said. 'I'm starving.'

'My pleasure,' said Francesco, adding salt to a vat of water for boiling. 'I like to cook for you.'

They continued with their supper like nothing untoward had been said.

*　*　*

'Argh!' cried Penny, clutching at where the towel had clipped her leg. 'You bastard! That one bloody hurt!'

'You said not to go easy on you,' Francesco said, jumping

from one foot to the other, the offending weapon in his hand.

'You're not normally this good at Tea Towel Warfare,' Penny said. 'If I didn't know any better I'd say you'd been practising.' She moved her own wrist in circles, like Francesco was doing, so that her damp towel coiled around itself and she could snap in with a flick at Francesco's legs.

'Missed me,' he said, laughing and moving side to side. 'Missed me again!' he cheered, almost walking into the pot-wash.

'Sorry Ollie,' he said.

'It's okay,' said Ollie.

'Okay,' declared Penny. 'Next one, the loser is responsible for washing up after supper.'

Francesco slowed down. 'Sorry, I actually have a date,' he said. 'I've gotta go in five.'

'You have a date? At 10 p.m.? I didn't know you were doing that. Dating. I thought you were maybe just . . . I don't know. I knew you saw Caroline for a drink or whatever. I didn't know it was . . .'

'What?'

'Nothing. It doesn't matter.'

Francesco shrugged. 'I'm not seeing Caroline. I mean, she's nice and everything. But I was at The Boot with Charlie the other night and got chatting to this girl – this woman – and so I got her number. It seemed like the logical thing to do.'

'Well good for you,' Penny said, trying to sound like she meant it. 'I'll cook pasta for one, then.'

'You aren't seeing Priyesh tonight?'

'I might do, now, actually. I guess I'd started to think of Tuesday night as our night, or something. I'm being silly.'

Francesco studied her. 'Okay, well.'

'Well,' Penny repeated, and Francesco put down his tea towel, their game over. Penny knew she should wish him a nice night, but she didn't.

Movie night? Priyesh texted Penny, a bit later.

You know what? Penny texted back. *I'm actually truly exhausted. Later in the week?*

Sure, he typed back. *Can I drop anything by? Candles? Hot water bottle?*

You're sweet, said Penny. *But I'm good, I think.*

Penny retired upstairs to the flat, commandeered candles from the living room, ran the hot tap on full, and the cold tap just a little, and located her Jo Malone bath foam instead of the usual Radox. It felt like a Jo Malone bath foam kind of a night. She said a small prayer for sisters with big salaries and generous gift-giving tendencies.

Soaking in the tub, listing to Matthew McConaughey reading a bedtime story, she examined her feelings. She'd felt funny when Francesco said he was going out on a date, and she wondered what he might be doing right now, and who with. Surely he wasn't laughing with this other person the same way he laughed with her. As soon as she thought that, though, guilt washed over her – why would she play compare and contrast? She should be thrilled he'd found somebody. She didn't even know that he and Charlie went to the pub together. He deserved to set up his own life here, after all.

Jealous.

Was she jealous?

She knew she didn't have any right to be.

Francesco was her friend, and that's because she'd made it that way. If he wanted to go out for dinner with somebody else, or kiss somebody else, or spend the night with somebody else, that was up to him. It didn't diminish their friendship. Although, of course, she didn't really want to know about his sex life, even if he was a friend. She just . . . didn't.

She closed her eyes and let the bedtime story wash over her, inhaling the scent and feeling the smoothness of her own skin. Maybe she should have seen Priyesh tonight – she just didn't want it to be reactionary, like she was using him because Francesco was busy. That didn't seem fair. Especially when Priyesh continued to surprise her. The sex was potentially the best she'd ever had. He didn't mind bodily fluids or noises or bumping heads. He was a man totally at ease with himself, no need to 'prove' his masculinity like other men Penny had been with. In fact, he didn't always come when they had sex – he seemed to get pleasure simply from them being together, exploring each other's bodies. He was patient, and they'd even managed to find common ground over the past two months – she didn't think he was boring anymore. He was educated and knowledgeable, and endlessly inquisitive, too.

Penny opened her eyes and reached out of the bath, first for a towel to wipe her hands, and then for her phone. She pulled up Priyesh's number.

No, she advised herself. *I can't call him just because Francesco has a date.*

Her finger lingered on the call button.

She put the phone back down.

18

'What? Are you kidding me? Yes, yes, yes!' Penny squealed. 'I'd kill to see Lizzo live! Thomas!'

At the other end of the phone line Thomas let out a pleased laugh. 'I was hoping you'd say yes,' he told her. 'I'll have Chris email you everything you need, and I'll see you here Thursday night then? Just give them your name at the door and they'll show you through.'

Penny sensed Francesco observing her from the other side of the pass and looked up, grinning. She pulled a face to signify her excitement, but Francesco raised his eyebrows in question.

'What's happening?' he mouthed.

'Can I bring somebody?' she asked. 'My friend Stu? He's been looking after the café, and I'd love to say thank you to him. He's as big a fan as I am.'

'Totally. Bring him. Listen, I've got to go. But I'm excited that you're excited. You'll stay with me? At The Langham? Does Stuart need digs?'

The Langham! Penny couldn't believe the luxury she was

being offered. She'd once gone to the bar there for a drink with Clementine and a round for two had cost a hundred quid. 'No, he's in my old apartment. It's just me. I'll drop my bag Thursday afternoon and see you there.'

'I can't wait,' Thomas said.

Penny put her phone into her apron pocket and walked to the pastry section.

'What was that?' Francesco said. 'Aside from obviously very good news?'

'I,' said Penny, sashaying comically on the spot. 'Am going to see,' she wiggled her hips seductively. 'Lizzo! Backstage passes baby!'

'What?' said Francesco. 'When? How!'

'Her tour manager comes to eat here sometimes,' Penny said, noting to herself only after she'd said it that, *Huh, that was a version of the truth.* But, it wasn't any of his business, really, was it. Especially not after how he reacted to Priyesh.

'When are you going?' asked Francesco. 'And am I your plus-one?'

Penny's face fell. She didn't want to disappoint him.

'Pen, relax, I'm kidding. I heard you ask about Stuart. I think that's a really nice gesture now I understand where you're going. By the way, has he told you he finally asked out Safiya? She told me the other day. She quite fancies him, it sounds like.'

'What?' said Penny, excited for her café employee and his endless crush on their bread supplier. 'He didn't! All the more reason to invite him, now. I can meet Lizzo, *and* get the inside scoop on how he finally plucked up the courage. That's very cool. He's liked her for ages, you know. At least a year.'

'You're such a blatherer,' Francesco said. 'You can't keep a secret to save your life.'

'It's hardly a secret now they're dating, is it? But. Even if I am a gossip, I'm a gossip who also needs a favour . . .'

'Go on,' Francesco said, returning to his pan of spinning sugar.

'I feel really bad asking this but – will you keep an eye on the place here? Keep me in the loop with what's happening? The gig is Thursday night. I can have Manuela fill in as head and get a temp in as sous until Saturday lunch, so I get a proper break, and then I'll be back for evening service on Saturday night. It's just – everyone loves you here, and I know you'll do right by me.' She smiled at him. 'What do you think?'

'Of course,' said Francesco, simply. 'And don't forget Charlie is the most competent front of house manager in the history of front of house managers, so if I were you I'd be zero per cent worried. Go. Enjoy. Bring us back some over-priced merchandise.'

'Ahhh,' said Penny. 'Thank you! I'll get you a t-shirt *and* a keyring. Cheers, pal.' She let out another squeal.

Francesco admired the shapes he'd made on the baking trays in front of him and asked, 'Won't this be the first time you've gone back to London since you took over?'

'I try not to let myself think about that,' Penny said. 'Because I miss it. I thought I'd at least get Christmas there, but I celebrated here and in Cornwall didn't I so yes, it will be my first trip back. I'm going to see Lizzo, get a coffee at Ozone, go to Arket in Covent Garden to maybe buy some new trousers . . .'

'Your version of heaven, then,' Francesco said.

'Yup!'

'Well please eat a bagel from Zobbler's in my honour, okay?

Oooooh, and maybe have an Old Fashioned in The Standard. You can't get drinks like theirs up here. Or anywhere, really.'

Penny looked at him at the mention of the hotel they'd stayed the night at together, but Francesco already had his head in the fridge. It was obviously only her who had memories of their romance. Although, by now they'd been friends for about four times as long as they'd ever been romantically involved, so maybe he really didn't remember their romantic dalliance. It occurred to her that she was foolish for even lingering on the thought.

'Okay,' she said, fishing out her phone again. 'Let me give Stuart the good news.' She put a hand on Francesco's shoulder and said, 'Really. Thank you.'

Francesco put his hand over hers and replied, 'Penny. Anything for you.'

'So,' Stuart said as they descended the escalator to get on the Jubilee line to The O2 Arena. 'Francesco is there day in and day out. Francesco with the hair and the eyes and the sex toys Francesco?'

'Honestly, we are so far beyond that,' Penny said. 'He's like my brother now, or something. It's not like *that*. We're best mates. And I'm his boss. He needed a job and a change of scenery and I need the help for the Bib Gourmand, so it's changed all the rules.'

'You're friends, but he's pissed off about you shagging the wine merchant?'

'Only in a protective way,' Penny reasoned. 'I'm protective over him, too. Like I'm protective over you with Safiya – I'll kill her if she hurts you.'

Stuart beamed. 'Can you believe my luck?' he asked. 'Me, dating Safiya Abadi . . .'

'I'm happy for you,' Penny said. 'She is very lucky to have you.'

'Thank you. And wait – let's not get distracted. Francesco. He's watching the pub as you come down here to hang out with the tour manager that you are also shagging?'

Penny rolled her eyes. 'I'm not shagging him now, am I? He's been all over Europe with these tour dates.'

'I'm just not buying it,' said Stuart. 'The second that man walked into the café the air changed. It was you, it was him, it was freshly baked bread. That doesn't just *go away.*'

'That's the thing though,' Penny said. 'It hasn't gone away. It's . . . changed. We hang out a lot and talk and laugh, but it's friendship. It's a really beautiful friendship. And I need that. It was lonely up there. I miss London something crazy. It's hard enough that I need a friend on my side, and that's what he is. I couldn't do it without him.'

'Mmmmmm,' uttered Stuart, unconvinced. 'You just sound greedy to me.'

Backstage, there were dancers and crew, other guests and a handful of celebrities.

'F-me, I think that's Blue Ivy!' Stuart hissed. 'Look!' They were both beside themselves with excitement. It was all terribly glamorous, with dancers and celebrities and hangers-on milling about everywhere, and access to as much champagne as they wanted.

Penny spun around. 'With Solange! Damn. Be cool. Be so cool.'

Solange and Blue Ivy walked past them, Solange making eye contact long enough to say, 'Hey, how are you,' but not as a question.

Penny turned to Stuart and did a fake scream face, making

him laugh hysterically, at which point Thomas turned a corner and clocked her.

'Good scream face or bad scream face?' he said, amused.

'Hey, you!' Penny said, going in for a hug to his kiss so that they ended up in a physical touch mis-match. 'Oh, sorry,' she said. 'I'm so clumsy. Ha.'

Extracting her limbs from his, Penny pulled away awkwardly and said, 'This is Stuart, who is looking after the café for me this year.'

'Hey,' Thomas said, shaking his hand.

'This is so awesome,' Stuart said. 'Thanks so much for the invite.'

'Of course,' Thomas said. 'Any friend of this one is a friend of mine.' He winked at Penny. Stuart saw and looked to Penny for her reaction. She swooned.

'Well,' Thomas continued. 'There's a green room just down this corridor,' he gestured to where he'd come from. 'Lizzo will come by and say hi after the show. For now she's in vocal warm up in her dressing room.'

'We'll get to meet her?'

'You will,' Thomas said. 'But,' he lowered his voice. 'Is it cool if you don't tell her how we know each other? You know – that we hooked up. Just say you're a friend from back home, yeah?'

'Right . . .' said Penny, feeling uncomfortable at the instruction. Before she could ask why, exactly, Lizzo had to be shielded from the truth of their relationship, a woman dressed all in black and carrying a clipboard and a walkie-talkie interrupted to whisper something in Thomas's ear.

'I've got a fire to put out,' he said, when she'd finished. 'If you'll excuse me?' He went to give Penny a kiss on the cheek. 'Enjoy the show, guys. I'll find you after.'

Penny and Stuart looked at each other once he'd gone. Neither spoke.

Finally Stuart said slowly, 'Is your man . . . sleeping with Lizzo?'

Penny pulled a face. 'I want to say no, but also . . . why can't I tell her who I am to him?'

'Because he's sleeping with her and she doesn't know he also has a little Derbyshire baby tucked away in the dales?' Stuart supplied.

'No,' Penny said. 'Surely not . . .'

'Sorry about it,' Stuart replied. His tone changed. 'But also, not sorry, because Francesco is obviously "The One". How have you not figured that out yet? Although of course, Francesco can't get us backstage passes.'

'You don't actually think he's sleeping with her, do you?' Penny said.

Stuart looked at her like she was stupid. 'Let's go and enjoy the show,' he replied, gently. 'Maybe let's get you a drink, too.'

'I don't know if I am more upset to know who I'm sharing him with, or that I'm basically his secret.'

Stuart handed her a glass of champagne from a small catering table down a side corridor.

'Ethical non-monogamy though, remember? He told you upfront what the deal was.'

Penny downed her glass. 'I suppose so,' she said, hurriedly adding: 'Anyway. I'm here for the music. Let's go find our box seats.'

The morning after the concert, Penny stood in the walk-in shower of Thomas's hotel room, remembering the look on Stuart's face as he shook Lizzo's hand after her show, and just how loudly he'd screamed in between singing along to every single song – exactly as Penny herself had done. It had been a superb night, and Lizzo had been lovely to them afterwards as well, although she was still none the wiser as to Thomas's relationship to her. Wrapped in a big bath towel Penny walked through to where she thought Thomas still slept, humming one of Lizzo's songs.

'Morning sunshine,' Thomas said. The table by the window was overloaded with food: pastries and juices, cooked eggs and jugs of bearnaise sauce. Thomas sat in his boxers.

'This is breakfast?' Penny said in awe. 'All of this just for us?'

'I didn't know what you might want,' he yawned, 'so I ordered a bit of everything. You made me work up quite the appetite.'

He craned his neck to give her a kiss, which she accepted.

'Mmmmm,' she replied. 'Get your energy up and then maybe it will be my turn to come,' she said, settling into a chair beside the table laden with food. She'd meant it to sound sassy, but it came out sour. Priyesh always put her pleasure front and centre, and she couldn't hide the fact that Thomas's selfishness last night had irritated her.

'Okay, grumpy,' Thomas said, unfolding a napkin.

She didn't say anything, popping a blueberry in her mouth instead.

'What shall we do today? The whole city is our oyster.'

She thought about it. 'I'd like to walk around,' she settled on. 'Maybe down through Southwark to The Tate? I'd even like to go in, walk around there too.' She bit wistfully into a pain au raisin. 'So much culture, everywhere,' she marvelled. 'That's what I miss most, I think. There's just so much to do here, no matter what the hour, no matter what the day. It's not like that up there, is it?'

'Ahhhh,' Thomas replied, pouring himself a coffee. 'You see when I'm on the road what I miss is the countryside, and the hills, and Havingley.'

'How lucky you are to have both,' Penny said. 'I feel like for me I have to choose one or the other.'

'Not long now though, right? Didn't you say you were going to give it a year?'

Penny tore into a second croissant. 'A year until I ask Uncle David what the new plan is, yeah. I'm enjoying it, I mean – most of the time – but I am keen to get back down here. I don't like to bring it up to him though. No point guilt-tripping him.'

'Let's make the most of it whilst you're here then,' Thomas said. 'Addressing, of course, the most important thing first.'

'And what's that?' Penny asked.

'Did you really not have an orgasm?'

Penny held up her hands as if to say, *nope.*

Thomas put down his coffee and in a flash leapt onto the bed, dragging her with him.

'Come here then!' he screamed, and Penny squealed in delight.

They walked through London all day, the cold air making their cheeks rosy, stopping for hot chocolate and red wine and lunch and eventually dinner. They racked up twenty-five thousand steps and with every single one Penny felt herself get more and more nostalgic for the city that she missed all the way down to her bones. She felt free in London. It wasn't anything to do with Havingley, or Derbyshire. It was everything to do with the fact that it wasn't her choice to be there. The Red Panda wasn't her choice. But to be in the place that felt most like home, for a few days, with Thomas, who was so good at adventure and making his own rules – well, it awakened something within her. It awakened a desire to regain control of her life, and to make her own rules, too. Francesco had said that's what inspired him about her. It wasn't like her to simply coast, and she had been. She didn't like that. Thomas had helped her remember.

'Listen, I want to tell you something,' Thomas said, as, on Penny's second night, they lingered by the Thames and darkness fell.

'Tell me,' said Penny, buzzed from the bottle of wine they'd just shared.

'I want to tell you,' Thomas said, 'that you being here has been the highlight of this tour for me. I told you the road was home for me as much as anywhere else, but . . . I have a great time with you. Have had a great time, but also: I always do.'

Penny smiled. 'I like our little adventures as well. I like how you show me things. Places.'

Thomas leaned in for a kiss.

'Shall we keep doing it?' Thomas said. 'Adventures? Unofficially official?'

She considered it. If they were unofficially official, and Thomas was never going to expect her to be monogamous because he'd never be monogamous himself, she could have these exciting adventures with him, and back at the pub keep having mind-blowing sex with Priyesh. It was quite the arrangement. Did that make her non-monogamous herself? She'd have to talk to Sharon about it. She'd never had more than one man on the go before.

'Yes,' Penny replied. 'Let's keep doing it. Unofficially official.'

She thought about what Stuart had said about her being greedy. But who said a woman couldn't have it all? She headed back to the pub feeling like the cat who'd got the cream.

Francesco stirred his sauce on the hob as Charlie put their head around the corner of the kitchen and said, 'That's us done. See you tomorrow.'

'See you tomorrow,' Penny said, waving. 'Thanks again for holding down the fort this week!'

'No worries, Pen. I'm glad you had a good time.' Charlie's statement was loaded. They knew exactly what Penny had been up to.

'Bye, bitch!' Francesco said to them in a funny voice.

'Bye, bitch!' Charlie repeated, laughing.

'I don't get it. What even is that?' Penny asked as Francesco scooped up his spoon and told her to taste what he was making. His face was encouraging, clearly expecting only compliments.

'Good, huh?' he said. 'I love this time of year for meat.'

'What pasta are we having with it?' Penny asked, watching Francesco as he tilted his head upwards, as if coming up to the thought.

'Fettuccini, I think,' he replied. 'This one would be good with the fettuccini.'

Penny went to the dry store to locate it, returning triumphant and doing a little dance of celebration.

'You've been like this all day,' Francesco said. 'Walking on a Lizzo high.'

'I had a great time,' said Penny. 'Lizzo was amazing, and I got to hang out in the city a bit, and Thomas was on form, too.'

'He's the one who gave you the tickets?'

'Yes.'

'How do you know him again?' Francesco opened the pasta and poured it into the pan of salted boiling water he'd prepared. He didn't use the bowls to measure out how much to use – he said it was the Italian in him that could judge how much to put in by sight. 'Pasta should be cooked in water as salty as the sea,' he'd once told her, and now he added in extra, just in case. Penny felt like she'd never cook pasta without thinking of him ever again.

'He has a house around here. We've hung out a few times.'

Francesco paused. 'As friends?' he said, trying to sound nonchalant.

'Well,' Penny started. 'Sort of. I mean. It wasn't serious.'

'Oh,' said Francesco, putting the salt back and resuming cooking. 'I didn't know that. Does Priyesh know?'

'It was before Priyesh.'

'And to think you told me you were lonely up here.'

Penny took a step back from him. 'I beg your pardon?' she said.

'This Thomas guy, Priyesh . . . doesn't sound very lonely to me, is all.' He didn't look at her. His eyes were on his pan.

'That sounds like slut-shaming.'

'Are you a slut?'

'I'm going to pretend you didn't just say that to me, Francesco.'

They stood in silence, Francesco faffing about with his food and Penny staring at him, waiting for his apology.

'You know what,' he said, turning the gas of the hob off and throwing down his towel. 'I'm actually not that hungry. Help yourself if you want it.' He banged the door on his way out.

Penny stood in the empty kitchen. She wasn't sure what had just happened, but she knew she felt the beginnings of total fury bubbling in the pit of her stomach. What right did Francesco have to get cross about a bloke she'd been seeing before he'd even arrived? Not to mention the fact that it took him the grand total of half a second to move on once she'd said she was leaving Stoke Newington. She stared at the pasta. She wasn't hungry now either, and so angrily poured it into the colander and pulled out a plastic container so it could be stored in the fridge. As she moved around the kitchen she got angrier and angrier. Even if Francesco was mad, how dare he walk out on her? That was just disrespectful. Downright rude. She flicked the lights off in the kitchen and went upstairs to her flat.

'Francesco,' she grumbled to herself. 'Bloody Francesco.' She showered, climbed into bed, and lay staring at the ceiling. She waited to calm down, to let the feeling subside, but it only got stronger.

The next morning Penny stood at the window of her front room and waited to see him coming down the hill opposite so she could intercept him at the door. She hadn't slept, and it was his fault. She fully intended to give him a piece of her mind. She wouldn't be spoken to like that and then shut out. It was totally inappropriate, especially since she was his boss.

At exactly ten to the hour he came over the hill and Penny picked up her phone to call him. She watched through the glass as he answered.

'Hello,' he said. He sounded gruff.

'Can you come straight up to the flat when you get here please?' Penny said.

Francesco sighed. 'Fine,' he said.

Penny expected him to be contrite and apologize from the

off about storming out on her. As far as she was concerned, she had every right to be furious, and only him saying sorry would do. Except the Francesco who came through her door wasn't sorry at all. If anything he was as angry as her – he was almost shaking with anger. If she'd tossed and turned in fury all night, it was apparent that he had too.

'No,' he said, as Penny went to speak. 'Me first. I get to talk.'

Penny was taken aback at his tone. He didn't sound hard in his rage. He sounded sad with it.

'You need to do some soul-searching, Pen,' he began. 'Because you don't realize your capacity to hurt people and it's making you not very nice.'

He stood opposite her, so furious it looked as though he was moments away from smoke escaping from his ears.

'Why don't you understand how loved you are?' he continued. 'Why can't you see what's right in front of your face?'

He looked at her, his eyes bright with craving. It hit Penny hard when she got what he meant.

'You?' she said.

'Yes me,' he replied. 'Come on, Penny. This is so stupid.'

'Don't call me stupid.'

'I didn't. This – the situation – that's what is stupid.' His tone was softer, now. He was calming down, like the pressure that had built up in him was slowly being released.

'We're supposed to be friends,' she said, barely above a whisper. 'Why are you saying all this?'

'This isn't friendship.'

Penny looked up at him.

'It's not, is it? These other men – the Lizzo guy, Priyesh. You don't have with them what you and me have.'

Penny shook her head.

Francesco carried on: 'Penny, I love you. And I think you love me too.'

'You're supposed to be my safe person,' Penny croaked, spooked. 'I don't want you to go anywhere.'

'That's the point,' he said, softer now. 'I'm not, am I? I love you.'

'I can't say it back,' she said, shaking her head, tears threatening to spill over.

'Do you want to say it back?' Francesco said.

'No,' said Penny. 'Because I know what you did.'

'What I did?'

'The day I left. The woman. The woman with all that hair.'

Francesco looked like he'd been slapped. The colour drained from his face.

'How did you . . .?' he began, taking a step towards Penny with his hand out, as if he was going to reach for her wrist, or her waist.

'Don't,' said Penny, taking a step back and bumping into the sofa. 'Don't touch me.'

'I need to explain.'

'I don't care.'

'Yes you do. Is this why we didn't speak? Is this why you disappeared? Because you saw me with Valentina?'

Penny went wild. 'Do NOT say her name to me. Don't you dare say her name!'

'I'm so sorry, Pen. I am so, so sorry if you thought . . . for all this time . . . that . . .' He stumbled over his own words, trying to decide where to start. 'She's nothing to me. That was my ex. It was messed up. She was there, somehow. I didn't know she still had me on Find My Friend. You know the app? We did it when we were together so she could see when I was on my way home from work. She'd been using it to see where I was going and that's how she knew I was at Bridges a lot. I told you she wanted me back, that she wanted to make it right after cheating. She thought I had a new job, I think, so went there looking for me. She was there right after you left, and I don't know . . . I hate her for what she did to me so much, and I hated you for leaving, and she was apologizing to me, telling me how much she needed me, wanted me, and for a tiny second I could believe it was you saying those things.'

'I came back for you,' Penny said. 'I turned the car around and in the thirty seconds since I left all this happened?'

Francesco shook his head, mortified at what she'd seen. 'Penny. I was so stupid. I wanted you to ask me to come with you so much.'

'I hated you for months,' Penny spat. 'You broke my heart and you promised me you wouldn't do that.' Francesco launched himself at her before she could object, pulling her close. She pushed her face against his t-shirt and he held her, tightly, stroking her hair.

'It's okay,' he said. 'It's okay.' Together they rocked back and forth.

'Are you telling me the truth?' she said, her voice muffled by his chest. 'If you lie to me . . .'

'It's the truth,' he said, pulling apart from her. He took her hand and they sat on the sofa, knees knocking and hands entwined.

'We're so good together, Penny. I think you've been fighting it because of what you saw, but what you saw was nothing. It was a mistake.'

He kept stroking her hand.

'*This* is how it is supposed to be. You and me. You have to feel it too. This is what it feels like when it's good.'

Penny started to cry. She cried for Mo for hurting her, which was boring but no less true because of it. She cried for Uncle David – in fear that he'd been sick, and in relief that he was getting better, and in anger that he'd put her here, away from her friends and in the middle of all these men. She cried because she was tired, and because she wanted Francesco to be enough – for it to be safe to truly love him, but it wasn't. Was it? Could it be? What was the worst that could happen?

She crumpled into him and felt the weight of his hand at the back of her neck, and the rise and fall of him. Pulling her head back slightly, he looked at her, and she looked at him, and he gave her a chaste kiss on the forehead, which she gratefully accepted.

They looked at each other again and he gave her an equally-chaste kiss on her lips, just briefly.

They looked at each other some more and Penny stopped thinking and pressed her mouth to his and the length of her body to the length of his body. She melted into him and he surrendered into her and it was pure and beautiful and had been such a long time coming. Penny didn't have to think when they were like this. It felt pre-destined and safe. Her tongue explored his mouth and her hands ran the length of his body and even if she couldn't say she loved him, it felt a lot like love.

'We need to go down for service,' Francesco said, after a while. 'I don't want to, but . . .'

'I don't want you to let go,' Penny said.

'Two more minutes,' he replied, holding her tightly.

'I need an emergency pep talk,' Penny hissed at Charlie. 'Something happened.'

Charlie looked up from where they were polishing glasses behind the bar.

'Good happened, or help-me-bury-the-body happened?'

'Help me bury the body. No. Good. No, bad. I don't know.'

Charlie put down the glass and cloth. 'Aw shit,' they said. 'Okay. Tea?'

Penny nodded, and they moved through to the kitchen, threw a couple of tea bags in some mugs and filled them from the tap that gave out boiling water from the coffee machine, before reconvening in the bar.

'I kissed Francesco,' Penny said.

'What?' said Charlie. 'Well that's amazing! I assume you've officially forgiven him then?'

'I mean, sure. The woman I saw him with – it was his ex. And so much has happened since then that . . . you know. Bygones.'

'Right.'

'Was that a bad idea?'

'To forgive and forget?'

'No. To snog him.'

'Tell me why you think it could be a bad idea.'

'Well. For one, Thomas. For two, Priyesh.'

'Ohmygod,' said Charlie. 'You're not even in a love triangle. You're in a love . . . square!'

'I don't know what to do next.'

'Do you have to do anything?'

'That's why I need this pep talk! I don't know!'

Penny's mind had raced all through lunch service. Francesco worked at the opposite end of the kitchen and it was a busy shift, so they'd both been focused and in the zone. But as her hands moved and she plated up food and called out orders to Manuela, in her head she'd been somewhere else.

Priyesh was filthy and serious.

Thomas was adventurous and free.

Francesco was her friend, above all else.

Was it possible to feel deeply about three men equally, for different reasons, in different ways? Penny didn't know the answer, but half-resolved that maybe she didn't need to. She wasn't sure what would happen next with Francesco. It was only a kiss. But, he'd also said I love you. She loved him too, she just didn't know to what extent. Everything had changed now she knew that woman had been his ex. She knew how he felt about her – about Valentina. What she'd done to him when she cheated. There was no way he'd been seeing her again. Penny believed that much. 'The obvious question is: are you actually in love with any of them?' Charlie probed.

'I don't want to screw up what Francesco and I have,' Penny said. 'Since he's been here everything has felt manageable. Do-able. Even enjoyable. I like having him here. But do I think I can trust him with my heart? I want to. I think he looks after me the best he can but hasn't he proven that he doesn't deserve my trust?'

'Does that mean he doesn't get a second chance?' asked Charlie. 'If you want to give him one, that is.'

'You're being a pussy,' said Sharon, down the phone, after Penny had explained everything to her. 'Listen, lord knows I'm not his biggest fan. I was Team Thomas all the way. Well. Then I was Team Priyesh all the way. But if what Francesco says is true, my reasons for hating him on your behalf don't stand up. You've already wasted too much time treading on eggshells with each other. It's now or never! Team Francesco!'

Penny felt sick as she listened.

'You don't get to tell me you're scared, Penny, okay? You beat bloody cancer. You can tell a man you love him back. Because you do, don't you? I can tell. I think you've been in love with him this whole time.' Her voice softened as she said the last bit, knowing not to push too hard.

Penny sighed dramatically. 'You give tough advice, do you know that?' she said.

'You and Francesco could be really happy together. You just have to give yourself permission to trust it.'

'Hmmm,' said Penny. 'That sounds terrifying.'

19

Havingley had, for inexplicable reasons dating back hundreds of years, always celebrated Valentine's Day as a village event. The locals always looked forward to the street party and The Red Panda had, over time, become the unofficial hub of the events, which included fundraising stalls lining the road in front – which was pedestrianized for the occasion – an open-air performance from the am-dram society, and a variety of acts from bands old and new.

It started out as a bright, if brisk, day. The air was cold but the sky was blue, and after the lull of post-Christmas and New Year drudgery it was nice, before spring came, to have a big event that broke up the wait for lighter days and warmer weather.

'I always come back for it,' Thomas had told Penny over the phone from Germany. 'I'll be there,' he said. 'I've been going since I was a little boy.' Penny had called him to talk about Francesco, but she'd dilly-dallied over her words and he'd had to go before she'd explained.

I'll do it when he's home, she told herself.

Priyesh, unsurprisingly, had never attended the Valentine's Day celebrations, but after Charlie had told him about it when he stopped by with some samples of a white wine he was drumming up springtime interest for, pledged to be there. Penny had wanted to tell him about Francesco, too. She knew the honourable thing to do would be to end her other relationships before anything further happened with Francesco, but he'd come right in the middle of dinner service when Penny had twelve guests in the private dining room and everyone had ordered a different starter.

I'll do it before the party, she told herself.

Francesco had heard at The Boot that it was quite the affair, and he was excited as well. He'd spent the past two days making Italian sweets and pastries for one of the stalls whilst looking too long in Penny's direction and smiling at her like they had some beautiful secret. They hadn't slept together – they hadn't even kissed since the morning they'd talked.

Penny was nervous around him. Jumpy. She had all of these things she wanted to say but she wasn't ready, yet, and Francesco could tell. So he didn't push her, or goad her. He was patient, and it was an act of kindness Penny appreciated. He smiled at her often and occasionally lightly touched the small of her back, but otherwise let her arrive to her feelings in her own time. She knew he assumed she was finishing things with Priyesh, too, from the way he eyed up the bar area when he'd been in. He was basically being the perfect gentleman.

'It gets rowdier than a rugby players' changing room in here as it kicks off,' Charlie had warned Penny as they set up. Penny was quite looking forward to it, though. It was nice to feel a surge in the sense of community. She might have missed London, but Stoke Newington never did a village event like this. Penny threw herself into it.

By 3 p.m. the pub was buzzing and a light shower had turned into heavier drizzle, so the bands had set up in a small sliver of space down by the bottom of Bar Four, near the fire. In a hurry, everyone had dismantled stalls and stands outside, and Penny had turned on the outdoor heaters so all the extra bodies could huddle under the shelter of the covered outdoor seating area, too. There were hundreds of people, and the rain was coming down heavier and heavier, but spirits were high and Penny was in the very best of moods. The high-spirits were catching.

'Penny, love,' one of the locals, Tim, said to her, a few hours into the celebration. 'I don't want to pry, duck, but it looks like the tiles over there on the outhouse are coming a cropper. You might want to get one of your lads to secure 'em down.'

Penny followed Tim's eye to the dusky skyline of outside. She saw instantly what he meant. The wind had picked up with the rain, and if she didn't get out there and secure the roof of the old coal store, it wouldn't take long before there *was* no roof.

'You're right. Thanks, Tim.'

'Here you are,' Tim exclaimed, on the approach of Thomas. 'This strapping young man will help you.'

'I will!' said Thomas, already quite drunk. And then, 'Hello, you. Help with what?'

'Those tiles,' said Penny, pointing. 'Do you mind? It won't take long, I don't think.'

'Lead the way,' Thomas said, downing the last two inches of his pint and handing the empty glass to Tim. 'Next round is on you,' Thomas said, to which Tim replied, 'And which round was on you?'

Penny and Thomas weaved through the throng of people in the bar and outside, and as soon as they stepped out of the huddle and to the side of the building, the wind hit them.

'Jesus!' said Thomas, his voice smothered by the weather. Penny could barely hear him, and he had to shout. 'Where did this all come from?'

'It was so nice this morning!' Penny yelled back.

'What are you doing out here?' came a voice from across the car park, and Thomas and Penny saw Priyesh climbing out of his Land Rover. 'You'll get blown away!' he said, and he was shouting, too.

'The roof!' said Penny, pointing to the small outhouse. 'Wanna help?'

'Sure!' said Priyesh, taking off his watch and putting it in his pocket, pulling out a Barbour jacket from the boot of his car and slipping it on.

Inside the pub, Francesco watched all of this unfold. He watched Penny standing in the rain and the wind with Thomas, and Priyesh pull up, and the way Penny was gesticulating to the outhouses. He could see that the tiles seemed unsteady, and it didn't take much to figure out that she was out there trying to secure them before the storm threatened to blow everything away. He grabbed his raincoat and slipped through the bar and into the kitchen, to take the back way out.

'Need a hand?' he yelled, as Thomas and Priyesh were manhandling a huge sheet of tarpaulin against the wind.

'Yes!' said Thomas. 'Take this!'

Francesco used his arm to help manoeuvre the middle part of the sheet, and Penny said, 'Here!' and passed him some bricks from the pile by the skip. They worked quickly and in harmony, securing the tiles as best they could. The rain came almost sideways, and Penny had to keep her face turned at an angle because the force it hit her with was almost painful. It was hard to see, but the men worked quickly and as a team, limiting any potential damage.

'I think that's enough!' she shouted into the elements. 'We did it!'

As they ran back to the pub the villagers crowded under the outdoor heaters cheered.

Inside the porch, the four of them – Penny, Francesco, Priyesh and Thomas – stood dripping in varying states of being soaked.

'Jesus,' said Priyesh, shaking his hands of water and peeling off his Barbour jacket.

'That was crazy!' said Francesco, his t-shirt stuck to him where his coat had flown open. 'I don't think I've ever known a storm like it!'

'Sorry-not-sorry lads, but—' Thomas said, taking off his sodden t-shirt. 'I'm wet through. Have you got a towel, Pen?' he asked, and Penny replied, without her eye wavering to his naked torso, that yes, she did. Thomas stood half naked and smiling, totally unabashed. It was typical Thomas.

Penny went out of the bottom of the kitchen into the restaurant part of the pub, to where they kept the laundry. She pulled out three towels and a handful of linen napkins, rushing back through to the kitchen to see, from one end to the other, the three men glistening and panting, adrenaline pumping through everyone's veins.

Priyesh didn't, technically, know about Thomas. Francesco knew about Thomas and Priyesh, in theory, but not since their kiss. Thomas knew better than to ask about Francesco or Priyesh, but could just about establish that situation if he used his imagination. Penny looked at the three men and knew the truth about her relationship to them all.

Not that it could last.

She was ready to make her choice.

As the four of them gathered themselves, drying off, there was a sudden moment of awkwardness. The three men didn't know each other well at all, and now that the adrenaline was winding down it was odd, really, to be semi-nude with a bunch of strange blokes. In the awkwardness, Francesco reached out to the back of Penny's neck – his port in the social storm. It was proprietorial, but he needed it as comfort. Penny looked up at him and he grinned at her, and she didn't know how to tell him now wasn't the time to lay claim to her. He could do that later, once they'd talked. She hadn't even told Priyesh or Thomas what she wanted, yet.

Priyesh clocked Francesco's hand on Penny, and didn't like it.

'Darling,' he said, taking her hand. 'Let's get some dry clothes from upstairs.'

Francesco looked at Priyesh in surprise. He didn't like that he was talking to Penny – his Penny – in such a familiar tone. And why was he holding her hand? He lightly tugged at her neck, pulling her towards him.

Priyesh pulled her towards him.

Francesco pulled again.

Penny deftly retrieved her arm from Priyesh's grip and bent down to take off her sodden trainers, releasing Francesco's hand from her. Thomas shook his head of blonde curls, combing his hair out of his face with his hands. As he did it he caught sight of Penny, hair in loose damp waves around her face and rain caught in her eyelashes and exclaimed, 'Pen, you look well fit right now.'

Priyesh looked mildly confused at that, but Francesco understood what he'd said loud and clear and immediately sent him daggers.

'Oh,' continued Thomas, clocking both men's reactions. 'It seems I'm not the only one who's thinking it . . .'

Priyesh frowned. 'Penny?' he said, and the way he said it made Francesco understand he felt they were somehow still involved.

'Ah,' Francesco said. 'I'm sorry, mate. Hasn't she told you?'

'Told me what?'

'That we're . . . well. Not "back" together, but . . . you know . . . together.'

'What?' said Penny. 'We're not back together.'

'Right,' said Francesco. 'Except. Well. These past few days. Not to mention everything before that.'

'Francesco, let's not do this now?'

Thomas piped up, 'This is why I don't put any rules on you, babe,' he said.

'Babe?!' said Priyesh and Francesco in unison.

Francesco narrowed his eyes. 'Penny – are you still seeing . . . all three of us?'

Penny looked from Francesco, with his earnestness and kind eyes, to Priyesh, with his chin held high, self-confident and certain, to Thomas, with his youthful charisma.

'No,' she began. 'I mean. Not on purpose. I don't know how this happened . . . you make it sound like I did something wrong, but . . .'

'Wrong?' said Priyesh. 'I thought we were falling in love?'

'In love?' countered Penny, genuinely perplexed. They had hardly sat and had long, deep, meaningful chats over hours and hours. They'd been sleeping together with a little light pillow talk every now and again. Did Priyesh think it was more than that? Her stomach lurched at the thought of having accidentally led him on.

Thomas patted Priyesh's back. 'You make love sound finite, mate. She can love more than one person.'

'Oh, do me a favour,' said Priyesh. 'That's just something little boys say so they can sleep around.'

Thomas held up his hands in surrender. 'Bit harsh,' he said.

Francesco stepped forward. 'Pen, come on. Us. Our history, and the kiss . . . the pasta . . . Don't you want that?'

Penny looked at him, water settled in droplets on his thick hair, big brown eyes searching hers for reassurance and confirmation. She did want those things. Two minutes ago she was certain of it. Her and Francesco. But now, with him asking her to say it, it was a lot.

Penny didn't know anything. She'd have to be so certain to make a choice, and before this moment she thought she had been, but now, confronted with a ticking clock and six eyes boring into her for her answer, she didn't want to decide anything. She didn't have it in her.

'I don't know what to say,' she stated, simply. 'Maybe I shouldn't be with any of you. I don't know. I'm scared.'

'This is bullshit!' cried Francesco. 'I do not accept what you are saying. Don't be so afraid, Penny. I just can't get my head around this. It's you and me. There isn't anything else.'

The presumptuousness of him enraged her, flipping a switch in her brain that told her not to be pushed around.

'You can't tell me what I feel,' she said. 'You don't understand. You think you do, but you don't. And that's just it, isn't it? As long as you think you know what's best for me,

260

you will never be what's best for me! Get your head around *that*!'

'Listen,' said Thomas. 'I don't want to get in the middle of anything here, okay? Penny, you're a babe, I enjoy knowing you, you know how I feel . . .' he trailed off. Penny appreciated that he knew when to back away.

'I'll call you,' she said. 'To explain.' She was pleased he knew how to take the temperature of a situation.

'Do that,' Thomas replied. 'I'm just going to have a nip of brandy to warm up, and then I'll be gone. Maggie from the fishmongers has been flirting with me anyway.' He picked up his things and headed, topless, into the throng of customers.

Priyesh stepped towards her. 'Penny, what is this? We've been having such a beautiful time together. If you're afraid, that's okay. I'm afraid too. If you need space, just say the word. But you and me . . . you can't deny it is special.'

Penny was shocked. She nodded, thankful to him for his kindness, but she hadn't realized he'd felt so deeply about her.

'I have so much respect for you . . .'

Priyesh smiled at her. 'I like you a lot,' he said. 'I know there's the age difference but I think you like me too.'

'Priyesh,' Penny said. 'It's just physical though, isn't it . . .?'

'Ah, sod this!' Francesco said, loud enough that people in the closest vicinity to them turned to look, and enough did so that the people behind them, too, turned to look as well.

'I'm not competing for your affections,' he said, his voice rising. 'This isn't the Penny Olympics. You're not a prize. I don't want to be the last man standing.'

Penny's jaw went slack at his outburst. Almost the whole pub had ceased talking amongst themselves in order to crane their necks to see what was happening.

'I am so angry at you,' he carried on. 'So, so angry. And I'm hurt. I am hurt, and I am angry, and it's not fair that you're shirking responsibility for that, like you don't know how it happened. You *know* how it happened!'

Penny was shaking her head, a mix of pleading with Francesco to stop and a way to disagree with what he was saying. She hadn't meant to upset him, or cause a scene. All she'd wanted was more time. A minute to think. This was all unravelling too fast. She looked to Priyesh apologetically, but he stood with his head bowed, lowering his eyes as if politely averting his gaze from Francesco's frenzy. She hadn't expected that from him. It was as if he was embarrassed to be near the whole thing.

'I have loved you since the very first day I met you,' Francesco continued. 'I don't understand why you think you aren't worthy of that love. It's here. I'm holding it right here in my hands for you, desperate to give it to you, and not because I'm selfish and want to claim you or own you. I want to give this love to you to free up my goddamn hands, so I can hold all the love you give me. Because you do. You love me. It couldn't be like this between us if you didn't. You. Love. Me. And I love you!'

A man stood near the bar put his pint down to clap, slowly at first – *clap, clap, clap* – and then the woman beside him joined in, and then somebody else, until the whole pub was whooping and cheering and somebody shouted, 'Kiss him, Pen!' and Penny turned and looked at all these well-wishers, and she froze. She couldn't say anything, couldn't do anything. Every sad thought about herself came flooding back – men leave, nobody sticks around. Nobody sticks around for *her*, anyway. She looked at Francesco – he deserved a woman who could give him his own kids, a woman who wasn't broken or lost, a woman who could trust him. It was all too much. She was better on her own. No matter how close she'd come to letting herself love him she couldn't take that one last step. She knew how to be on her own. She didn't know how to give in to this feeling with Francesco.

She looked back around, thinking of Priyesh, feeling self-conscious at what he'd just heard, but he was gone. Instead there was only Francesco and, in that moment, even seeing him was too much for her.

'I can't do this,' she said, panicked. 'I'm sorry.'

Penny pushed through the throng of people to the stairs that would lead her to her flat. She took them two at a time and locked the door behind her. After five minutes of hyperventilating, desperately trying to get herself to calm down, she could hear the noise in the bar get louder and she knew she had to go downstairs to help. They'd be totally overwhelmed without her. She pulled herself together, engaging the 'I am the boss' muscle it would take to head back downstairs. She splashed her face with cold water, found some dry shoes, and joined Charlie behind the bar.

'You okay?' they said, clocking her ashen face and fake smile.

'Nope,' said Penny, teeth clenched. 'Not one bit.'

She let herself assess who was still in the pub, but there was no sight of Francesco, or of Priyesh. She just caught the back of Thomas's head before he ducked around a corner with Maggie from the fishmongers. She didn't care.

20

The cemetery was quiet. Penny didn't even see the groundsman, but she didn't know how unusual that was because she hardly ever actually came to the physical grave of her mother. Before she'd died, when she'd known that it was terminal, Hermione Bridge had pulled her daughters Penny and Clementine close to her in bed, one of them either side, and whispered, 'You can talk to me whenever you like, even when I'm not there. Anything you say I will hear.'

Penny wondered if that's why she spent so much time recording voice notes. Sometimes they were for the recipient, but some of them were really just prayers for mum. *What must it be like to live around the corner from your mother, or pick up the phone to hear her voice whenever you wanted?* Penny wondered. *What a luxury,* she thought. *What a privilege.*

'Hi mum,' Penny said, as she took off her scarf and used it to kneel at the side of the grave. It had a white granite headstone, engraved with the fact she'd left two beautiful daughters behind, and Penny reached out to stroke it, as if by doing so she'd wake up the spirit of her mother, who might then respond.

'Sorry I haven't been in a while. I guess I feel like I don't have to come here to tell you I'm thinking of you. I think of you all the time. I really do.' She took a breath. She hadn't come here to keep crying. She'd come here so she'd stop.

'I feel in a bit of a mess actually, mum. I thought you'd know what to do. There was a man, and I made it too complicated, I think, and now he's mad at me. So, so mad.

'There's another man who I think could love me, but am I settling? He's too old for me, at the very least. How do I know if it's settling, or if it's right? And I don't want you to think you left behind a slutty daughter or anything, but there's also been this other guy, too, but . . . well, did they have non-monogamy in your day, mum? I mean, it was the seventies, of course they did. Did you ever do that? Because this man, Thomas, he's shown me this whole area, all things I didn't know or hadn't seen or had forgotten, and he makes me laugh, and he's exciting, but he travels so much and is hardly here and when he is sometimes he doesn't really show up. I don't think I want to be in an open relationship. I mean – I know I don't. I want one person, one love, one main partner who I choose and who chooses me and together we are against the world.

'I want somebody who puts me first and thinks of me and looks after me and I want to have one person, above all else, who I do that for too.

'That's what I want. I do.'

Penny stopped talking as she watched a woman with two small children walk through the graveyard, silently weeping but still smiling. She was carrying flowers, and the children looked solemn and serious, like they understood now wasn't the time to run or play or act up.

'I love you mum. I'm just trying to make you proud, you know? But it feels hard, lately. I feel like I've strayed from my path or something, and that makes me sad. I think because I know it would make you sad, if you knew.'

Penny started to cry again now.

'I wish I didn't feel like this,' she said. 'I wish you could tell me what to do.'

She stayed by the grave for forty-five minutes, waiting for a sign. It didn't come. Penny understood she had to figure it out for herself.

Over the next few days, the tension at The Red Panda was such that it interfered with Penny's leadership. Lunches were made and evening shifts came and went but she was distracted and made mistakes. Francesco's cold shoulder was so extreme that Penny didn't dare suggest a bowl of pasta. Francesco didn't really say much at all, until one day he did.

'We need to talk.'

He'd appeared at the bar where Penny was stood talking to Charlie about the benefits of the Kiehl's Turmeric and Cranberry scrub versus the Elemis superfood glow mask.

'I just can't afford to stain yet another towel yellow,' Charlie was saying, when Francesco interrupted. He looked wan and pale, and like he hadn't slept.

'Morning, bitch,' Charlie said to him, but all he replied with was, 'Hey.' Charlie looked taken aback, and quickly understood he was finally going to have it out with Penny.

'Shall we go outside?' Penny asked Francesco, understanding the same thing.

'I think that would be wise,' he replied, and Charlie and Penny exchanged a loaded look as he led the way.

The pair walked through the pub to the back decking, and

Penny studied Francesco's face. It was the first time she'd seen more than a side profile of him in days. She pulled out a chair that was damp from earlier rain and sat, hoping he'd pull out the other one, but he remained standing.

'I'm leaving,' he said, simply. 'I can't stay.'

Penny nodded. She'd wondered if he might decide that. He'd made no attempts to make things right between them, or to even open up the space for Penny to try. He was furious, and did his job each shift and then left wordlessly. Every time Penny tried to make even light chit-chat, he'd shut her down. It made trying to move forward really hard, being met with an emotional brick wall that way.

'I'm not happy about leaving,' he said. 'But I don't know what else to do.'

'Where will you go?' Penny asked, after a beat. He wouldn't look at her. He was looking at his shoes. Penny wanted to fix it, she wanted to take away his pain. But she knew she couldn't. She'd messed this up, and her punishment was the look on Francesco's face.

I can't say that I love you, Penny thought. *I just can't.*

'My grandmother,' he said. 'She has a Pasticceria in Bologna. I'll stay with her. Learn some new recipes. Decide what's next . . .'

Penny felt sick at the thought of him leaving Havingley, let alone to another country.

'Italy?' she said. 'Oh, Francesco. This is all my fault. I'm sorry. I wish I could tell you not to go. I wish I could undo Valentine's Day, and everything that happened.'

'Don't,' insisted Francesco. 'Let's not do this again. We've been here before. It shouldn't be this hard. If it is, then . . .'

Penny swallowed. She knew she had no right to get emotional. Not really. She'd turned it over in her mind and she knew, deep down, she didn't trust Francesco. How could he say he loved her when the whole time he'd been here he'd been dating other women? The goddess woman, the woman he'd met at The Boot – his words and his actions hadn't lined up, so why should she think they were now, even if he'd said he loved her? What were words anyway?

She couldn't trust him.

She couldn't trust herself.

It was better if he went.

I can't say that I love you.

She'd loved having him at the pub but it had all been pretend. They'd pretended to be friends, to be pals, to be buddies, but it was always going to end in tears, wasn't it, exactly like it did that morning in Stoke Newington. It was a short-lived romance limping on, masquerading as something more and exhausting them both.

I can't say that I love you.

'When will you go?' she asked.

'Is two weeks' notice okay?'

'Sure,' she replied. 'Though I'm sure I can find somebody else before then, if you want.'

Penny said softly, 'We really screwed this up, didn't we?' and it made him finally look her dead in the eye.

'No, Penny,' he said, plainly. '*We* didn't screw this up – *you* did. You were right: you're too broken for me to fix, and I'm not a good enough man to be a pick-me-up who doubles as a toy.'

Penny was shocked by the level of his anger. His words came out strong and practised, like he'd rehearsed them in his head and designed them for maximum impact.

'You are selfish, and uncomprehending of the games you play with grown men's emotions,' he continued. 'I said I loved you, but now I have thought about it I don't know if I could love somebody who would be so cruel. So thoughtless. You are an animal, trapped in her own pain, lashing out at anybody who dares come close enough to show you some kindness. I say this because I care, and because as soon as I have finished talking I will not care any longer. Get help. Go to therapy. Sort your head out. Because you will never find true contentment until you do, okay? This victim routine you have is mind-numbing. It's time to grow up. It really, really is.'

Penny felt like she'd been slapped. Francesco was talking as though he hated her.

'On second thoughts,' he said, untying his apron. 'I hereby retract giving you two weeks' notice. You can stick your job up your arse.' He tugged the apron over his head and handed it to Penny. 'All the best.'

And then he walked away.

Penny stood shaking in humiliation. She knew she should go after him. She knew she should beg him to listen to her, to let her explain how she felt, to tell him she did trust him, actually, or she could, if he helped her, but the truth was that she had no idea what she felt. Who was this person she'd become? She'd strayed so far from who she thought she was that it was almost as if Francesco was right: she didn't deserve his love.

And so she didn't deserve to chase after him, either.

'I couldn't do it,' she told Sharon over the phone. 'I just froze. I'm an idiot.'

Sharon tutted at the other end of the line, kindly. 'You're not an idiot, darling, I promise you. This isn't anybody's fault. Maybe he won't even go?'

Penny sniffled and reached for a tissue. 'I think he already has,' she said. 'Charlie saw him packing up his car.'

'Oh.'

'Yeah. Oh.'

'Well, you don't have to do anything just now, okay? If you're hurt, be hurt. If you don't know what to do next, don't do anything for a moment. None of us is fucking up like we think we are, okay? So just be. I'm here if you need me, okay?'

'Okay,' said Penny. 'Thank you.'

'I love you.'

Penny pulled out some Ben & Jerry's from the freezer and flicked on *The Notebook*. She used a tablespoon to shovel the food into her mouth without tasting it, the sugar hit barely making her high. She didn't want to be alone, but she didn't want to be with anybody else, either. She watched Noah and Allie swinging into the river and riding bikes and snogging up against walls, and her whole relationship with Francesco played like a movie montage in her mind: how'd he'd looked that first morning in the café, the way it felt to see him at Dofi's restaurant. She thought about him standing in stocking feet in her kitchen making brunch, kissing her by the reservoir, taking her to a hotel with a bag of toys. The endless chats, the midnight snacks, the way she felt more capable with him than without him.

I can't say that I love you.

'We're staging an intervention.'

Penny had opened the door to the back step of the kitchen for her afternoon smoke to find her sister and Rima stood on the decking. She hadn't been expecting them – had no idea they were coming at all – and so the first words out of her mouth had been, 'What are you doing here?' That had

271

been Clementine's response: that they were staging an intervention. Penny didn't have a clue what that meant.

'Are we okay to go through to the bar?' Clementine asked, after giving Penny a big hug and taking a good look at her face. She refused to acknowledge her sister's confusion, as if there would be an 'all will be revealed' moment if only Penny were patient enough.

'Sure,' Penny replied, shaking her head. 'Go ahead.'

It was the only time in her life she hadn't been pleased to see her sister.

'Charlie!' Clementine cheered, seeing them through the archway to the bottom bar. 'Oh, I'm so pleased you're here! I was hoping I could introduce you to Rima. Rima come here,' she said, turning to her wife. 'This is Charlie. We used to go to school together. Charlie—' with this she turned back to Charlie, 'this is Rima.'

'It's so nice to meet you,' Charlie said, reaching a hand out. 'I'm so pleased you came.'

Penny scowled. Had Charlie been expecting them?

'Oh, no handshakes!' Rima said. 'Give me a hug!'

Everyone watched them wrap their arms around each other, smiling and making squealed exclamations. Penny couldn't get a handle on what was unfolding. She couldn't stand how happy everyone seemed, how okay they all were. Didn't they know she was hurting? Didn't they know not to be demonstrably happy in front of her breaking heart?

'You guys are making me feel really stupid,' Penny announced. 'This feels like an ambush and I don't know what about, except that I feel a bit like I'm in trouble.'

As soon as she said it she felt a wobble in her throat. She'd been like this for ten days now, since Francesco had walked out. She felt guilty he'd gone, panicked about getting a replacement for him, sad that she'd made him sad, somehow like she'd failed . . . And here her sister was, making her feel an inch tall for reasons as yet unknown.

Rima and Charlie parted. Clementine took off her coat.

'Sit down,' Clementine said. 'Charlie, is it okay if Rima helps you make some tea?'

'It's not an ambush,' Clementine repeated, sat beside her sister.

'So why do I feel overwhelmed when I should just be pleased to see you?' Penny asked, glumly. It was obvious she wasn't okay.

Clementine reached out for her hand. 'I should have told you. I'm sorry. I was just worried you'd tell me not to, and I figured it was easier to get forgiveness than permission if you were feeling . . .'

'Shit,' supplied Penny, fiddling with a salt shaker.

Clementine nodded. 'Charlie mentioned you've been a bit upset. They weren't gossiping about you, I swear. I called to book a table for Uncle David's visit, because you weren't replying to my voice notes. I specifically asked if you were okay, because not hearing from you was scaring me. You always tell me everything, and since Francesco left you've told me nothing.'

Penny shrugged. 'Nothing to tell,' she said, when what she meant was: *how do I even begin?*

They drank their tea and ate their biscuits, and eventually Penny said: 'I miss him.'

As she blinked, a tear spilled over and ran down her face. She used her fingers to blot it away and the others didn't say a word, knowing that on the verge of confession the best thing to do is simply listen.

'I just . . .' Penny looked around the room as a way to distract herself. It was getting lighter noticeably later recently, and the promise of spring – her year's end – was near. And then what? She felt like she'd thrown a hand grenade into her time in Havingley. She'd wanted to leave proud of what she'd done in transforming the place to its fully-booked, profitable incarnation. Now she'd leave knowing that above all else, what she'd done was get distracted by a bevy of men, like a horny teenager, and spoiled everything she had with each of them.

'I guess . . .' She looked up at the ceiling. 'I don't know . . .' Now she looked down again at her lap. Clementine stood and moved to sit beside her.

'It's shit that Francesco has gone,' she supplied. 'I can't imagine how that must feel.'

Penny nodded. 'Yeah,' she said. 'I miss him, you know? He was my friend, and then he got so mad at me, and . . .'

'Is that all? He was just your friend?'

'I don't even know,' Penny said. 'I can't figure it out. I think he is. We'd talk about who I was dating, and who he was dating, but then we kissed and I panicked . . .'

Charlie added, 'And then he flew off the handle. Like, he barely spoke before he walked out. Just came for his shifts, made his desserts, and then left. I don't know how well you two knew him, but that was so weird for him. I'd never seen him like that before.'

'He didn't even say goodbye,' Penny said, suddenly letting out a huge wail of a cry.

Clementine put her arm around her. 'It's okay,' she said, stroking her hair. 'It's okay, Pen.'

Rima said, 'And he's gone to Italy?'

'I think so,' Penny nodded. 'I don't know. I feel so, so sad that I hurt him. I think . . . I think I really did. I think I really hurt him, and I didn't mean to. I don't think I've been a very nice person . . .'

Clementine rubbed Penny's back and Penny closed her eyes, thoughts of Francesco swimming in her mind. It had all spiralled out of control. It had all gotten too dramatic, too crazy. All these men, dictating her fate: her uncle asking her to move in the first place, Thomas walking into the joint and asking her out, Priyesh being at her Christmas party and Francesco showing up on her doorstep and *staying*. Everyone wanted something from her, and Penny realized she didn't know what she wanted for herself. She'd been so caught up in everyone else's needs and wants and agendas, escaping from herself and making a mess of her life, when what she actually needed was to look inward and figure out what was important to *her*.

'God, I'm sick of myself,' Penny proclaimed, finally. 'If my life was a movie I don't think it would pass the Bechdel test, you know. All I do is talk about bloody men. Even sat here with you right now – I'm not asking about Stella, or the non-profit, Rima. You and me, Charlie, we should be talking about podcasts and the movies we've seen and what we think about the local government. When did I become this person? This woman that only talks about her love life? It's so un-interesting!'

She was interrupted, then, by Priyesh's voice sing-songing through from the top bar.

'Hellooooo,' he said. 'Anybody there?' He appeared in the archway, a bouquet of flowers in hand.

'Oh,' he said. 'You're having a party and I wasn't invited?' He meant it jovially, but he'd misread the mood of the room.

Penny stood quickly, dabbing at her cheeks. 'Priyesh!' she said, fixing a smile. 'What are you doing here?'

'I just wanted to drop these off,' he said, studying her face. If he could tell she'd been crying he was sympathetic enough not to mention it. 'I haven't really heard from you since Valentine's Day.' He turned his attention to the others sat around the table. 'Hello,' he said. 'I'm Priyesh.'

Clementine's eyes widened slightly at his name, understanding who he was. 'I'm Clementine,' she said. 'Penny's sister. And this is Rima, my wife.'

Priyesh walked to the table. 'Hello, Charlie,' he said, acknowledging them too.

Penny took the flowers from him, and as she did he leaned in for a kiss. Penny offered up her cheek.

'Well,' said Priyesh, addressing Penny. 'I didn't want to interrupt, I just wanted to give you these.'

'I'll walk you out,' she said.

They walked in silence to his car, and then Priyesh began, 'It's okay. All of it – it's okay. I knew you and Francesco were close. I didn't let myself understand how close. But, you and him – that makes a million times more sense than this. I can see that. But I'm not going anywhere, okay. Take your time in any decision you make.'

'Priyesh,' Penny said, softly.

'Oh,' he said, his face dropping. 'I see.'

'It's not you, it really isn't.'

He paused for a second. 'Right. That's . . . disappointing.'

'It's not like I'm going to be around for much longer anyway, you know? It's been ace, spending all this time with you, but I was never here to stay.'

'You stopped talking about leaving, though,' he replied. 'I suppose I thought maybe you'd change your mind.'

'My life is in London. You are charming and so clever and honestly, the sex we've had has been out of this world. This really is all me.'

'And I can't change your mind?'

'You don't want someone whose mind you have to change, do you?'

Priyesh offered a lop-sided smile. 'No,' he said. 'You're right.' Penny opened her arms for a hug.

'No hard feelings?'

'No hard feelings.'

21

'Penny Bridge,' she said, into the buzzer microphone at the front door. 'Here for a 9 a.m. initial consultation.'

'Come in Penny,' a sober voice said at the other end. 'We're upstairs and to the left.'

The lock sounded and Penny pushed her way through into the terraced townhouse that, from the outside, could have been somebody's home. On the other side of the door, though, it gave itself away as a corporate space, furnished with carpet tiles, strip lighting, and a fire extinguisher. It was chilly. Penny gingerly climbed the stairs, found the waiting room, and took a seat. On the table in the middle were various leaflets.

Post-Traumatic Stress and You.

You Don't Have to Do This Alone.

CBT and Psychoanalysis: What's The Difference?

A woman with short grey hair sat flipping through a copy of *HELLO!* and a student in a hoodie sat picking at the skin around his fingernails. Penny felt as if everyone was looking at her, assessing what her secret might be, but she was doing exactly the same in return. She wondered if the woman was weathering a divorce after years of putting up with a husband who never appreciated her. Maybe the student had questions about his sexuality. What would they say if they knew what Penny's problem was? *Oh, boo-hoo, you had three men fighting over you? How awful.*

'Penny?' a woman said, appearing in the doorway. Penny stood and followed her into a stark room painted cream, with a cream sofa and a cream chair Penny recognized immediately as IKEA. There was a small table beside the sofa with a box of tissues on it. She couldn't see a clock.

'Can I get you a cup of tea, or some water?' said the woman, who wore a name badge that read 'Christina.'

'No, no, I'm fine,' said Penny, sitting on the sofa. 'Thank you.'

Christina nodded. 'And what brings you here today? This is our first time together, so I'll be making notes as we talk. Is that okay?'

Penny nodded.

'Thank you,' Christina smiled. 'So. What's on your mind?'

Penny thought about how to begin. With Uncle David? Francesco?

'Everything just feels a bit of a mess,' she settled on, which was as good a summary as any. 'And I'm having a hard time untangling myself from it, I think.'

'Okay,' said Christina, her voice slow, her tone neutral. 'In what way does it all feel a bit of a mess?'

Penny shrugged. 'I just don't feel very happy, I suppose,' she said, and saying that out loud to a stranger made her voice crack, like it had done when she'd talked to Clementine and Rima and Charlie. 'And I don't know what to do about it.'

Christina nodded. Her eyes were sympathetic but her face didn't give away any kind of feeling about what Penny was saying.

'That sounds like it would be a very heavy thing to carry around with you,' she said.

'It is,' Penny said.

Christina let that hang in the air. She wasn't desperate, it seemed to Penny, to drive the conversation forward at all or fill in the gaps after Penny had spoken. It made Penny nervous. Was she supposed to keep talking? Or was Christina just thinking about what to say next? When Penny had been to counselling throughout the cancer it was a bit more talkative than this, a bit more informal. Christina didn't seem to want to go in for the role of a Chatty Cathy.

'I feel like I'm letting everyone down,' Penny continued, the thought just occurring to her in the space Christina's silence had made. 'I rely on my sister too much, and don't support my uncle enough – he's basically my dad, because dad left. Mum died. And I've been sleeping around a bit. Not sleeping around – god, this isn't nineteen-fifty – but maybe I've been farming my self-worth out to men, like they might make me feel like it all makes more sense, or something. I don't know. My friend Francesco said I was hurting people. He said he loved me, but then he said he changed his mind because he couldn't love somebody who hurt people. Do I sound like a sociopath? Wait. Is sociopath the one who manipulates people? Maybe I mean psychopath? Narcissist?'

More silence.

'Penny,' said Christina, after a beat. 'Can I ask you one question? You don't have to answer it now. It can be your homework, in fact, if you think you'd like to continue with these sessions.'

Penny wasn't sure if she wanted to continue – they hadn't really done anything. Penny had basically come and recited a monologue for forty-five minutes and paid thirty pounds for the privilege. She could have done that on a voice note.

'Okay,' Penny said, uncertainly. 'What's the question?'

'My question is this,' said Christina. 'What is it that you want?'

Penny blinked. What was it that she wanted?

'Well,' she said. 'I want to be happy, obviously. That's why I'm here.'

Christina smiled.

'Take some time. Maybe go for a walk, or for a coffee on your own. Sit with your feelings. And ask yourself: what is it that I want? Because I suspect you already know the answer, and that really, you're here for permission to want it. Most people are. But that's okay. We can work on that together. First – just spend some time with the question, okay?'

Penny nodded. 'Okay.'

Penny exited the townhouse and blinked in the morning sun. The showers from earlier had cleared, and her first instinct was to pull out her phone to record a Personal Podcast for her sister, but then she thought better of it.

Go for a walk, or for a coffee.

Penny texted Manuela and asked if she'd be okay setting up for service without her. It was a Tuesday, and it was still only 9.30 a.m. Manuela texted back right away, saying: *no problem.* Penny put some more money in the parking meter and looked around. She didn't know this part of town very well, so it was a case of picking a direction and following her nose. She looked across the road at a tree-lined avenue

282

that seemed to have signs of life at the other end. She walked.

The cool air felt good against her face – Penny hadn't realized how warm she'd gotten at the therapy centre, like her emotions had been pressed up against her skin, asking for a way out. She tried to focus on the sensations in her body over the thoughts in her mind, but that lasted all of ten minutes before her tummy rumbled – she hadn't had break-fast. She pushed through the door of the first café she saw, ordered a coffee and a croissant, and slipped into the window seat right as another woman was leaving. The woman smiled at her.

'Enjoy,' she said, even though Penny didn't know her.

'Thanks,' Penny replied, slipping off her coat.

Penny sat in the coffee shop, cradling her oat milk latte and alternating between watching the hum-drum of the café play out, and idly watching the world pass by.

She thought of Bridges. The café she was in was similar, but bigger. Behind the counter was a young woman who looked as much of an art graduate as Stuart always had, managing to steam milk and grind beans and find extra ice when the other woman – plainer, more serious, her Levi's so high-rise they almost reached her chest – navigated the till. People moved in and out. Two women in Lycra leggings debated loudly about sharing a scone, a middle-aged man with a very tiny dog ordered two almond croissants that looked crunchy and crispy and delicious enough to make Penny wonder if she should get one, too – even though she'd already had a chocolate one – and at one point a red-headed man in chef's whites and an apron came out of the kitchen door carrying two plates of eggs.

'Sorry, Aaron,' the serious-looking girl said. 'We had a rush on.'

'It's alright,' said the chef, delivering the food to a couple sat looking at a laptop screen together, pointing at things and musing over numbers and colours.

Penny missed Bridges, and ached to be back there soon. She had to admit, she'd enjoyed Derbyshire more than she thought she would – Penny knew she'd improved her skills, and her ability to manage a team. It hadn't been easy, but she'd done it. Apart from Uncle David falling ill in the first place, she wouldn't change having been there. It made her appreciate the life she'd made in London all the more, and it had been pretty fun, in the end, until it wasn't. What did she want? She wanted to be back in London, living the life she had designed for herself and not the one her uncle had given her, the one she'd felt powerless to refuse.

She thought about Francesco. If she'd never had to come to The Red Panda, would they have stayed together all this time? Penny weighed it up. It was entirely possible that they would still have tortured each other, still caused one another pain. Before she'd met him she was about to start a family, on her own, happily. He'd confused things. Without him, it made her path to parenthood clear. She could go back to the original plan. She was going to do it alone before him – why not do it now he'd gone?

As if on cue, outside on the pavement a mother stopped with her toddler in a pram, another child attached to a board at the back, similar to a skateboard attached width-ways, so he didn't have to walk. The older child hopped off and bent down to pick something up off the ground, and therein commenced a seemingly rather intense discussion with his mother about something that made Penny understand that the mum was taking it all very seriously, when what was being discussed was undoubtedly not very serious at all. The kid came up to her knees. It was hardly world economic policy they were dissecting. The love in her face was like a punch to the heart for Penny.

A family.

Kids.

She ran a hand over her stomach. It seemed wildly unfair that she'd never know what it was to carry her own child, but at least she had her embryos. She also had a sister who, once upon a time, had offered to help.

Penny wanted it, deeply. In her late teens and early twenties, becoming a parent had never really occurred to her. And when the choice was made for her with the cancer, the early menopause, and having the biological right taken away from her, it had all made her realize how much she did want it.

She looked around the café. Yes, she missed her own. And more that, what she missed was something she hadn't actually yet known. A child. Motherhood. Babies and toddlers and prams and serious discussions about what had just been picked up off the pavement.

The issue outside of the window was resolved and the little boy hopped back onto the two wheels behind the pram so his mother could keep pushing.

That's what I want, Penny thought to herself. *And I want it now.*

Her eyes welled up with the knowledge of it.

Yup, she thought. *I really do.*

She'd put everything on hold for The Red Panda. For her sick uncle, who had given her everything. She'd done her duty. She'd even had a little excitement on the way – and, of course, a little heartbreak. That was life. But Penny wanted her agency back, now. She wanted to take back control.

I can't believe I've buried this feeling all year, she texted Clementine as she finished her coffee. *I'm ready,* she said. *My time here is almost up, and I know what I want next. I don't care about a man. I want that baby!*

22

Hey friend, Penny typed into her phone. She couldn't stand that he was out there, mad at her. She needed resolution. Surely she could make him forgive her – surely he wouldn't ignore her forever.

Clementine had gently suggested that maybe he hadn't ever been a friend, but Penny didn't know where that left her now. She was desperate to make things right.

She deleted what she'd typed.

I miss you, she wrote instead, before deleting that, too.

Knowing he existed in the world, cross and hurt, weighed her down. What could she do?

Nothing.

She pulled up her web browser, instead. *Having a baby as a single mum,* she typed in, settling in to scroll through the results.

23

Running late, Thomas's text said after Penny had gathered everything they needed. *Meet after instead?*

Penny held the phone in her hand and took a deep breath. She hated that he'd ducked out of helping her without even saying sorry. There was a bees nest in the car park that needed a special powder sprinkled over it to encourage the bees to leave and make a home somewhere else, which was important because Penny couldn't have a bees nest outside as it continued to get warmer. A thought barraged its way into her brain: *Francesco would already have done it.*

Penny sighed. She shouldn't have been relying on Thomas in the first place, since she was about to break off whatever they were to each other.

'Look what the cat dragged in,' she said, when Thomas finally arrived. She'd taken care of the bees nest herself, spraying it with the industrial strength stuff she'd got online and not suffering a single sting in the process. She looked ridiculous doing it – just in case, she'd had not an inch of skin on show with her joggers tucked into her socks and gloves pulled up over her long sleeves. She'd even wrapped an old scarf around her head, leaving room only for her eyes and nose, and held it all in place with a woolly hat.

'Ahhh come on,' Thomas said. 'I've only just got back. Don't be like that.' He looked at Penny pleadingly, his eyes big and adorable. He knew she wasn't really mad, and that even if she was he'd soften her up in seconds. He was just too charming.

'Just,' said Penny, walking from the door she'd let him in from back up to her flat, peeling off her layers as she did so. 'Don't say you'll do something and then not do it. Don't agree in the first place. Like, have some self-respect, you know?' It came out harsher than she'd meant, but it was too late. She'd said it.

'Self-respect?' Thomas said, pausing on the stairs.

'Yeah,' said Penny, changing her tone. 'Just be a man of your word.'

'Hey,' Thomas said, making her stop and turn around. 'Are you okay?'

Penny nodded. She shouldn't be picking a fight. She knew why she was doing it – because an argument was easier than a mature discussion about no longer sleeping together. 'I'm fine. I'm just saying, it's not cool to have your actions mismatch your words.' She walked up ahead and flopped down onto the sofa. It took Thomas a minute to come and join her.

'Well this is a side of you I've never seen before,' he said. 'Are you sure you're okay?'

'I just told you – you've annoyed me.'

'Okay, well that doesn't make me feel great.'

'It doesn't feel great to me, either.'

Thomas stood there, scowling. 'This is going to be a fun hike then, isn't it?'

Penny picked up a magazine and began flicking through it. 'I don't think I want to hike today,' she said. 'I've changed my mind.'

'You've changed your mind.'

'Yes,' she said. 'I don't want to go. You go without me.'

Thomas came to sit beside her. 'Hey,' he said. 'Come on. I'm only off for a few days before I go again. Let's go walking, Pen.'

'I said I don't want to,' Penny snapped. 'Stop pushing it.'

'But you love the hikes!' Thomas said. 'It's like you're mad at me or something!'

Penny sighed. 'I'm not mad at you, Thomas. I'm tired. Really, really tired. So instead of walking ten miles I'm going to rest, because that is what my body is asking for. Okay?' It wasn't really a question.

'I was really looking forward to spending the day with you.'

'I know. But I just need one day to be in my own company. That's not a rejection of you. That's me taking care of myself.'

'Hmmmm,' said Thomas, not at all happy. 'I think you're mad at me.'

'I will be if you keep saying that. Text me later. Just . . . I don't want to go.'

Thomas nodded. 'Fine,' he said. 'But you're going to have to text me. See you later.'

She felt terrible once he'd gone.

'Shit,' she said to herself. She pulled on her shoes to see if she could catch him at his house before he left.

Penny knocked on Thomas's door, hearing a dog yapping on the other side of it. He answered wearing grey jogging bottoms that sat low on his hips, and a grey t-shirt that hung just a sliver above his waistband so that he revealed enough

291

flesh to distract Penny's gaze. He was a beautiful man, she'd give him that. Maybe she thought that now because it was the first time she'd seen him dressed in anything other than a label. He was obviously halfway through changing.

'Hello, you,' Thomas said.

'Hey,' said Penny, smiling. 'Hi. I was a bitch before, and I've come to say sorry.'

'Do you want to come in?'

Penny looked at him. 'Um . . .' she said, and in her hesitation Thomas's face softened. 'It's okay,' he said. 'You're not into this anymore, are you?'

Penny shrugged. 'I want to be, but . . . no,' she said. 'I'm sorry.'

'Penny,' said Thomas. 'That's okay. It's a laugh until it's not, right?'

'Right.'

'And you deserve everything your heart wants. Even if your heart doesn't want me.'

'I owe you a lot, though,' said Penny.

Thomas furrowed his brow in question.

'You showed me a side to this place that I wouldn't have seen otherwise. You got me out of the pub and into the hills, and other restaurants, and parks and pubs.'

'Well you know,' Thomas said, 'we can still do that. I like you, Penny – I'd love to see you when I'm back, hang out, catch up.'

Penny smiled. 'I'd like that too,' she said, understanding implicitly that she could be his friend, because she'd never felt that deeply about him as a lover. And, of course, the reason she and Francesco could never have simply been friends, was precisely the opposite: she didn't just love him. She was *in love* with him.

'I don't want to take up your day off,' she said. 'I just wanted to say . . .'

Thomas opened his arms to her. 'Don't say anything, Pen. It's okay. We're okay.'

Less than a minute after he'd opened the door to her, he closed it again, and Penny already felt lighter.

I should have treated you better, Penny typed into the text thread with Francesco. Everything she wanted to say to him was a variation of the same thing.

I screwed up.

I wish you hadn't left.

I'm sorry.

She stared at the text box, debating, like she always did, on whether to send it.

She didn't.

I think I want to have a baby, she typed. *I want a family. I'm excited!*

She deleted that, too.

24

It was two weeks later, in the middle of March, when Uncle David and Eric came to visit, along with Rima and Clementine.

'Look at it here,' Uncle David said. 'I hardly recognize it!'

'Yes you do,' said Penny, smiling. 'It's almost exactly as you left it.'

Her uncle took in the pub. Penny had, to be fair, put her stamp on it. Things were cleaner and more orderly. She'd added in more textures to the rooms – softer throws and pillows and different candle holders and linen napkins instead of paper ones. The fires were always stacked, even if it wasn't cold enough to light one, and the bar glistened and gleamed. Various members of staff made their way towards their old boss, genuinely thrilled to see him. Penny waited patiently as David asked after husbands and wives, children and parents, his rapport with his staff obvious and natural.

'Good to see you looking well,' Charlie said to him. 'You frightened the life out of us.'

Not one of them, though, asked if he was coming back. It was obvious to everyone that he wouldn't be – he looked so well, in fact, that a return to his old lifestyle would surely cause nothing but damage.

'It's the best thing we ever did, spending time down there on the coast,' he said to more than one person, riffing on how healing being near the water was, and how restorative the sea air.

Clementine, Rima and Eric had gone on a short tour of the area so that Penny and her uncle could catch up whilst Eric could check in on friends they'd not seen in a while to invite them for drinks later. Penny told Uncle David that Francesco had gone. She didn't know why she hadn't told him before. She wondered if saying it to him would have made Francesco's leaving seem important, and for weeks she'd tried to make out it wasn't so. She'd tried calling Francesco that morning before she'd even got out of bed and had chance to lose her nerve, but the phone issued a foreign dial tone and rang out. She didn't text to follow up: he'd see the missed call. That was enough.

'That's such a shame,' Uncle David said, looking around the flat and taking an inventory of what Penny had changed. 'I liked Francesco, very much. I liked him being up here with you, too.'

'Well,' said Penny, offering up a plate of biscuits. 'Let me tell you, he could be a real dick.'

Uncle David stirred cream into his coffee. 'Can't we all,' he said, mildly.

'No,' said Penny. 'But I mean like, possessive. Dark. Moody. And jealous.'

'Of you?'

'Yeah.'

Uncle David considered this information. 'And you?' he said, finally.

'What do you mean, and me?'

'Could you be dark or moody with him?'

Penny considered this. She had so seldom ever felt anything other than excited to be with Francesco, really. He made everything *seem* more exciting. Even in the kitchen, after hours, eating pasta. For a stretch, there hadn't needed to be anything else.

'I mean, I didn't put on a performance for him or anything,' she said, eventually. 'I was just who I am with him.' Saying it, she reflected immediately on how that sounded. She was able to be herself with him, which is a privilege so few are afforded.

'Hmmm,' said Uncle David.

'Anyway,' she said, changing the subject. She was boring herself with this post-mortem of him, and of her. Of them. There wasn't even a 'them' if he wouldn't bloody take her calls. 'How are you? You look a hundred times better than you have. Even since Christmas. It's really, really good to see.'

Uncle David nodded. 'I'm good,' he said. 'So much better. It's the sea air. And Eric – he's so much happier down there. He was done with the pub for a long time before I was ready to admit it.'

'I know how that feels,' Penny said, instantly wishing she hadn't. There was no need.

'I thought you'd be happier,' Uncle David remarked. 'I thought you'd thrive.'

'I've done my best,' she said, in a small voice.

Uncle David sighed. 'So I'm the only one who wants to be here,' he intoned. 'And everybody else is just my prisoner.'

Penny didn't know what to say. That wasn't too far from the truth, really, was it? He'd imposed his will on Eric, and then Penny.

'You don't ever want to sell it?' Penny said, gently.

'I suppose I had better start thinking about it,' he said, and Penny could barely let herself breathe in case she interrupted this train of thought. Had he really just said he would think about selling? Penny sat very still. She waited.

Finally he continued, 'It breaks my heart, but . . . I think it's time, isn't it?'

Penny shook her head. 'I can't make that choice for you,' she settled on.

'It's fine,' David said. 'I've expected too much from you. Every week I've got better is a week you've sounded less like yourself. I really thought I was doing the right thing. I really thought you'd love it here. I really thought you'd get the Bib Gourmand and it would make you hungry for more.'

'You can't come back?'

'I need to think about the best thing to do. We're so happy down in Cornwall – Eric is so happy in Cornwall. I'm finally treating him like the priority he should be, instead of making the pub the top of my list. Clementine said I've been unfair on you. Do you think I have?'

'I don't think anything, Davvy. I'd go to the moon and back for you.'

'That doesn't mean I should ask you to,' he smiled. 'I'm so impressed by what you've done here, you know,' he continued. 'Can you tell me that you understand how impressive what you've done is?'

Penny shrugged. 'We all worked hard,' she said. 'And we all feel proud, I think.'

Eric appeared at the door of the lounge.

'What are you two whispering about?' he said, playfully. He added, 'Oooh, coffee – great. I need a warmer.'

Uncle David shot Penny a look.

'Never you mind,' he said, before adding, 'Did you catch anyone? Who can come for a drink later?'

Penny felt about eighty different emotions. She felt excitement about what David had said. She felt regret that she hadn't ever felt different about being there. She felt relief that David had made the decision for her. And she felt blind panic, too, because without the excuse of the pub to hold her back, what was stopping her from starting her family now? Everyone knew the old adage that there is never a *great* time to do it, but it seemed to Penny that this was about as good as it was going to get for her. She could go back to Bridges, back to her flat, keep the cover chef on part time for when the baby came and then . . . well. And then she didn't know what. She'd work part time? She'd get childcare? She'd live frugally and have the café look after itself for a while? Whatever the decision, she had options. And for the first time in ages Penny understood what that meant. Choices. Decisions. She was, finally, back in the driving seat of her own destiny and so the time was, terrifyingly, exhilaratingly, perfectly, now.

'I need to talk to you,' Penny said to Clementine. 'I'm having some thoughts and feelings.'

'Shocker,' said Clementine, smiling.

'Uncle David just told me he's selling.'

'What?' said Clementine. 'Really?'

'Yes. I can go back to Bridges. I'm free!'

Clementine hugged her sister. Still keeping her voice low she said, 'When?'

Penny shrugged. 'Probably not for a while, but he's going to put the wheels in motion.'

'I see,' said Clementine. 'Well. God. That's so good for you!

I mean, don't take this the wrong way but obviously I'm sad this place won't be in our family anymore. It's the right thing and everything but like, it's where we grew up, isn't it?'

Penny understood what she meant. 'Yeah,' she said. 'But.'

'But,' Clementine said, nodding.

'It's not my job to protect that.'

'It really isn't,' said Clementine.

They both sat with that realization.

'Will you still be my surrogate?' Penny said, eventually.

Clementine turned to her. 'You're sure you're ready?'

Penny let out a little whoop of glee, careful not to let their uncles hear. 'So ready!' she said. 'Now that I am free!'

'And how does it feel,' Christina said, 'now that you have been truthful with the men you have been seeing?'

'Lighter,' Penny said, sat again in the IKEA-furnished room of her therapist, a tissue in her hands. 'I was crying a lot before. Like, I would cry if I burnt my hand in the kitchen, which, well, I'm a chef, so that happens all the time and we're literally trained to withstand it. Or I'd cry at what was on TV, not just the movie or whatever, but the adverts too. Since everything happened I haven't cried once. I think it's just . . .'

'Go on,' said Christina.

'Life can be overwhelming, can't it?'

'It can.'

'And I think I have been really, really overwhelmed. And not very good at asking for help. And feeling bad for needing help, which is a real head-spin. I felt better after talking to you, even that first time.'

'I'm pleased to hear that,' Christina said, writing something down on her clipboard.

'And I did what you asked. I thought about what I want

and I'm scared of the answer but more than anything it's a baby. So.'

'Yes?'

'I've been talking to my sister.'

'And how does that make you feel?'

Penny smiled. In theory she could have these conversations with a friend or her uncle, but in reality it was the very fact that Christina had never met any of the people Penny talked about that made it so easy to be honest.

'It makes me really excited,' Penny said. 'Like I am actually taking charge of my future, and that I deserve to.'

'You do deserve to.'

'I don't think I have believed that. I think literally ever since the cancer I've let things happen *to* me. Maybe even before then. Even becoming a chef happened *to* me. I stumbled into it.'

'I don't think that is unusual. Many people prefer to be passive in their happiness because it feels safer.'

'That's awful,' said Penny. 'I don't want to be like that.'

'Well the good news is,' said Christina, 'I don't think you are. Not anymore.'

25

'I lost my head,' Penny told Sharon, who'd finally come up overnight to visit. 'I lost my head because I was bored, and needed a distraction, and now all of my distractions have gone and I'm back. I'm focused.'

'Focused for what, exactly?' Sharon said. They were taking a short walk around the village so Sharon could see the area Penny had been living in for the past year. They passed dog-walkers Penny knew and waved through shop windows at the grocers and people in the Post Office. It made Penny proud. She'd made a home out of a place she hadn't – as everyone in her life knew – been totally sure of.

'You can level with me, you know. I won't hold it against you. If you are still not okay, we can talk about it.'

They circled back around the lane where the pub sat in the distance, and Penny kept her gaze on it as she talked.

'A baby. I'm going to do it. Clementine is having the tests this week to see if she's okay to be surrogate and presuming she is . . . well. We're going to go for it. Everything is lined up.'

'Oh, babe,' Sharon smiled. 'Come here!' She stopped walking and pulled Penny in for a hug. 'This is amazing news. Oh, I am so, so happy for you. Over the moon! After everything you've been through – this year, your whole life – I think this is brilliant. You've talked about it for so long.'

Penny grinned. 'Thank you,' she replied. 'Even Uncle David has accepted it, you know. I think he feels a bit guilty that he pulled me away from what I really wanted because he was worried for me. But he gets it, now – I don't want to take over the food world. I just want to be a mum.'

'And dare I ask about Francesco?'

'Still nothing. I WhatsApped him a few times, but got no response. I didn't know I'd hurt him that much, you know. I guess I thought he was having a tantrum that wouldn't last.'

'And he's in Italy?'

'Last I heard, yes. So, I guess that's what they call closure.'

The pair used the front entrance to get into the pub, even though, when closed, Penny normally consigned herself to the back entrance. As she pushed through the old front door, Charlie flung open the second door that led through to the top bar.

'O-M-G,' they said. 'Bib Gourmand.'

'What about it?' said Penny, before adding, 'Sharon, Charlie. Charlie, Sharon.'

'Pleased to meet you,' Sharon said. 'Penny says you've been a lifesaver here.'

Charlie thrust an envelope into Penny's face. 'A lifesaver,' they said, 'and deliverer of good news. Look! Look at the envelope.'

They all stepped through into the bar proper, and Penny saw the Michelin guide logo stamped onto the envelope, next to a postmark.

'Shit,' she said.

'Good shit, or bad shit?' Sharon said.

'Amazing shit,' Charlie said. 'It's about the award we've been chasing.'

Penny held the envelope in front of her, staring at the logo.

'It's not going to be bad news, is it?' Charlie said, reading her mind. 'They aren't going to write if they've been and hated it.'

Penny nodded. 'Right,' she said. 'Sure. Of course.' She turned the envelope over and started to tear it open. She was shaking slightly, and it made Sharon reach out and put a hand on her shoulder.

Penny slid the single piece of paper out of the envelope and unfolded it. Sharon hung on her left shoulder, Charlie on her right. The three of them read it together.

'YES!' screamed Charlie. 'YES, YES, YES!'

'Oh my goodness,' said Penny, looking up. 'We did it. WE DID IT!'

Sharon looked from Charlie to her friend. 'You did it?'

Penny nodded and leapt up to her feet. 'WE. DID. IT!' she screamed, lurching to Charlie for a hug, and then to Sharon, and then the three of them were hugging all together and jumping up and down and screaming over and over, 'We did it!'

Penny pulled away. 'I can't believe it! I really can't believe it.'

'Can't you?' said Charlie. 'Because I can. Look what you did to this place, babe. You really made something of it. You made it next level. I knew we'd get the award. Honestly. I really had a feeling.'

'Have you got any idea who? When?' Penny turned to Sharon to explain, 'Nobody ever knows who the inspectors

305

are, what they look like, nothing. You can't prepare for it. You only find out afterwards if they liked it.'

'I have no idea who it could've been. There was a woman in maybe two months ago who asked a lot of questions about the specials, like really specific questions, but I just thought she was one of those people who'd once read a Nigella cookbook and so wanted to show off what she knew. But maybe it was her?'

'Well god bless her,' Penny said. 'Praise be!'

'Are you going to tell him, then?' Charlie said. 'Go call him!'

Penny wished Francesco was here to see the letter himself. She'd have to photograph it and send it to him. Maybe that would be enough to make him reply.

'I hope it doesn't give him another heart attack, though,' Charlie continued, and Penny realized they were talking about her uncle.

'I'll call him now,' Penny said, suddenly deflated. She thought this was her excuse to finally get through to Francesco, but she'd have to call her uncle first. 'He'll be over the moon.'

He was.

In Bologna, Francesco was taking an afternoon *passeggiata* with a friend through the arches of the town centre when his phoned beeped. The terracotta-coloured buildings hummed golden in the afternoon sun, holding in the heat of the day to make it feel warmer than it was. Lucia had welcomed him back to the city he had been born in with open arms, but she knew her oldest childhood friend was deeply sad.

'What's her name?' she'd said when they met for apperitivo in her favourite piazza. It was the same piazza Francesco had had his first and only cigarette in – on a visit back when his family had lived in Germany – the same piazza he'd kissed Guilia Fernando in when he'd visited in between Germany and the UAE, and the same piazza he'd come with Lucia to play chess with the old men from their town, silently plotting manoeuvres around a black and white board and listening to the stories the men told of lives well-lived.

He finished the last mouthful of his *pistaccio* gelato, savouring the smooth, nutty taste as it went down. Lucia had seen somebody she knew and had veered off to give kisses and grand hellos, and Francesco wiped his hands and deposited the *copetta* in the bin. He pulled out his phone and saw her name on his screen. Penny.

He took a breath.

There was no message, only a photo of a piece of paper.

At the top of the screen it said the word 'online' under Penny's name.

At The Red Panda, Penny sat at the bottom of the stairs clutching her phone, watching as the message got delivered to Francesco, one tick for sent, a second tick for received, turning blue as he came online and read it.

In Bologna, Francesco zoomed in on the letter. The Bib Gourmand. The Red Panda had been awarded the Bib Gourmand with a whole sentence about the dessert menu. *A concise and complete exploration of taste, texture and imaginative flavour on offer to end the meal, crafted with knowledge and love.*

Crafted with knowledge and love, he marvelled.

Penny watched as the word under Francesco's name changed from 'online' to 'typing'. For an agonizing minute she waited for his message to come through. Maybe he'd say congratulations. Maybe he'd ask her not to text again. Maybe he'd offer to come back, if this was the sort of thing they could achieve together.

'Francesco, *vieni qui*,' Lucia requested of him, from where she stood with her friends. They were two women, one of whom was blushing profusely. Francesco locked his phone and put it back in his pocket as he wandered over.

At the bottom of the stairs Penny saw 'typing' change to nothing. No message. No longer on his phone. No longer connected to her from wherever he was.

*   *   *

The pub went on sale almost immediately, valued higher now that they had the Bib Gourmand. Uncle David had said any pound over what they thought they'd get could go to Penny, for everything she had done – but she said she wouldn't hold him to that. Uncle David and Eric temporarily moved up to The Red Panda to get affairs in order, with Penny splitting shifts with David so that he didn't work full time. They closed Sunday night through to Wednesday morning, and then he took daytimes, and she took evening dinners. After Sunday service she'd headed down to London to check on the café and start to organize herself for what came next, scheduling in appointments at the clinic for then, too.

Clementine came with her and had check after check to ensure her womb would be a hospitable home for Penny's embryos, and it was startling, really, how in sync her life felt. Clementine was allowed to take a six-month-long paid sabbatical from her job after Stella heard what she was doing and supported the idea completely. Clementine would act as a consultant and take maternity leave at full pay for two months and half pay after that if she needed it. Penny had spent so long fighting against herself, and her circumstance, that the simple-ness of the next few months could almost have been a trap – except she didn't stop long enough to think about it. Her mantra was: *I accept all the good that comes to me in life.* It was woo-woo, but she was determined that every choice she made and every step in the direction of her new life she took, she would embody this.

What if it is supposed to be easy? she dared ask herself.

Clementine had to call the clinic on the first day of her period so that she could go in for a scan to check her womb lining. Then she got checked every few days, and on the twelfth day the doctor said it was time.

On the day of the first embryo transfer, Penny had resigned herself to it not working first try. She didn't want to get her hopes up, or stake everything all at once. If life was going to be easy, that meant understanding that the plan would unfold as it needed to, and gripping on any harder wasn't going to alter its course.

'Well, this is all quite no-nonsense,' the doctor had explained. 'Because your eggs have already been fertilized it's a case of simple transference. It's a bit like a smear test, really: no anaesthetic, you'll be awake, and after five minutes you can get up.'

'And what about after?' Clementine had asked. 'If I stand or go for a wee . . .?'

The doctor smiled. 'You mean, will the embryo fall out if you do those things?'

Penny burst out laughing.

'What!' said Clementine. 'Don't laugh! If you haven't noticed this is quite an important job I've been tasked with here! I don't want to screw it up!'

'You'll be fine afterwards,' said the doctor. 'Just go about your day.'

'Okay,' said Clementine. 'I'm ready. Let's do this.'

'I'll give you your privacy to get changed. Take off your bottom half, swing into the stirrups and try to put your bum as close to the edge as possible, like you did in your MOT. Put this piece of paper towel over you and I'll be back in two, okay?'

'Got it,' said Clementine.

Penny read the posters on the wall as her sister changed. 'Are you nervous?' she asked. 'Can I do anything?'

'Nope,' said Clementine. 'Honestly, I feel super calm. Are *you* okay?'

'I'm okay,' said Penny. 'I think.'

There was a light knock on the door. 'Can I come in?' the doctor said.

'Yes!' the two women harmonized.

'Okay Clementine, if you could bring your bum down even more please . . .'

Clementine moved down the chair.

'I'm now going to place the catheter through your cervix and into your uterus, which might feel slightly uncomfortable but should be pain-free, okay?'

'Okay.'

My eggs could take and make a baby, Penny thought to herself. *Any minute now I might be making a baby.*

'And that's everything!' the doctor said, almost right away. 'Just sit here for a few minutes, and then you can get changed.

And listen: try not to read anything into any changes you think you can feel, your breasts or gas or anything. It could all just be a side effect of the hormones, and as such it is imperative that you do not take a test at home. It's possible to get a false positive, and when emotions are this fraught it's better to leave it to us, okay? No matter how much you convince yourself you are pregnant. Come back for your blood tests in a couple of weeks – the nurse will let you know when.'

The two women nodded. That was it.

'I am quite in awe of how she suggested we might relax, now,' Penny said, as the pair left the clinic. 'Like this isn't potentially the biggest thing that has ever happened.'

'Well, I know I should be nervous and everything but to be honest,' Clementine replied, 'right now I am simply starving. Do you want to go get some food?'

Penny nodded. 'Yes. Absolutely. I would say let's go and raise a glass of champagne to this, except, well, obviously we can't do that. You know, just in case . . .'

Clementine smiled. 'Come on, I'll treat us to Berner's Tavern.'

'No, no, no!' Penny said. 'Obviously lunch is *my* treat!' She looped her arm through Clementine's. 'This way,' she guided her sister. 'I know a shortcut.'

The pair turned the corner onto a quiet, mews-like alleyway, and directly in front of them stood a tall, olive-skinned man.

'He looks like . . .' Clementine started to say.

'Hello, Francesco,' Penny interrupted.

They'd seen him before he'd seen them, and the shock registered on his face as it went totally devoid of colour.

'Penny,' he said.

Clementine looked from Penny to Francesco.

'I thought you were in Italy?' Penny asked.

'I was,' he said. He didn't offer anything beyond that. It was like he didn't want to talk, but he didn't move to walk away either. He looked, quite frankly, stunned.

'Are you here for a holiday, or . . .?'

'I had a job interview. I miss London.'

'I know what that's like,' Penny said, trying to make him smile. 'I'm coming back here too, actually. Uncle David is selling the pub.'

'Oh,' he replied – still almost totally impassive. 'Well. You must be very happy,' Francesco added. 'You wanted that.'

You could cut the tension with a knife.

'Francesco—' Penny started to say.

He held up a hand. 'Please don't,' he said. 'I'm only just getting back on track again. Just – don't, okay?'

Penny nodded, biting her lip.

'I have to go. See you. Bye, Clementine.'

Clementine whispered a small, 'Bye, Francesco,' and he continued in the direction he'd been walking before they'd seen him. They stood for a moment, processing what had just happened.

'You know what?' said Clementine. 'How about Deliveroo at mine? I think I'd prefer to be at home.'

'Yeah,' said Penny. 'Fine.' She turned to watch where he'd walked. 'Gah!' she said.

'Yeah,' Clementine agreed.

At home, the sisters lay on Penny's bed in Clementine's guest room, their feet in the air against the wall and pillows under their heads.

'Are you okay?' Clementine said.

'Me?' said Penny. 'Are *you* okay?'

'Mate, I'm peachy,' said Clementine, ever the chilled sister. She rubbed her belly. 'Come on, tummy!' she said to it. 'Make a baby!'

Penny leaned across. 'May I?' she said, asking permission to touch her sister.

'My body is your body,' said Clementine. 'Course you can.'

'Come on, tummy!' Penny said. 'Make a baby!'

The two lay there.

'Do you think we should say a prayer or something?' Clementine said.

'What, to like, god?'

'Or whatever. Whoever.'

'Yeah,' said Penny, thinking about it. 'Like, we can put some vibes out there, can't we? Some good vibes?'

'Yeah,' said Clementine. 'Here, hold my hand.'

Penny rested her arm down by her side and Clementine laced her fingers around her sister's. 'Okay,' she said. 'Dear . . . whoever, or whatever, can hear us.'

'Mum,' said Penny, simply.

Clementine turned her head to look at her sister, who looked right back at her.

'Mum can hear us,' Penny said, and Clementine squeezed her hand twice, a little double pump.

'Mum,' said Clementine, her gaze drifting back to the ceiling. 'You're here with us, now. We can feel it.'

'We've felt it all day,' said Penny.

'And we love you – we'll never stop loving you, and we know that you're beside us every single day, and every single day we say a prayer for you and hope we're making you proud. If we could, though, ask just one small favour from

313

you – you know, if you don't mind . . . We wondered if you could make sure Penny's baby grows in my tummy, nice and big and strong and healthy.'

'Any help you can lend to that would be really cool of you,' said Penny, trying to keep the mood light.

'Yeah,' said Clementine, starting to cry. 'It'd be a real baller move to keep the old bloodline going.'

'You'd be the MVP.'

'The VIP.'

'Mammy Big Balls.'

'Thanks, mum,' Clementine said.

'We miss you,' Penny said.

'I really do feel her, you know,' said Clementine, turning to her sister again. 'She's here with us. I feel all protected and okay.'

'Me too,' said Penny. 'I feel protected and okay because you're here, as well. Thank you will never be big enough for all this.'

'Hush,' said Clementine. 'You don't have to keep saying it for me to know.'

Penny's phone buzzed. She reached for it absentmindedly with her free hand, the other one clutched to her sister.

'It's Francesco,' she said, sitting bolt upright. 'Ohmygod. Should I answer it?'

From where she was lying Clementine said, 'Of course you should answer it. Take a breath first though. You're okay, okay?'

'Okay.'

She slid the bar across the screen to answer it.

'Hello?' she asked.

'Hi,' Francesco said. 'I didn't know if you'd pick up.'

'Of course I'd pick up,' Penny replied.

'Okay,' Francesco said. She could hear him breathing down the phone like he was out of breath, somehow, like maybe he'd just run up some stairs or for a bus.

'Did you hear about the job?' Penny said.

'Not yet. Maybe tomorrow,' Francesco replied. 'Listen. I kind of can't believe I saw you earlier. I'm glad I did.'

'Me too.'

'It reminded me of how we bumped into each other at Dofi's restaurant opening that night. How it was a second chance.'

Penny held her breath.

'I shouldn't have said what I did to you, Penny. When I left. It was really awful of me. I was just so . . .'

'It's okay,' interrupted Penny. 'I hardly behaved in a way that my mother would have been proud of.'

Another beat.

'I'd like to see you,' he said. 'Do you think . . . that's possible?'

Penny looked at her sister, who had leaned in close to try and hear what Francesco was saying. Clementine nodded, furiously, as if to say, *yesyesyes – say yes!* But Penny couldn't imagine what they might say to each other. Unless she did it – unless she told him how she felt. But her sister could literally be pregnant with her baby, and so what good would that do, now? She'd declare her love for him whilst also telling him she was potentially having a kid? It was hardly a seductive offer, was it? She'd already picked her path.

'Okay,' she said, in a small voice. 'If you like. But can I tell you something first?'

'Okay.'

'Clementine had IVF today. With my embryo. As my surrogate.'

'Wow.'

'Yeah.' Penny could feel her sister's eyes on her. 'I just wanted you to know,' she said. 'I know it's weird.'

'Okay. Thank you.'

'Let me know when you'd like to meet up,' she said, implying that if he didn't want to now she was going ahead with the surrogacy, this was his get-out-of-jail card.

'Are you in London for long?'

'For two days now, and then I'm back again next week for two more days. By May I'll be back here full time, I hope.'

'Tomorrow then?'

Penny inhaled sharply. 'Yes. Okay. Tomorrow.'

'Let me think of a place and I'll text you,' he said, before hanging up the phone.

Penny didn't sleep. Clementine could be pregnant. She was meeting Francesco for breakfast. Her uncle was at the pub with Eric, conducting the last parts of the paperwork for a potential sale that meant she stood to get a cash injection of almost thirty thousand pounds – enough for more or less two years' maternity leave when the time came. She was due to return properly to Bridges in a month, and had ideas about new dishes for the summer menu. It would be so wonderful to go back to working only days.

'You awake?' said Clementine through the crack in the door. Penny was staying over since Stuart was still in her flat. Plus, Penny had wanted to be close to her sister.

'I have been all night,' Penny said.

'Me too,' said Clementine. 'So much is happening.'

'Do you have those undereye patches I can borrow? The ones that will get rid of my bags?'

Clementine handed over one of the mugs she was carrying

316

and sat on the bed beside her sister. 'You bet,' she said. 'But first: coffee.'

'I like your style,' said Penny. 'Thanks.'

Penny deliberated on what to wear from her suitcase, eventually dipping into Clementine's wardrobe to steal something she'd bought with her discount from Stella McCartney. She studied her reflection in the mirror: jeans, a short-sleeved sweater, and Veja trainers with her rain mac. It reminded her of her first date with Francesco, which felt like years ago now. She'd fussed at the mirror for a full fifteen minutes to perfect a 'no make-up' make-up look so she was fresh-faced without looking like she'd tried. If Francesco was meeting her to say goodbye, she wanted to look dignified and refined as she received it. But if maybe there was one final sliver of a chance that she thought he might take her back, forgive her, she wanted to look elegant, too.

'Good morning,' she said as he approached. He was in jeans and trainers too, but admittedly looked a little pale. 'How are you?'

'Tired,' he smiled. 'I feel nervous.'

Penny swallowed. 'You do?'

'Did you order?'

'No, I was waiting for you.'

Francesco signalled to a nearby waiter and asked for a cappuccino and sparkling water. 'What do you want, Penny?'

'The same,' she said. 'But with oat milk. Thank you.' She turned back to him. 'Why do you feel nervous?'

He looked at her. 'Because I don't know what I'm doing.' He continued: 'I'm pleased I saw you yesterday. But, you know, I was embarrassed, too.'

'Embarrassed?'

'I shouldn't have spoken to you like that. I've been so mad at myself. It wasn't right.'

Penny shrugged lightly. 'It's okay. I think I understand now.'

'What do you think you understand?'

'That we weren't ever really just friends.'

'Yeah,' said Francesco, and the waiter appeared with their drinks. They watched her unload them onto the table in silence.

'Did it ever mean something to you though?' he asked, wide-eyed and earnest. 'You know. You and me.'

Penny's eyebrows shot up. 'Francesco, yes. Of course it did. If I could go back in time I would have asked you to come with me right from the start, even if it was after only three weeks of dating. Or, I should have got out of the car when I saw you with that woman and asked you what the hell was going on, in the moment. Or, I should have asked you afterwards instead of ignoring you and then holding you at arms' length as I slept with other men and fell in love with you.'

'You fell in love with me?'

'Yes. I see that now. Everything is better when you are there. I know I made no secret of how taxing this past year was but the months when you were there, with me – just being in the kitchen with you after service – it was perfect. I understand the point of everything when you're around.'

Francesco looked like he might cry. 'Urgh!' he said. 'You drive me crazy! I have been so, so mad at you!'

'I didn't know how to fix it. I felt like I deserved being ignored, because that's exactly what I'd done to you.'

'So what do you suggest now?' He was sort of laughing and crying, and Penny wanted to get up and kiss him. Instead she reached out across the table.

'I want to commit to you,' Penny said. 'This is messy and weird and god, we've already started the IVF, so that's a whole other thing to discuss. But I want you. I do. And I promise I will show up to that commitment every single day. I won't run away, or try to hide, or push you away. I promise to let you see me, even when it hurts to be seen. I will be your partner, and eat whatever you make, and I will continue to fall in friendship with you, whilst also being madly, and truly, head-over-heels in love.'

Francesco stood and came to her side of the table, slipping onto the bench beside her.

'I promise all of that too,' he said, leaning in for a kiss. 'Penny, I love you.'

Penny pulled away and put a finger to his lips. 'Just, one teeny tiny thing,' she said.

Francesco sighed playfully. 'Are you joking?' he laughed.

'The IVF.'

'I think it's great,' he said. 'We can totally figure that out.' He leaned his forehead against Penny's.

'I'm not asking you to be a father,' Penny said, softly. 'That would be . . . weird.'

'It would,' Francesco said. 'But I can commit to you as a mother. It's unconventional, but so is everything about you . . .'

'This is the first thing I have done for myself – properly for me, knowing in my gut that it is right – and so, you know. Potentially – *hopefully!* – it won't just be me soon . . .'

'I get it,' said Francesco. 'I understand. I know what I'm letting myself in for.'

'It's not a deal-breaker?'

He looked up to the sky, frustrated that he hadn't snogged her face off yet and said, 'No. I know you've wanted motherhood for a very long time, and it was basically the plan right before you met me, and then this whole past year took you so off-course, and I disappeared . . . The last thing I want to do is to pull you off course again. I won't. If it's you and a baby then it's you and a baby. I can be Uncle Francesco.'

Penny laughed. 'Maybe not *uncle*.'

Francesco brushed her hair from her face and behind her ear and lowered his voice to say, 'Penelope Hermione Bridge, you are the least traditional woman I have ever met and we can make up our own rules. Together. Okay? We can defy convention together.'

'I love you,' Penny said.

'Then let me bloody kiss you,' Francesco whispered.

26

Two weeks later Penny waited in the consultancy room of the fancy Harley Street clinic with her sister.

'I can't believe there might be a baby in here,' Clementine said.

'Don't,' Penny said, whispering. 'It probably won't happen first time. Let's not get excited. Just – go steady.' Penny surprised herself at being the level-headed one in the situation. Normally it was Clementine who kept everyone calm.

Penny had no idea what the doctor was going to say. Clementine had been excitable for the past two weeks, even though she'd tried to hide it.

Penny's phone vibrated in her bag. Out of habit she reached for it – it hadn't even crossed her mind that now was the time for it to be on silent.

'FRANCESCO,' it said.

'Are you doing it?' he said, as soon as she'd answered. 'What's happening?'

He'd asked if Penny wanted him there, but she hadn't. This was for her and her sister. They'd entered into this together, and Penny wanted the appointments to be made up of just them, too.

'We're just waiting for the doctor to come back into the room,' she said.

'Put me on speaker!'

'Okay. But don't say anything.'

'I promise,' he replied.

The doctor returned and sat in the chair opposite them. Penny's phone with Francesco on the line was resting face-up on the desk between the sisters and her white coat.

'Well,' she said. 'I am very pleased to tell you that you are pregnant, Clementine. Penny, you're going to be a mother.'

Penny's mouth fell wide open and Clementine launched herself on her sister.

'I knew it!' she said. 'I could just feel it. I knew it!'

'You're having a baby,' the doctor said.

'I'm having a baby?' Penny said.

From the phone, on the table, Francesco's voice loomed large.

'Shit! Penny! You're having a baby!'

Penny pulled away from her sister's embrace. 'How is this possible?' she said. 'Nobody ever gets pregnant the first time.'

The doctor smiled. 'Well, it was a forty-four per cent chance since you fertilized your eggs so young.'

'But chance isn't ever on my side,' said Penny. 'I didn't think this would happen.' She was shell-shocked, her whole body tense.

Clementine beamed. 'I've felt so sick these past two days. And my boobs already feel bigger. I didn't want to get your hopes up, but . . . I think we can believe this, Pen.'

'I'm going to be a mama,' Penny said, smiling.

'You're going to be *the best* mama,' Clementine said, going in for another hug.

'I'm so happy for you, Penny!' came Francesco's voice, still on speakerphone. 'This is exactly what you wanted! And you deserve it all!'

Epilogue

Hermione played on the mat laid out on the café floor. Chubby, smiley, an easy baby who slept through the night, Penny couldn't have been luckier with how the first twelve months of her baby's life had gone. They'd been a unit, a team of two, right from the moment she held Hermione's tiny, six-pound-two-ounce body in the hospital ward, crying – sobbing, really – and knowing, right in that moment, that everything she had hoped for herself had materialized through a pathway she could never have imagined.

'One year old, I can hardly believe it!' Uncle David said, arranging glasses and a big ice bucket for the champagne on the counter of Bridges. Eric stood beside him tying helium balloons to the backs of some chairs, spitting the odd swear word when his manly fingers proved too chubby for the fine work of knotting the latex.

'Darling, how many times are you going to say that today?' Eric said sweetly, finally getting a knot in a green one.

Uncle David scowled, making Sharon and Luke laugh.

'What's funny?' asked Mia, from where she played with

Hermione and Jonny on the playmat they'd put down in the corner.

'Uncle David, Mia,' replied Penny. 'He's getting all emotional, and it isn't even his birthday!'

Faint music came over the café sound system just then, and Stuart said from near the coffee machine, 'Music maestro, at last! It's not a party without some music!' Safiya, his new wife, stood beside him.

'You're so clever, baby,' she said, in a teasing tone. He grinned at her. She grinned back.

'Oh, amazing,' said Sharon, as Francesco came out from the kitchen with two platters of finger food. 'Look at that! God, it's sexy that you can cook, Francesco.'

Francesco chortled. 'Oh, I know all about finding chefs sexy,' he winked, and Penny pulled a face that was the exact opposite of sexy.

'There she is,' said Francesco. 'My hot girlfriend, looking her best.' He wandered over and gave her a kiss, Penny accepting it gratefully.

It had taken Penny some time before she was here, in this moment, to figure it all out – life, and everything like it – and to say out loud what she wanted. It had taken her time to understand she could have boundaries, and that saying no is as important as embracing a yes. It had taken hard-fought lessons to arrive at herself, but with Hermione against her naked chest that very first time – skin to skin contact to encourage bonding from the off – Penny knew: taking time is the whole point. She could see it now. Life is about how you handle being thrown off course, not discounting yourself from the race because you were thrown off course in the first place. And look where her life had brought her.

'Knock, knock,' came a voice at the doorway, 'I come bearing presents . . .'

Hermione looked up at the familiar voice, sunbeams shooting from her smile. It was Auntie Clementine and Auntie Rima. 'Look who I found loitering near the station, too,' Clementine added.

Charlie appeared beside them, triumphantly holding up the arm of the man beside her.

'I got him here!' they cried. 'I got Priyesh here!'

Priyesh, dressed for a child's birthday party in a suit and tie, smiled. 'You hardly dragged me here against my own free will, Charlie,' he said, soberly. 'I wanted to come and meet the baby. And see the other baby – the café.'

Penny stood and kissed everybody, scooping up Hermione so that they all got baby cuddles, despite the fact that Hermione was very much in an independent phase and didn't like to be picked up. It was like she knew everybody was there for her, and so for this one Sunday afternoon she allowed herself to be passed from auntie to uncle, friend to friend, gurgling and chattering.

Penny's phone rang, vibrating against the table with a start. Francesco picked it up and passed it over.

'Thomas!' Penny said, swiping open a FaceTime. He appeared on screen, pixelated at first and then slowly coming into focus, sat in what looked like a dressing room next to a woman with big hair and a bright pink dress on.

'Lizzo and I just wanted to say sorry again for being unable to make it,' he said.

Lizzo waved down the camera. 'Hey Penny,' she said. 'Happy birthday to your baby girl!'

'Thank you guys!' said Penny, scanning the room for Hermione. 'I actually don't know where my baby is. She's being smothered with cuddles left, right and centre! But thank you for the gift. A full playhouse was *very* generous.'

Thomas laughed. 'That's okay. Sorry again. You were very sweet to invite us. We'll make sure you all get tickets to the next London shows, okay?'

'Okay! Have a good show, Lizzo!' said Penny, waving goodbye and putting her phone back down, drinking in the scene of the room. Her uncle and his love, her sister and hers. She was pleased she and Thomas had stayed friends. He called by at Bridges when he was around, and always had an outrageous story to tell from life on the road.

Dofi, the owner of the restaurant Penny and Francesco had met in that night, slid in to the chair next to her and said, 'I'm so happy for you, Penny. Look at all this! Look at your life!'

Penny grinned.

'Thank you so much for coming,' Penny said. 'God we've got so much to catch up on.'

Dofi made a murmur of agreement. 'We do,' she said. 'And not that I'm not desperate to hear your news but first, can you tell me more about the man in the suit? He's hysterical – he just had me in stitches with a joke about three penguins and a llama.'

'Priyesh?'

'Anything I should know?' Dofi said. 'Because I think I'm going to ask him how long he's in London for and maybe get him out for a coffee.'

Penny looked from Dofi to Priyesh. She could see it. It made sense. 'I want you to know we dated for ten seconds when I was up Havingley, and it feels like a million years ago, but other than that . . .'

'Oh, I'm zero per cent bothered by that,' Dofi replied. 'Anything else?'

Penny shook her head. 'He's a really good guy. Do it.'

'Okay,' said Dofi. 'I'm going to do it right now.' She stood up and Francesco slipped into her place. Penny issued him with a kiss, for nothing other than the fact that he was here, at what was now their café, a joint venture since they worked together so well, offering to feed her family and friends and her baby. His open heart made her softer. His ability to savour small moments rooted her in the present. His daily pledge to be her partner made her want to do him justice, too.

'I love you,' she said into his neck.

'I love you too,' he said, smiling.

'And I respect you,' she said, playing their favourite game.

'I respect you too,' Francesco replied.

'And I think you're the hottest mama on the planet.'

Francesco smiled even broader. 'It goes without saying that I think *you're* the hottest mama on the planet . . .'

A loud crash came from around the playmat, followed by an almighty wail from Hermione.

'Whoopsy!' said Safiya, in a high-pitched voice. 'I think I built the tower too high.' She swooped in to pick Hermione up, walking over to find Penny. 'We just hit ourselves in the face with a tower of cuppy cups, didn't we?' Safiya said, still in her baby voice. 'We didn't mean to do that, did we?'

'Oh my darling, my baby!' Penny said, standing and opening her arms for her daughter. It was heart-breaking to hear – every single time, whatever the need – and yet she loved – deeply enough that as she lay in bed at night holding her breath to hear her own child breathing in the bassinet beside her – being needed. She loved being Hermione's person.

329

Penny raised her close and whispered that she loved her. 'You're okay,' she continued. 'You're okay.'

Francesco came to see if she was okay too, fussing over her with Penny.

'Da,' Hermione said, reaching for him with pudgy fists. 'Daddy.'

Penny looked at Francesco and shrugged. Francesco shrugged back.

'There you go, da,' Penny said, passing her daughter along and watching her nuzzle into his chest. She watched him hold the back of her head with his hand, how Hermie settled easily when she was with him. It was exactly how Penny felt with him, too.

'Daddy,' Penny said, smiling. 'I think we should make it official.'

They'd talked about it before, the idea that he might adopt her. But Penny had come this far alone, and always delayed a conclusion. She couldn't delay it any longer, though, because it was true: Francesco was Hermione's father as much as she was her mother.

Francesco nodded, careful not to wake the baby as her eyes drifted closed in her father's embrace.

'I'd like that,' he said. 'I'd like that very much.'

And in Bridges café on a back street of Stoke Newington, family that were friends and friends who were like family – all dented in their own way by love and grief and uncertainty and disappointment – came together and celebrated, choosing to try again in their imperfect humanness, thankful for everything that had happened before that meant there was so very much to look forward to in their futures.

Penny grinned at her boyfriend and her daughter.

'I'd like that very much too,' she said.

Acknowledgements

Ever since I read Elton John's autobiography I've been *dying* to try out acknowledgements like he did. At the end of *Me* he has one line that says, 'Thank you to everyone who jogged my memory and who contributed to my amazing life.' That's it. How baller is that! Not to mention funny. However, on reflection, I don't think I can pull it off like he does – and besides, a shout-out here is the least I can do when I stand on the shoulders of giants.

There's a lot of work that goes into a book. Aside from the hours that stretch into days, weeks, and months wherein I sit at home eating biscuits and imagine various witty exchanges between friends and lovers – as well as the odd afternoon crafting a titillating sex scene – there's scores of people who contribute to what happens after that. I want to list them all here because it's the right thing to do, but also it could be interesting for you, or your daughter, or your nephew, or your neighbour, maybe, to know how broad a range of jobs publishing offers. I teach writing, sometimes,

331

and it always comes up: that there's more than one way to contribute to a book. Loads of publishing houses are now opening up regional offices, so you don't even need to be London-based to pursue a career working in publishing. It can get lonely for me, working solo, but remotely becoming part of Avon, the imprint of HarperCollins this book is made under, has been like becoming a member of the most positive, accomplished, 'can do' team possible. I am proud to bear witness to their #BDE. (That's one of those annoying private jokes we have. I apologize.)

Anyway. To the credits.

When we published my previous book, *Our Stop*, it reached more readers than I could have ever imagined. Katie Loughnane is a commissioning editor who inherited me from her co-worker, and when that happens it can be a disaster for the author. Not with Katie. Right from the second we began working together she championed my work louder and harder than anyone ever has, and what *Our Stop* did is testament to the way she ran the gamut. Developing my first full novel with her, *The Love Square*, has been an honour, and I'm excited to work alongside her forever and ever. She writes notes that make me think harder, pushes me to be a better storyteller, and still, somehow, has the vim to get her colleagues excited about what we are making, too. She's badass, and also very nice. I like that in a person: extreme competency and total thoughtfulness. Give the woman a raise!

Sabah Khan, head of publicity, is unrivalled in what she does. Thoughtful, committed and innovative, she magically sees opportunity everywhere. Every time her name appears in my emails I genuinely let out a little cheer, because I just love knowing her. Her author care is second to none – rare in the world of promotion! Combined with my straight-talking, deal-wielding, brass-balled agent, Ella Kahn, these three women make up the core of my publishing posse, making this wild a ride one in safe hands. Thank you, gang.

To everyone at Team Avon: do you mind if I swear? Because *fuck me* are you good at what you do.

Beth Wickington – Editorial Assistant
Caroline Bovey – Key Account Manager
Charlotte Cross – Key Account Manager, International Sales
Ellie Pilcher – Marketing Manager
Hannah O'Brien – Marketing Director
Hannah Todd – Digital Commissioning Editor
Helen Huthwaite – Publishing Director
Molly Walker-Sharp – Assistant Editor
Oli Malcolm – Executive Publisher
Phoebe Morgan – Editorial Director
Sanjana Cunniah – Marketing and Publicity Assistant
Tilda McDonald – Senior Commissioning Editor

Katie doesn't so much speak highly of you as much as she does single out every single person's contributions so that I know *exactly* the ways you've helped make my books what they are. The same goes for the folks working within the wider business:

Ammara Isa – Marketing Manager
Anna Derkacz – Group Sales Director
Ben Hurd – Trade Marketing Director

Catriona Beamish – Production Controller
Ellie Game – Senior Designer
Holly MacDonald – Deputy Design Director
Kelly Webster – Key Account Director, Digital Sales
Laura Daley – Digital Sales Manager
Melissa Okusanya – Publishing Operations Director
Mia Jupp – Film & TV Team
Rebecca Fortuin – Audio Editor
Robyn Watts – Production Assistant

Whether you've stayed late to work on proofs, been the one who came up with the 'tagline' (Holly, you understood the essence of Penny Bridge's dilemma better than I did!), were in the room as titles were thrown around, bonus content ideas were floated, or cover designs fussed over . . . whether you were selecting actors for the audio, convincing bookshops to order more copies, leveraging brand partnerships or talking to journalists, know that I appreciate every single contribution and I wish there was a way to put all our names on the cover, because I meant what I said about standing on the shoulders of giants. I write the words but you get them read, and that's what makes this worthwhile. Thank you.

To everyone in international sales and territories:

Ben Wright – International Sales Director
Emily Yolland – Rights Assistant
Iona Teixeira Stevens – Rights Manager
Zoe Shine – Head of UK Rights
. . . and the **HCUK Rights Team**
Brigitta Doyle – Publishing Director, HarperCollins
    Australia

. . . and the **HarperCollins Australia Team**

Peter Borcsok – Sales Manager, HarperCollins Canada

. . . and the **HarperCollins Canada Team**

Emily Gerbner – Digital Marketing Manager, Harper360

Jean Marie Kelly – Affiliate Publisher, Harper360

. . . and the **Harper360 Team**

If the name of my game is to find readers who care about the same stories that I do, you're the ones helping that to happen beyond the UK. To think these books get to go global – that is staggering to me, and anytime you need me to take a business trip to, say, Toronto or Sydney or NYC, you just let me know. It's the least I can do to say thank you for representing worldwide! (That's partly a joke, and partly a plea to rack up some airmiles to places I've never been before . . . International book tour, anyone?)

When I was developing *The Love Square* my planning co-incided with fundraising for my grandmother's nursing home. I auctioned off the chance to have a character named after anyone who donated £1 or more, and the winner was Sharon Harris. Sharon, I hope Sharon in the book is the kind of woman who does you proud! Thank you everyone who contributed to that, too – I wanted to raise £500 and we ended up raising over four times that. What a feat!

Thank you to Jamie Varon, for being my beta-reader and fellow Gemini-psyche-exploring-other-women-aren't-the-competition soul sister who knows just what to say to get me to push myself that last little bit. Lauren Mahon, thank you for sharing your stories as a breast cancer survivor with me. Google her brand GirlvsCancer! Lauren was served lemons but made lemonade after her own diagnosis, and she inspires me madly. Thomas Hardy – I loosely borrowed the plot of *The Love Square* from *Far From the Madding Crowd*, and Penny Bridge is absolutely modelled on Bathsheba Everdene, so a big shout-out for representing complex and three-dimensional female characters all the way back in 1874.

Finally, there are the true loves of my heart: the booksellers, and the book bloggers. I hope I've made a book you like here, because the way you had my back with *Our Stop* made me so grateful, and I want to please you forevermore. Writing reviews online or in stores, putting what I made in window displays, on tables in the middle of the stores, pressing it into people's hands when they asked for advice on what to buy or sending them to a blogpost you did . . . You're the most important piece of the publishing puzzle. Thank you for every kind word, social media tag, email. Thank you for making me feel like I'm okay at this gig.

And to you, the reader. I never thought I'd end up writing books about women's love lives but the truth is, it fascinates me. Our romantic lives reflect our wider lives, so when we talk about feelings of self-worth, self-respect, fears of being seen, the need for our friends, how our relationships with our primary caregivers impact our adult behaviours . . . What we're really talking about is love, period. Romantic love, yes, but familial love, platonic love, sexual love, love for the self. I suppose what I mean is: 'women's fiction' is just human fiction, and I love having the space to explore that humanness. Thank you for buying my books, for telling your friends about them, for leaving reviews on booksellers' websites, for posting about them on Instagram, and for coming out to events to say that you, too, enjoy exploring humanness. It's a funny old thing, isn't it, trying our best day after day. My characters and I are right there in the trenches of learning with ya.

Here's to having the self-respect of Francesco, then, and the curiosity of Thomas. I want to strive for the emotional insight that Priyesh has, the humour of Sharon, and the open-heartedness of Clementine. Mostly, I want to forever allow myself to right a wrong path, like Penny. Deciding what we want in this life and then making it happen is the best way to know we're not just living – but alive. Because of these imaginary friends of mine, I feel a little bit more ready to give the world hell. My hope is that you will, too.

Don't forget to check your boobs,
Laura x

Nose in armpit.

Elbow in back.

Not every romance starts with flowers . . .

Don't miss the international sensation *Our Stop* – a not-quite-romance of near-misses, true love, and the power of the written word.

Available in paperback, ebook and audiobook now.

THIS IS NO LONGER THE PROPERTY
OF THE SEATTLE PUBLIC LIBRARY